The Tabernacle Bar

The Tabernacle Bar

a novel by

Susan Palmer

For Madison Thomas
Thanks for sharing
the concept of a "concentric
rings" relationship to the church
Best
Susan Pal

SIGNATURE BOOKS
SALT LAKE CITY

The Tabernacle Bar was printed on acid-free
paper and was composed, printed, and bound in
the United States

© 1997 Susan Palmer
Published by Signature Books. Signature Books
is a registered trademark of Signature Books, Inc.

2001 2000 99 98 97   4 3 2 1

Epigraph quote from "The Soul of the Night,"
by Chet Raymo

Quote from *All the Strange Hours* by Loren
Eisley © 1975, reprinted with permission of
Schribner, a division of Simon & Schuster

Library of Congress
Cataloging-in-Publication Data
Palmer, Susan
  The tabernacle bar : a novel / by Susan Palmer.
    p.   cm.
  ISBN 1-56085-096-5
  1. Mormons—Utah—Fiction. I. Title.
PS3566.A5428T33   1997
813'.54—dc21   97-28907
                                          CIP

for
Nancy, Liz & Jay

who know
how, where, and why

Fifteen

billion

years

ago

there

was

nothing.

Then

God

laughed.

—Chet Raymo

One

If you were catering the weather for a mid-June funeral in Willow Valley, up in the Rocky Mountains that run like an arthritic spine through the arid state of Utah, you'd have a breeze handy. Five thousand feet above sea level, tucked beneath the craggy peaks of the Wasatch Range, Willow Valley is the sun's own darling. Summer shimmers hot and bright. One good look at the William Moroni Cannon clan, standing by the open grave in the ninety-degree heat of midday, and you'd have had a little compassion for them as they sweltered through William Moroni's interment. You'd have blessed the mostly devout assemblage with a slight breeze, a breeze to flutter shirt sleeves and send a touch of coolness to slippery armpits, a breeze to lift blouses from the small of delicate backs and brush against sweaty nyloned or trousered thighs, a breeze as gentle as a benediction, carrying the throaty calling of a dove. This you would do unless you were one of the capricious weather gods of the West, who, during the interment in question, held the breeze but did serve up an annoying cacophony of magpies. So much for ambiance.

The Cannon family could be forgiven for cutting the graveside ceremony short. William Moroni, ninety-five-year-old patriarch, hadn't ever stood on ritual anyhow. A quick prayer, a brief song—so long, Grandpa—and the fruit of the old man's loins headed for the cool bliss of Aunt Claire and Uncle Alden's air-conditioned living room for a light lunch and the reading of the will.

A string of mid-sized American cars and vans threaded down the narrow cemetery road and onto Main Street in Bridger, green jewel of a town in the heart of Willow Valley. A beat-up tan Toyota Land Cruiser tailed the discreet display of wealth, square and grungy with an angular, grumpy person behind the wheel. Jessie Cannon, thirty years old in this particular year of our Lord, 1982. A lanky, dark-eyed bundle of nervous energy, Jessie would not be your average smooth-skinned, Nordic-blond, empty-eyed Utah gal, guaranteed to inspire wholesome thoughts, all the while breeding like gangbusters. No. The way she manhandles the Land Cruiser bespeaks some other energy, a restlessness, a rage. Short, dark curly hair ruffled by wind through the open window, small brown eyes, big mouth, broad shoulders, narrow waist, well-set hips, good-sized hands and feet—a catalog of the various parts of Jessie Cannon as she drove to her Aunt Claire and Uncle Alden's house, wondering how soon she could reasonably cut out and get back to her own life.

From a toddler's perspective, the post-funeral gathering was all long legs and well-heeled restraint. And should a toddler become enchanted by the iridescent glass egg on Auntie Claire's coffee table, happily reaching all ten fat fingers toward it, why the squat bundle of trouble would find itself swung up into someone's arms and plopped down among various other siblings and/or cousins far, far from any of the good stuff.

Jessie had a lot in common with the toddlers. She picked up the glass egg and passed it absently from one hand to the other, wondering why she bothered to show up at these tribal gatherings. Funerals, yes, all right, she could see funerals. Respect for the dead and all that, and, in fact, her grandfather had been one of the few people in her family whom she did respect. But already this summer there had been a family reunion, a wedding, the return of a missionary from the mission field (her own devout brother, Daniel, twenty-one), and a baptism. Each event required the assembling of the family forces—same faces, same stories, same overwhelming certainties. God is on our side, by God, and everybody else can ride at the back of the bus.

Jessie told herself she came for her mother's sake. She told herself she endured the tunnel vision of sixty-plus devout Mormons because she had cheated her mother of everything else a Mormon mother wants: daughter married in the temple to a returned missionary and spewing grandkids like some overactive volcano, mired in church work, obedient to her husband, and happy—let's not forget that— happy to be a homemaker in Zion.

Jessie had pushed away from that feast of opportunities when she was nineteen, and nothing anyone had been able to say or do could prevail upon her to come back to the table.

Had there been skirmishes to that end? Oh, yes. Let us count the ways the family had warred over Jessie's various declarations of independence. The tears, the rages, the long sieges of silent treatment, the sly manipulations, the overt threats. Troops might have been withdrawn from the battle front in recent years, but scars still marred the landscape on both sides.

Standing in the corner of her Aunt Claire's living room, she watched the family God had seen fit to provide her with engage in one of its more smug pastimes. Everyone was taking a turn describing some positive spiritual experience they had shared with their now-dead grandpa. A subtle form of one-upmanship flavored the event.

Clutching the egg in her hand, Jessie sidled over to her Uncle Alden, black-sheep ally in the otherwise virtuous fold.

"You know the one thing I always wanted to do with Grandpa?" she whispered in his ear. He tilted his head to hear her better. "I always wanted to get tanked with him. Don't you think he'd have been a hell of a righteous drunk?"

Alden snorted fruit punch through his nose. Jessie's parents—John and Dorothy—looked over in her direction.

"Care to share your thoughts with the rest of us?" her father asked.

"I always liked arguing with Grandpa. He was a clean fighter. Direct. Didn't sneak up on you," she said.

Alden disappeared in the direction of the kitchen, coming back a few minutes later with a big platter of cold cuts to set on the table. Jessie considered disappearing, herself. She'd done her family duty, after all, but she was curious about the will. Might as well just stick around and see who got the bulk of the property. The only thing she had her eye on was William Moroni's slab of an oak desk, but since her grandfather had engendered so many additional humans for the planet to absorb, she didn't think she'd see anything moving in her direction.

The story-telling round robin ended with knots of family asserting territorial rights around the food. Eventually Claire, the oldest of William Moroni's four children, insisted that it was time to get down to it. Whereupon her children (all-grown-up Denny, Lisa, Raylene, and Carol, and respective spouses) and her brother John and his wife, Dorothy, and their children (Daniel and Jessie, no respective spouses), and her sister Chloe and husband Frank and their children (Hyrum, Frank Jr., Stacy, Melinda, LuAnn, Judith, and Carmela and their respective spouses), and baby brother David and his wife, Margene, and their children (Rebecca, Bryan, Elizabeth, Dora, and David Jr., and their respective spouses) all crowded into the ample but now stuffed living room, while their offspring—too numerous to name—tore out into the back yard to trash Claire's hydrangeas and heave rocks at the noisy longtailed magpies flickering in and out of the branches of Alden's apricot trees.

Claire read through the formal language, but when she got to the punch line her voice did funny back-up-and-start-over things, all "ahhs" and "ahems" and "what have we heres" in a cadence of disapproving wonder. Because the devout William Moroni Cannon, patriarch in the Church of Jesus Christ of Latter-day Saints, whose wife, Madeline, had preceded him to the Celestial Kingdom, had left everything he owned to Jessie.

To wit: The house (an eighty-year-old landmark in the heart of the historic downtown district), a peach orchard (sixty acres of producing trees at the south end of Willow Valley), and everything in the house and in the bank.

Jessie remembered afterward the quality of the silence in her aunt's living room. These were people who'd been raised with the Walt Disney dictum: If you can't say something nice, don't say anything at all. As a result they had managed, over the years, to develop the skill of saying the most dreadful things in the most exquisitely pleasant manner. But just then they simply looked at her as though she'd broken all the fine china.

And Jessie sailed out of the room and out of the house in the way a thunderhead scuds past the rim of a mountain. She swung into her Land Cruiser, catching the edge of her dress and tearing it on the door frame. Alden reached her before she fired out of the driveway. "Call me tomorrow," he said.

She stared past him and kicked the vehicle into reverse.

"Do it," he said.

She squealed out onto the street.

He went back into the house and made a phone call to one Nephi Jones.

———

Driving the Land Cruiser, Jessie forgot her limitations. She could climb mountains, ford rushing streams, barrel down rutted dirt roads, and thumb her nose at more pedestrian vehicles. Jessie drove the Land Cruiser because she needed the assurance of the quick getaway, and to her that didn't mean screaming one hundred miles an hour down a highway, but slipping off behind a bluff somewhere. It meant outwitting her pursuers. Not that anyone pursued her. Not that she was involved in nefarious and illegal practices which made escape an imperative. This was a Jessie quirk. "They'll never get me," she often muttered to herself, but she never defined who "they" were or why "they" might be after her.

She was right about one thing. Her family didn't get her. They didn't get her at all. While she careened up the mountain road that laced its way through Bridger Canyon, the bewildering noise of her

4

own confusion wailed like a bad country music medley in her head. *It's fabulous news. It's some new kind of family bullshit. Christ, I sell that orchard to some developer, I'm rich. What in the hell was he thinking? Oh, man they'll contest it. I know they will. They better not mess me up over this. I wonder how much I can sell the house for?* And so on.

Back in Claire's living room, the family wondered if William Moroni had grown senile before he died. No evidence for it but the will. Lawyers might be needed.

At the moment, however, the question was unassailable, especially since flower-spattered youngsters had begun to straggle in whining, "Mamaaa, I wanna go home." William Moroni had not explained why he'd given his estate to the only one of his grandchildren walking a different corridor, and, barring miraculous revelation of some sort, he couldn't very well do it now. So the Cannons broke up into satellite families, each with its own small universe of concerns. As evening slipped down over the valley, they found their various ways home.

———

From the surrounding peaks, the night lights of Bridger appear to wink and blink with the nodding of the trees. Backpackers braving the steep trails of the Thunder Mountains see the lights twinkling starlike as branches sway to the tune of a canyon breeze (which turns up every summer evening, when the temperature has dropped twenty degrees and the dark air whispers delicacies in willing ears).

Bridger sported no high-rises on the orderly grid of its downtown streets. It did own an imposing religious edifice, a Mormon tabernacle, three stories high in the center of town, buttressed and pinnacled, suggesting reverence. The town harbored a less noble building that might be said to be its namesake—though you'd want to be careful who you reminded of that fact. It was the Tabernacle Bar, midway down an alley across the street from the gathering place of the Latter-day Saints.

It had opened in the 1950s, a hole-in-the-wall kind of drinking establishment that didn't make a big deal about itself. Its owner, an atheist who lacked a sense of irony as well as a sense of reverence, had named the bar for convenience more than anything. "It's by the Tabernacle," he'd say in the bar's early days when he was still drumming up business and when he still thought he'd name it after himself. But for some reason, Anthony's Place hadn't caught on. And when one day he overheard a couple of guys in the hardware store talking about "that Tabernacle bar," he'd gone back to his little establishment and quietly

5

stenciled the words on the door. Since it was down the alley and obscure, nobody who would have objected to it took much notice.

Ralph Bates, a one-armed former mill hand who anchored a bar stool daily from 4 p.m. till closing and was the joint's unofficial historian, would recall periodically (whether you asked him or not) that a city council member had tried to shut the place down in the late 1960s on the grounds that its name was blasphemous. But at the time the council had been trying to lure an east-coast piano manufacturer into building in the valley and they needed all the bars they had, to demonstrate a certain worldliness. And so the Tabernacle Bar survived, dispensing the watered-down brew that passes for beer in the Beehive State.

Thus you could hear folk of profoundly different persuasions on the streets of Bridger say, "I'm headed for the tabernacle," or "See you at the Tabernacle," meaning quite different things.

It was one of the delightful aspects of Bridger that it harbored folk of profoundly different persuasions. You had your pioneer descendants, the great-great-grandsons and great-great-granddaughters of the contingent of Latter-day Saints who'd come to wrest the sweet valley from the Indians and mountain men who knew its rich streams, mild summers, and plentiful game. You had your more recent immigrants, factory workers attracted by the lumber mill up at the north end, and the piano plant east of town, not to mention the vegetable cannery belching steam into the air and dirty water into Bridger Creek.

You had a closeknit group of Mexican immigrants—peach pickers, cherry pickers, bean and pea pickers—living on the southern skirt of town in a broken-down mobile home park lively with children, music, and the rage of its under-paid and overworked folk.

And up, riding sides of the Wasatch Mountains where the view over the valley pushed up real estate rates, fine Bridger State University, a land grant school with a reputation for excellence in various fields, which brought in students a little too liberal for Brigham Young University down south in Provo, and professors from all points of the compass. The university gave Bridger a touch more intellectual sophistication than your average Utah town. Mormon at its core, it was nicely fringed with other enticing elements.

Living in Bridger was sort of like listening to a good soloist with a decent group of backup singers. Of course, sometimes the music devolved into rank noise, and sometimes the soloist's voice seemed annoyingly one-noted. But there were options, other voices, differing points of view, the Tabernacle Bar.

Jessie—wanting not to be corralled into some narrow paddock of her grandfather's design, but also wanting the money—took the brunt of her feelings out on the road, then steered back into town, parked the Land Cruiser in front of the tabernacle, and went down the alley to the Tabernacle Bar. She perched on a bar stool, ordered up a pint of beer, and was not surprised when Nephi, long dark locks flowing down over his shoulders, high Shoshone cheekbones beneath the clear dark eyes, wandered in, jack-knifing himself next to her, tipping his hat onto the counter, and snorting down the beer set in front of him before Jessie could say, "You know what that wily old man has gone and done?"

"Yeah, I do," he said.

"Well, shit, Nephi. Do you think they're just going to stand around like cows and let it ride? They'll be hauling that damn will through the courts and tying up that property for years, until nobody but the lawyers will get anything. What in God's name was he thinking? That he could just sit up there in heaven and watch the battle for entertainment's sake?"

Nephi thought it might be a rhetorical question.

"Maybe he thought there'd be some sort of spiritual force field to his property that would bring me to my knees," she said and jumped off the bar stool the better to wave her arms in the air. "You know that would be just like him. Maybe he plans to haunt the place. Maybe he thinks ownership would have some kind of emotional impact on me, like I care about an orchard and a drafty old house." She flung her arms wide when she said the word "orchard" and Nephi leaned out of her way.

"Listen to me, I could sell off that property tomorrow and I'd be a rich woman. And I'd do it, too. Just like that."

She wiggled back onto the bar stool and drank down the rest of her beer. "Just like that!" she said again for emphasis and ordered another.

"Nobody in my family does anything without an ulterior motive," she said. "I want a new family. I want a family where I wake up in the morning and nobody's after my immortal soul."

The wiggling continued.

"Go pee," said Nephi.

She went.

He sighed. So much noise. So much energy. It made him tired. But he understood something about Jessie nobody else seemed to get. It mattered to her what her family thought of her. She minded her "other" status. She didn't want to be like them, but she did want to be liked by them. He heard the noise this created in her, this war of the worlds as she defined herself in opposition to her only context. It made his head hurt. "'Nother beer," he said to the bartender and opened his throat to let it run straight down.

When she came back he said, "Let's get out of here," and they headed for his rusty green '68 Chevy pickup. He drove out to the last twenty acres of his father's once substantial ranch. He pulled to a stop along the northwest corner of his small range, where the valley rose to meet the mountains in gentle ascending tables that the locals called benches. They pulled a couple of sleeping bags from the bed of the truck and spread them on the ground. Nephi gave her the only consolation he could think of, a tender, frenzied sort of passion in which her first response seemed angry and aggressive. When she suddenly went passive on him, he stopped the wild ride and brought her an orgasm like an offering of eternity, and then they held each other the way they had when they were seventeen and bliss was splendid and new.

That's how Nephi's horses found them the next morning, spooned together, breathing evenly.

Two

Dawn teases light into the sky. Watch how midnight blue inches toward sapphire, how sapphire splays itself across the heaven, washing up to robin's egg blue. It's the same sexy dance morning after morning in the Utah firmament. Dawn toys with those who wait. Dawn, in fact, is a bitch to the truckers hauling cattle, wheat, and other produce through the tricky entrails of Bridger Canyon. Will they beat her to town? Will they be able to stop at King's Bakery for a giant cinnamon roll and five cups of coffee, or will they lose time crawling behind a motorhome on the switchbacks and have to haul it straight on through to Salt Lake City, settling for the burnt brew that HoJos pours?

On the June morning that found Nephi's horses nudging Jessie awake, the truckers were not held back by a black '79 Corvette with gray interior. The Corvette came blitzing through the canyon like a bat, sonar working well, thank you. It contained a suitcase, a pair of binoculars, several dirty Styrofoam coffee cups, and a driver. In the suitcase were three pairs of jeans, three blue work shirts, six T-shirts, six pairs of boxer shorts, one pair of sandals, a comb, a dog-eared copy of *Penthouse*, a Robert Heinlein novel *(Stranger in a Strange Land)*, some ribbed Trojans, and a stack of letters wrapped with a rubber band. The owner of this collection, his nerves tingling, his heart throbbing life to his limbs, his brain humming a Willie Nelson refrain, was Maxwell Logan. A tangled mess of macho elegance and sleazeball, Max had two goals as he roared through the canyon. Foremost, he did not want to die before getting laid. Also, he never wanted to be surrounded by men again. Having just wrapped a ten-year stint in the Navy (nuclear powered submarines: long, dark, phallic), he knew all he wanted to know about men's voices. The sound of men at work set his hair on end, cut agonizing grooves across his soul, and, on at least one occasion, had driven him into such a confounded fury, he'd had to be restrained in the process of popping the top, so to speak, on one of Uncle Sam's nuclear deterrent death machines while it was several hundred feet under water. Max could get out of control.

9

From Groton, Connecticut, submarine capital of the world, he made a beeline for Bridger, Utah.

Why? Not for the sunlight spilling down the peaks of the Thunder Mountains to the west of Willow Valley at dawn. Not for the charming wide maple- and sycamore-lined streets of the little burg. Not for the water gurgling down the gutters of the streets that made it seem so clean each summer morning. Not for the monotony of daily sunshine or the grandeur of the Wasatch Range east of town. Nor the pale green of spring wheat fields that surrounded it. These were aspects of the valley he had yet to know.

Max was making his beeline for the university. Bridger State (he wasn't the only person amused by its initials: BSU), home to a particularly well-known Department of Home Economics and Family Life, where women from all over the country studied for careers as nutritionists, family counselors, wives and mothers, and child-care workers. Hundreds of women.

And that sounded good to Max. He had learned about this upstanding school in the heart of God's country from a clever little piece in *Penthouse* about college campuses with great-looking coeds. He didn't know (and *Penthouse*, bless them, never bothered to mention) that many of the women attending Bridger would have shot Max dead before giving up the prize of their virtue.

Blissful in his ignorance, he had been driving nonstop for about three days, wired on his own excitement, free of the military at last. He had paused now and then to load up on caffeine and carbs, following the truckers to high-calorie, low-priced food joints on the interstates.

The sunrise gods introduced him to Bridger in the pale blue-gray of dawn, right before the sun popped up above the mountains. He came around the last bend and spied Willow Valley, sleepy, serene. He pulled his car to the side of the road and stared at what he saw. Even streets, swaying trees, twinkling lights, the smell of something green. Cool, dry air ruffled through his open window, touching his temples. Then ten eighteen-wheelers plowed past him in a whining flash of noise and dust. He followed them to King's Bakery, the word "home" maneuvering around in his mouth. He had to admit he liked the way it tasted.

On almost any other morning he would have run into Jessie Cannon at the bakery, but she was shaking Nephi awake and saying, "Let's get a move on here. I've got to get going."

Wiping horse spit from her face, she rolled him over.

"Come on, come on. I gotta go."

"Take the keys," he muttered and danced back into his dreams, so she left him there surrounded by his horses and drove into town, to her smart condo just below University Hill, where she changed into clothing a real estate broker might wear and called her secretary.

"Harry," she said, "are the McKays there yet? No? Listen, call them and see if you can postpone that 11 a.m. showing until this afternoon, and can you take the Hinkels over to the place on Tenth East? ... Harry ... Harry, don't whine about this, just do it," she said and hung up. Then she dialed another number and said, "Fred? Hey, it's Jessie. Listen, I think we can do that deal. You want to meet me over at King's in, say, forty-five minutes?"

She drove to her lawyer's office, bypassed the receptionist and the secretaries, and went straight on through Marianne Meecham's door.

Marianne looked up, frowning, from her computer. "Don't you knock? Don't you phone? Don't you know the etiquette of the appointment book?"

"You know you love it when I drop by," said Jessie.

Marianne took off the large-framed glasses that distorted the shape of her blue eyes. "Well?"

"Well, my grandfather died and I just found out he left me everything he owned."

"Congratulations," said Marianne. "Will I be seeing some of that action?"

"I don't know. Maybe. I've never won any popularity contests in my family and this doesn't help. Not that I care," said Jessie. "But maybe they'll figure I coerced him or something. Maybe they'll contest it."

"Did you coerce him?"

"Oh, please."

"Don't give me that," snapped Marianne. "I've seen your work."

"Yeah, well, but William Cannon wasn't senile. He was still running his life. You couldn't talk him into a bowl of soup if he didn't want it. And anyway, talk about coercion, the last year of his life he was always on *my* ass. 'Come back to church, Jessie. Read the Book of Mormon, again, Jessie.' Etc., etc., same old same old. But I figure if the old man wants me to have the property, then I'm willing to fight the rest of them for it." She tossed her head back as she said this, glanced out the window, and then looked at Marianne.

"OK, then. Get me a copy of the will. But make an appointment next time you want to talk to me. I swear I'm going to start billing you by the minute."

—

Fred Baugh, an old high school buddy of Jessie's, had inherited the Tabernacle Bar from his alcoholic father, Anthony, who'd died young and thereby relieved Fred of the burden of constructing his own future. Fred took over managing the place before he was old enough to drink in it.

Jessie contemplated the deal she thought she could strike as she drove to King's Bakery. Fred was waiting for her. Over coffee and warm croissants, they haggled. They were both good at it, the conversation looping from hard money talk to weather predictions, to nostalgia for misspent youth, back to money and another round of coffee. Slowly bottom lines on both sides emerged, both of them quiet but stunned by the enormity of their mutual good fortune. They shook hands across the table. Jessie promised to get the paperwork drawn up and meet him again in a couple of days.

And in a couple of days Jessie had thrown together a nice wad of cash for Fred, and had managed, on the strength of her newly acquired peach orchard and house, to nail down a loan to cover the rest of the deal. Thus it was that Jessie laid claim to the Tabernacle Bar.

They signed the various papers one sunny afternoon in the presence of Ben Cody, Korean war-veteran-turned-mystic-bartender, who watched the proceeding gravely and then poured the wherewithal for a toast.

"To the future," said Jessie.

"Indeedy," said Fred.

They clinked their glasses together, nodded at Ben, and drank.

"You remember my ex-wife?" said Fred.

"Caroline? Yeah, she was a couple years behind us in school wasn't she? Redhead? Had sullen down to a fine art?"

"You remember!" said Fred. "Listen, if she ever comes in here, I want you to pay attention. I want to know every single thing she says and does. Expressions on her face. The whole nine yards. And then I want you to write it all down in a letter and send it to me at this address." He slipped a piece of paper to her across the bar.

"But if anybody asks, you don't know where I am. Don't know what I'm doing. Don't know how to get in touch. You can lie pretty good, as I recall. OK, sweet knees, I'm outta here."

"So long, compadre," Jessie said as he walked out the door. She looked at the crimped writing on the slip of paper he'd handed her. It was a box number in Cheyenne, Wyoming. She stuffed it in her shirt pocket.

For all her buying and selling of real estate, Jessie had never purchased anything she lusted after until now. She walked the narrow length of the bar, sweeping a hand across the cracked old leather of the booths along one wall, pausing at the juke box to play a little vintage Hank Williams, taking a turn around the tiny dance floor, rolling the cue ball across the faded felt of the pool table. A powerful sense of something seeped into her. Some damn thing. She couldn't name it. All the profits of ten years hustling real estate summed up. I own the bar, she said to herself. I own it. Me and the bank.

Except for the laconic Ben Cody—redheaded, freckle-faced, barrel-chested, loping past fifty but wearing it well—the bar was empty. As Cody passed another glass her way, he said, "Talk to me."

She looked into his green eyes and found strange emotions queuing up in her, things yanking her one way and another, something giddy, something foreboding, a noisy convolution of stuff. She surprised them both by opening her mouth and letting loose a belch.

"I see," said Ben.

Three

Max Logan discovered the reason the rooms at the Norseman Motel cost next to nothing when a freak west wind blew the stench of the Bridger sewer ponds through his open window. He'd planned on sleeping till noon, but this olfactory wake-up call roused him. He hauled himself out of the narrow bed, showered, and dressed. He tossed his belongings back into his suitcase, noticed the bundle of letters, pulled them out, and hurled them against the flimsy motel wall.

"Damn it," he said, but without conviction, and went into the bathroom for a drink of water. A tired face looked back at him from the mirror. That face—pale at the moment, sidling up on the rugged end of ugly with its close-set hazel eyes, prominent Greek-type nose (let's call it a stalwart nose), and full lips. They seemed out of place below that particular nose. They looked as though they might have preferred a patrician nose, even an upturned nose. They might have said "welcome home" to a broken nose, but in fact they were stuck with the Greek number, and they did their best. They got along better with the high cheekbones and the tough-guy jaw.

There were circles under the eyes and five days of stubble on the chin. The mouth drooped.

Where was she, anyway?

The letters lay on the floor as passively as they could manage. He picked them up and slipped one from the bundle. The postmark said Evansville, Wyoming, 1981. The writing was back slanted.

The pissed-off voice in his head said, "DON'T DO THIS. DON'T DO THIS. DON'T FUCKING DO THIS." Maybe one of the reasons it was always pissed off was that he never listened to it.

The letter was close to falling apart at the creases. He fingered it open.

"Lover," it began, "I feel like a part of me is dying." He fingered it closed. Slipped it back into its envelope. Tucked the envelope back under the elastic band. Chucked the whole mess into the waste basket, snapped his suitcase closed, and went out the door. The room stood empty, waiting.

Logan came back in, fished the unwanted letters from the trash, and got into his dusty car. The pissed-off voice in his head said, "Happy now?"

To which Max Logan of the sensuous mouth and tired eyes replied, "No, but I am starving," and he headed toward the bakery where he was about to collide with Jessie Cannon.

They converged on the only empty table. He said, "Mind sharing?" She said, "No problem," and pretty soon they were sitting across from each other taking in the highlights, the lowlights, the shape of palms, the cheek hollows, tousled hair, their minds chugging down the same narrow groove.

Just then Nephi trotted in, parked himself beside Jessie, got a good sniff of the air, and said, "Who are you?" at Max in a let's-not-jerk-each-other-around kind of voice.

Not the best voice for addressing Logan, who, having fought and whored his way from Singapore to Olongopo, figured he wasn't gonna take any crap from any Utah wimps. Still, fighting over a woman whose name he didn't yet know seemed even more tiresome than old letters that began "Lover." So he stuck out a hand and said, "Max Logan."

Nephi turned his dark eyes upon Jessie. "I'm running a couple of mares up to Tremonton. Want to come?"

"No," said Jessie. "I got appointments up the wazzoo. But meet me later at the Tabernacle? I've got something I think you'll get a kick out of."

Nephi stood up. "Nice day," he said at Logan and was gone.

Max and Jessie commenced eyeing each other.

"You've got that look about you," Jessie said.

"Which look is that?"

"It's that road look," she said. "You've been driving for days. Where'd you come from?"

"Another planet," he said.

She was only mildly disappointed with this answer, but then again, let's not be hasty. She could see from his eyes, there was some truth in it.

"Just passing through?" she said.

"No, going to school here in the fall."

"Got a place to stay?"

"Nope," he said.

"Well," said Jessie. "I own a condo near campus and a house a few blocks from here. I'm about to move into the house, and I need to rent the condo."

A condo near campus. A condo. He hated the word. But near the campus sounded good. Lover, I live in a condo near the campus where beautiful babes stroll languidly by and parts of me are reviving.

"When can I see it?" he asked.

"Now would be good," said Jessie.

She showed Logan her place. They argued some over the rent. She agreed to get her stuff out by the end of the week. He talked her into letting him crash there until she did. She left him standing in the middle of the small living room, arms at his sides, his wide fine hands running absently down over his hips as she closed the door and went down to her Cruiser, punched Kris Kristofferson into her tape deck—something dark, as the lanky crooner even now pointed out, singing in her veins.

—

Max was reconciled to his dreams. He'd been having them a long time. They'd lost their capacity to startle him into wide-eyed terror, but they weren't any less dreadful. He'd brought his few belongings into the condo, had taken a walk along the periphery of the university, keeping to the paths skirting the fine old buildings, now in bright sun, now in dappled shade. Students swirled out around him and then disappeared at a class change. Secretaries on break sat on benches as the fiery sun reached its zenith in the sky. Max felt good. And then Max felt sleepy. And soon he was snoozing the afternoon away on Jessie's couch, where his dreams gave him something that he couldn't give back.

In these particular dreams bodies did not explode into bloody wrecks before his helpless eyes. Odd body parts, bloodless, floated around him. They bumped him. He pushed them away, a toe, a nose, an arm, an ear. They were suspended in heavy air. He waved a foot away from his face. Another chamber of his mind said, "It's a dream," and Logan came up through a few layers of sleep. The dream stayed behind. He turned over, tucked his face into the back cushion of the sofa, and drifted down again where no dreams followed.

—

Jessie met Alden at William Moroni's house at three that afternoon. He had a six-pack. She poured herself into a beat-up wicker chair on the front porch and reached out a hand. He tossed her a beer and sat down on the long bench. They drank in silence. The shaded porch had been a popular family spot for more than forty years. Jessie had played house, built forts, met boys on the porch. She'd received her first kiss while standing on the porch. She'd laughed at her grandpa's jokes, argued religion with her father, and exchanged raw looks with her mother in its shaded recesses. It seemed that every momentous event in the Cannon clan had had its prelude or coda at William Moroni's house. Of all the things Jessie thought might happen to her, it had never occurred to her that she might one day own it.

"Strange twist of fate," said Alden.

"Nothing like the collective hatred of your family to throw you," replied Jessie.

"That wasn't hatred. Disappointment and envy, maybe."

"Well, how'd you like to be on the receiving end?"

"Are you kidding? In a heartbeat. I wouldn't mind owning this place."

"Me, either," said Jessie. "The question is, am I going to have to put up some kind of fight to hang on to it."

Alden rubbed the back of his neck, twisting his head sideways and grinned at her. "I don't think so."

"Why not?"

"Because when Claire dropped in to see your grandpa's lawyer about whether or not there was any hope of contesting the will, he handed her a letter that William Moroni wrote to her, in case she should come calling."

"No, really? That must have given her quite a charge. What did it say?" Jessie leaned forward in her chair.

"It suggested that she settle down and mind her own business. He said he knew what he was about and that she ought to trust his judgment."

"Now that's the $64,000 question," said Jessie. "What in hell is he about? I don't have a clue. But I'll tell you something, Uncle Alden. I don't care. I'll take the property. I ain't proud. In fact, I can use the money. His timing couldn't be better."

"How so?" he asked.

"I just bought the Tabernacle Bar."

"Oh, my sweet Daisy Mae," said Alden.

She leaned back in her chair looking satisfied.

Alden shook his head and stared at the beer in his hand.

"Let me guess," he said. "You mortgaged the orchard."

"And the house," she said, "bars aren't cheap."

"You are some piece of work, Jessie. What do you do, sit around plotting these parental assaults?"

"Uncle Alden, I bought the bar because I like the bar. And, hey, I got a great deal on it. It's prime downtown property. It's a good investment. Do you sit around wondering how your parents will react to every deal you make? I don't think so."

"My parents are lapsed Catholics," said Alden. "I'm not making deals with the devil, and I'm not doing it under their noses."

"Owning a bar is not a deal with the devil. In fact, it's a noble Mormon tradition. Joseph Smith owned a tavern in Nauvoo, Illinois. I seem to recall something about Emma threatening to leave him unless he shut the place down."

"I'll bet you didn't read that in the official church history books," said Alden.

Jessie laughed and shook her head.

"Well, there's repercussions," said Alden. "And I don't think you've thought them through."

"Repercussions? Look, I've been at the butt end of their disapproval for so many years, a little more isn't going to make that big a difference. And, anyway, maybe it's a good thing. Now, instead of sweating all the small stuff, they've got something big and solid, something worthy of all that negative energy."

"How's Nephi?" he said.

"Oh, Nephi's Nephi, what can I tell you? He's living in his little horse fantasy world, getting high, and running out of money," she said.

"You two should get married or get over each other," said Alden.

Jessie looked like she had something smart to say but changed her mind. She squinted toward the street where a couple of boys on skateboards practiced jumping the curb.

"I mean it," said Alden.

"On the principle that someone my age should be married?"

"On the principle that love anchors you, that it's about time you grew up. That the care and feeding of some kids would be good for you."

"Is this you talking?" she asked him, "Or is this Claire?"

"Claire and I agree on a lot of things," he said.

"Well, I'm as grownup as I care to be, thanks. Grownup enough to know that I'd make a lousy parent. I can't even keep house plants alive. And as for Nephi ... " She twisted the cool beer can around in her hands and peered at the logo on the front of it, as though it had something to offer. "As for Nephi, listen, you can't judge somebody else's relation-

18

ship on the strength of your own. You and Claire have this cool thing, OK? But that would never work for me. I need somebody in my life who can keep his distance."

Alden shook his head. "Here's the keys to this place, Honey. Claire says to tell you if you want any help going through your grandparents' stuff or getting rid of any of it, you should let her know. I've got to go."

He drove away, leaving Jessie in the shaded heat of the porch.

She unlocked the door and went inside. Hot stuffy air sat heavy in the living room. She opened the windows and turned on the ceiling fan, then went into the spacious old kitchen with its pale-blue papered walls and white cabinets, and put the rest of the beer in the fridge. In the middle of the quiet hovered the imprint of hundreds of noisy gatherings, of women crowding around the sink and stove, and children of all ages running in and tugging on them and wanting and running out again. Jessie moved to her grandparents' bedroom to open more windows. The big bed was made, Grandma's pink chenille bedspread carefully in place. Jessie sat down. She could see her grandmother's combs and brushes still laid out, as though she might be coming in soon to coax her long silvery hair up into a loose knot. It had been four years since Madeline's death. Jessie opened the closet and thought she detected a faint lilac scent from her grandmother's clothes, which still hung there. She felt a sudden urge to talk to her mother, something about the rush of nostalgia, of missing her grandparents and their composed smiles and their delicate fingers running through her hair.

But when she thought of her mother, she saw a stiffness and she knew what her mother would say: "Families are forever, Jessie," the unsaid portion being, "except for you if you don't shape up."

She didn't want that noise in her head and so she stifled it.

⸺

Max Logan unwound himself from his dreams. He opened his eyes. The slatted blinds cut sun in ribbons across him, gentle evening light. He felt stiff. The tiny, stark living room of Jessie's condo contained only bookshelves along one wall, no art, no television, no stereo, a big armchair in the corner by the window. Cream-colored walls, tan carpet, pale gray furniture. An open book on the floor by the armchair and near it a half-empty glass of wine. He reached out and picked up the book, *The Dancing Wu Li Masters*.

The kitchen, also small, was a mess of letters and bills stacked on the table, dirty dishes in the sink, and something in Latin painted in blue on the fridge door: *Illegitimus non carborundum.*

In the fridge were several bottles of wine and a ham. He poured himself a glass of something red and went looking for the bathroom. He found it tidy except for notes in lipstick on the mirror: "Alden, 3 p.m." "close on McKays." ... Mirror as appointment book? Well, it had a certain charm.

He wondered what the letters would think of all this. Max wished he hadn't thought of them as he wandered into Jessie's bedroom and found a low bed, a small stereo and a closet of jeans, plaid shirts, a skirt or two, one short black dress, boots everywhere, sneakers, one pair of black high heels. Max loved the smell of the closet; some musky cologne hung in the air. He sat down on the bed and picked up one of the books on the night stand, *All the Strange Hours,* by Loren Eisley. He liked the title and opened to the first page where he read: "Everything in the mind is in rat's country. It doesn't die. They are merely carried, these disparate memories, back and forth in the desert of a billion neurons, set down, picked up and dropped again by mental pack rats."

He read this bit because Jessie had underlined it. Snuggled in among her pillows, wine in hand, he let the book carry him into the long summer evening.

———

Jessie left her grandfather's house and walked the six blocks to the Tabernacle Bar. When she got there, Nephi was standing outside.

"What did you want to show me?" he asked.

"Let's go in," she said.

When they sat down at the bar, Ben said, "Hey, lady," in a way that disturbed Nephi. In all the years he'd been listening to Ben's greetings, he'd never heard him call anyone "lady."

Jessie was grinning like a madman.

"Get him a beer, Ben," she said. "On the house."

Nephi looked at her. "On the house?" he said.

"On the house," she replied.

He stared at his reflection in the smoky mirror that ran the length of the bar. He held the information being offered him at bay by noticing how the crow's feet at his eyes were deeper than usual, how the sun hadn't reached into the tiny grooves, which showed pale lines when the smile drifted down off his face. Nephi hated surprises more than he hated mornings. He also wasn't fond of Jessie's schemes, many of which he'd watched take flight only to later crash and burn when she lost interest in them.

"How can you afford it?" he asked. "I thought liquor licenses cost a small fortune."

"Well, a peach orchard can cook you up a nice mortgage."

Now Nephi liked the bar. He liked beer. He liked Ben. He liked Jessie. But he didn't know that he liked them all linked together. He didn't like the grin on her face. He didn't like the look on Ben's face, either, which he interpreted as possessive, perhaps paternal. What the hell did Ben have to be paternal about? Nephi's shoulders tensed up around his ears.

"Oh, come on, don't be weird about it," said Jessie. "Shoot some pool with me. Have another beer."

That seemed like a wise idea. Another beer he could deal with. In fact, he dealt with half a dozen other beers before the evening was over. He played terrible pool with Jessie, their games dragging on and on as balls caromed badly, nicking pocket corners or flat-out missing by a mile. Jessie didn't say much and neither did he. But in his gut bad feelings percolated.

It's that feeling you get when you know something is going to happen and you don't know what it is, but you know you aren't going to like it. Nephi had this sensation down, knew it well from long ago. It didn't leave him when Jessie suggested they go to her place and it didn't leave him when they opened the door to her condo and it didn't leave him when they went into her bedroom. But it did flower into a full-fledged rage when he saw the guy from the bakery curled up on Jessie's bed.

"Uh, oh," Jessie said and pulled Nephi into the kitchen.

"It's one of those situations," she said. "The sort where things look bad, but they're not. I forgot about him, just completely, Nephi. He needed a place to stay, so I'm renting him the condo and I'm moving into my grandpa's house. The Land Cruiser was on auto-pilot. I just forgot."

"Most landlords move out first," said Nephi. He reached into her cupboard and poured himself a tumbler of tequila, then propped himself against the fridge.

"Let's go to your place," she said.

He pondered the amber fluid in the glass. Jessie rarely forgot things. He himself rarely forgot things. Sometimes you can anticipate the past, he thought. He'd been here before. He pulled himself away from the fridge, added another finger of tequila to the tumbler.

"Jessie, do what you gotta do. But I just get tired of having to watch." And he found his way to the door.

Four

The sound of voices brought Max awake, a man's voice, then a woman's, then a man's. He heard a door close. He got up and found Jessie in the kitchen.

"What are you doing here?" he said.

"Just leaving," she said but made no move to go.

He sat down. He thought how real life rarely matched his expectations. You come to a new place and fall into the lap of a woman who is angular (not round), who is dark-haired (not blond), whose voice is deep with a raspy edge to it (not high, not bird-like), whose eyes do not flicker 'round the room but look right at you, nothing coy in them, no hidden messages flashing.

She came to the table, slumped over, and rested her head on her arms. The fine hairs along her forearm fluttered as she breathed. Her skin looked smooth and warm. He wanted to touch her skin, and before he'd finished the thought his fingers traced the length of her arm.

"Mmmmmmmmm," she said.

He liked the sound. Various body parts began to come awake. His toes sang. His shins tingled. Various messages arrived in his brain from kneecaps, shoulder blades, the small of his back, the center of his belly, the hollow at his throat. A body chorus of messages and all parts on key. He drew back.

Jessie's eyes fluttered open.

"I gotta go," she said and grabbed her keys and the bottle of tequila before disappearing out the door.

⸻

The urge to run hit Nephi hard. He wanted out of the valley. If he could have arranged to crawl out of his skin, he might have done so. In the morning he ran his horses to a neighboring ranch, promised his neighbor a fee he couldn't afford, loaded his pickup with the standard paraphernalia for a run down to Moab, and hit the road.

Who knows what it is between men and women? One minute you're in each other's arms, God help you. The next, you're staring at some stranger in her bed and adrenaline knifes around inside you looking for a way out.

22

He knew things must be as Jessie said they were. But he also knew the crease that formed between Jessie's eyebrows when she saw Max on her bed. The momentary frown going inquisitive, the line of sweat on her upper lip. He wasn't gifted in any para-deeply-psycho-mystical way. His forte was hindsight. He knew the innocence would be short-lived. And that was bad news for everybody.

For a moment he didn't know which of them to feel sorriest for, but Nephi figured that his was the most enviable position. Jessie would gear up for true love and go into ecstasy overload for a couple of weeks before spiraling down to the abyss of despair. Mr. Wonderful would go along for the ride, believing everything she said, but therein lay disaster. Because although Jessie did mean everything she said, she didn't always mean it for very long.

When at the end of a month or two the bottom fell out of her passion, the other man would discover both his heart and Jessie missing. All Nephi would have to endure, on the other hand, was a month or two of solitude, after which he would be required to forgive, forget, and take up their relationship at whatever stage of disrepair it had been dropped. At least he knew what his future held.

The first thing it held that midday as he headed out of town was a case of beer and a full tank of gas. Then he turned his Chevy south on the highway and ruminated for the zillionth time on the trouble with Jessie. The trouble with Jessie was that she wanted you when she wanted you and not when she didn't. She was emphatic on all points and no negotiating.

He slammed a tape into the tape deck and Jimmy Buffett sang to him in a Peter Pan voice, a voice that promised you'd never age as long as you listened. Nephi blended himself into the music, bellowing out the lyrics of some tequila tune, and thumping the outside door with his fist. His speedometer rose unnoticed. Nephi cruised along, willing himself into a lightheartedness that the sunshine and mountains abetted. He was startled out of it by a sudden resounding thwock as the body of a mashed magpie flipped up and over the hood of his truck. He slammed on the brakes, pulled off onto the shoulder, and stopped the truck. Damn birds.

There was a small dent in his rusty grill. Heat rose in glittering waves off the pavement. He squinted at the sky. Time for a little something. He reached into the cooler, grabbed a can and popped the top. Nothing in the way of shade near the highway. He stomped down a ditch, through the drooping barbed wire of an old fence and off toward a spindly stand of alders where he took refuge from the sun. One by one, Jessie memories eclipsed the present. Jessie watching him mount a troublesome mare when he was about twelve. She'd been afraid of horses then, but she'd grabbed the reins when the horse pulled away from him and hung on even when the mare had reared back. And she'd been brave when they were teenagers climbing Mount Bridger and she'd lost her footing near the top, slipping down into a gully and breaking her leg in the fall. Had she cried when he splinted the leg? No. Had she insisted on hobbling back to the trail where some college kids found them? Yes. And although she cried on the jeep ride to the hospital, had there been tears in the emergency room? No.

That toughness, he liked it. He envied it and figured that was why she meant so much to him. He himself was more a walking ganglion of pain. He had come into the world the son of a couple whose marriage rang hollow and empty, a marriage between adversaries shooting fierce silences at each other. Being the sole witness to that battle had sent Nephi running for cover at eighteen, straight into the Army, which shipped him off to the jungles of Vietnam. It would have been a green refuge in peacetime. In 1970 it was not exactly a haven from the scars of childhood. When you're the son of a quiet English father and an angry Shoshone mother, growing up is confusing on the best days.

Jessie's certainties, no matter how short-lived, somehow ordered his chaotic world. Then again Jessie wreaked havoc with equal aplomb. She'd left him five times (six times?) for other men. Once she'd damn near left him at the altar, breaking off their engagement a month before the wedding.

But whose letters parted the mists of horror, reminding him of a world that did matter to him while he was bent on the destruction of unknown Vietnamese? Yeah, but who had promised to meet him at Pearl Harbor on his way home and then hadn't shown up? Had got entranced with the concept of gambling in Elko and hadn't been able to tear herself away? Who hadn't left his side for three weeks after his father died?

The trouble with Jessie was she did what she wanted to do until she overdid it. Moderation eluded her.

Nephi finished his beer and went back to the truck, climbed in the cab, wound her up, and let her fly down the highway. The interstate took him south past the roar and commotion of Salt Lake City, past the refineries and their brown air, past Point of the Mountain and Provo. Dry foothills covered with sage and scrubby trees swept by him. The highway ran in slow curves, nothing but the occasional jack rabbit or vulture to distract him. He played more Buffett, and when he tired of Jimmy, he switched over to Bonnie Raitt because he was losing the battle against melancholy and figured he might as well roll with it.

Moab was lush with night when he arrived; soft air played about him as he stepped from his truck and unkinked the compressed miles from his back. He had returned to the Mexican diner he and his father had discovered when they were fresh from the pain of his mother's desertion. What had he been, eight years old? Nine? The chile verde went down hot and filling. His hand hovered near a beer. He couldn't help stalking the past.

When you are eight, your father seems tall. He seems invincible. The early morning sound of his boots on the kitchen floorboards sends you scurrying out of bed just to be near him before you're jostled into a school bus. The depth and echo of his voice fills you with assurance. His silence creates dread. It doesn't matter that your mother's voice is a high whining. It doesn't matter that some nights your home is enmeshed in a battle of wills that seems to rend your heart from your body.

The sound of your father, fresh from feeding the horses, sitting down to his own breakfast is impossibly reassuring. The day will go well. You will not be called upon in class to recite times tables. Your mother will not be drunk when you come home. There will be no battle at the dinner table. It's morning, and your father will smile as he eats his eggs and biscuits. He'll ask you about your softball game. If you tell him a joke, he'll laugh in the most untroubled manner. And if you're ready in time, he'll swing you onto his back, trot out to the end of the drive snorting like a stallion, and deposit you laughing at the bus stop where, for a while, you'll feel like a happy child in a safe world.

And then one morning you wake up, but there is no sound. Not your mother bustling about the kitchen. Not your father banging through the door. The silence carries a weight. You can't quite lift the blankets from your bed. You wait. And when your father comes into your room, he is no longer tall. He is a small man, and there is no color in his face. He sits on your bed, gathers you into his arms, and begins to cry, maybe for hours. You keep your arms around his neck and you bury your head in his chest and you know that she is gone and that she will always be gone. A part of you shuts down.

Nephi signaled to the waitress, and she brought him another beer. His father had been dead eight years, sailing his truck out into the blue

25

as though he hadn't even seen the hairpin turn in the road he'd been driving all his life. Had despair finally pushed him over? Perhaps it was possible to suffer fourteen years over a passion and in the end be consumed by it.

Nephi told himself he wasn't sure. He said to himself that most likely his father had been driving too long and fallen asleep at the wheel. But like most things connected with his parents, he faced a blank wall.

He dug in his pocket for cash to pay the bill and went outside. He was in no condition to drive. He'd had a few too many. He was an irresponsible citizen. But he got into his damn truck and stuck the damn key in the ignition, said, "The hell with you" to the responsible man who lurked in his brain, and drove out of town, heading for Castle Valley and the deep red spires of a canyon that had offered solace to him and his father when they were learning about the nuances of life without the woman they loved.

The desert and highway gods rousted themselves with a degree of compassion that evening, which is why Nephi didn't kill himself or anyone else. He maneuvered down the narrow road until he found the dusty track he wanted. He turned on it and drove along until everything seemed to stop, the motion of the truck, the voices in his head, the movement of the moon. So. He got out his sleeping bag, stuffed himself into it, and soon dreams fell in on him. The gods, with pressing business elsewhere perhaps, abandoned him then to be preyed upon by any number of creatures.

Melody Stardust was engrossed in a final exam on desert survival when she stumbled upon Nephi's truck. This wasn't some planned university course, but an exercise in the college of the real. She was really in the desert. She had really run out of water, and she was really lost.

Melody, what are you doing? said a voice in her head that sounded suspiciously like her mother's. Oh, gee, Mom, just lost here, just spending a miserable night in the dark all by myself. Probably die in the morning when the sun comes up and fries me.

Melody grew up the only daughter of Moondance Stardust (an acquired name). Her mother had never negotiated her way out of the 1960s, lingering in them by virtue of an uncanny gift for telling rich and famous people what they wanted to hear. She wore paisley caftans and piled her fine, wavy hair up on her head. The smell of rose incense permeated her Los Angeles apartment. She had started out an astrologer, but had moved on to trance channeling because she had a gift for drama. Movie stars, businessmen, even politicians didn't mind paying increasingly daunting sums to be given a window, however narrow or obscure, into the future. Anything to put them one up on the competition.

Moondance had smothered her daughter with an affectionate disregard, no mean trick, predicting marriage to a wealthy banker for Melody and handsome children. Though it might have been an accurate prediction, it failed a vital test: It wasn't what her daughter wanted to hear.

Melody heard Edward Abbey whispering in her ear. *Desert Solitaire* had been required reading in Melody's senior English class, and she had fallen in love, fallen in love with the crimson sunrise and the cliffrose and the granite and the sagebrush. She'd fallen in love with the sunflowers and the Indian paintbrush and the junipers with their pale berries. These images had intoxicated her without conveying their harsher truths, in the way television depicts the exhilaration of violence without relaying that all-important sensation of pain. Not understanding the complexities of canyons, not understanding the heat undulating down from the sun and bouncing back off sand and stone, not understanding that 80 percent of her own body was liquid and that the air would suck that moisture out through her pores, Melody plotted a getaway to the desert. It was a graduation gift to herself.

Blond-haired, blue-eyed, pretty little nineteen-year-old California girl on the run from Mom and the stunning shallowness of L.A., Melody sought an uncluttered place to explore the meaning of the world, a place where her future could unfold freely.

But her ignorance and curiosity had pulled her off the safety of the trail, and it hadn't taken the city girl long to lose herself in the folded twisting universe of red rock and sun. In truth, she wasn't far from the road winding through Castle Valley. But she didn't know that, and perception is everything.

When the first fingers of dawn illuminated a narrow track nearby, and on that track she spied a truck, her heart yammered happily in her chest. Deliverance! she hollered to herself. I am so lucky.

Nephi was not so lucky, and neither was the snake. Some squeaking little-girl voice in his ear, somebody shaking him awake. It's impossible to say whether he heard her first or the warning whir of the rattler balled up behind his knees. He jerked wide awake when he felt the stabbing pain in his calf and the pressure of the snake's jaws gripping his leg. As he tried to sit up, he felt the snake's fangs pull out of his leg and saw it struggle to loosen its grip from the sleeping bag.

Melody screamed. The snake lurched, sidewinding blindly into the truck tire and stunning itself long enough for Nephi to roll out of its way and shed the bag. He grabbed a tire iron from the back of the truck and beat the snake to death.

He conducted the carnage in nothing but his underwear. He'd used his jeans as a pillow. Melody watched as he leaned down to rub his calf, with its tiny twin punctures. She blinked as he struggled into his jeans.

"You've got to drive me into Moab," he said as he threw his sleeping bag into the back of the truck and then grabbed the cooler on the ground and stowed it as well. Melody watched him hobble around to the passenger side of his truck. He reached behind the seat, pulled out a blue bandanna, and tied it just below his knee, while she stood still, her breath coming shallow and fast. When he was finished, he looked at her over the hood of the truck.

"I'm snakebit," Nephi said. "You've got to drive me." He slipped into the passenger seat. She got in quickly behind the steering wheel, then looked at Nephi apologetically. "I've never driven a standard transmission," she said.

Nephi's shoulders slumped a little. "Push in the clutch," he said.

"What?"

"Push in the clutch—the pedal beside the brake."

She did it.

"OK, now turn the key."

The engine sputtered and caught. Nephi shifted into first gear for her.

"Now slowly let the clutch out and give ... NO! SLOWLY!"

The truck lurched forward and the engine gagged and quit.

Nephi turned to face her. "What's your name?"

"Melody," she said in a tone that was as small as she could make it.

"Melody," he said. "My leg is going to swell up like a watermelon. In a couple of minutes I could pass out. I don't know, you know? I don't damn know. You have to get me to the clinic in Moab. The sooner the better."

"Aren't you supposed to, like, suck the poison out?" she said.

"Well," he said, "if I could reach that part of my leg. ... You want to try it?"

"I'll drive," she said and fumbled her way into first gear and then second, and they got onto the road, the truck lurching and rocking as she tried and failed to get the feel of the action of the clutch. Nephi didn't pass out but stayed relatively alert right up until they staggered into the clinic where a doctor shot him full of painkiller and antivenin and sent him by ambulance to the hospital at Green River. At which point somebody finally noticed the pale and fading Melody, light-headed from dehydration and surprise.

Five

Jessie stood in the alley just outside the bar in the 11 p.m. darkness. A small light above the door gave the only clue to the bar's presence. It's not enough, she thought, as a couple of college students came out.

"Feel that canyon breeze," said one.

"Hey, there ain't no canyon breeze. Bridger sucks," said the other, and they laughed as they disappeared from sight.

She walked to the end of the alley and looked back toward the bar. Too demure, thought Jessie. As a customer she'd appreciated the bar's out-of-the-way placement. It was rarely crowded, even on Friday nights. You could usually get on the pool table, even if you weren't a great player, and there was always some place to sit. But as owner, her priorities underwent a shift. The Tabernacle Bar needed to increase its clientele.

She went back inside and watched Cody working his few customers.

"I didn't realize how dead this place could be," she said as he punched the cash register buttons.

"It has its moments," said Cody.

"Too few and far between," she said.

"Some people don't like a crowd," he said.

"Well, some people don't have a mortgage hanging over their heads," said Jessie.

"Fred used to say this town needed a place where you could sit over a quiet brew and hear yourself think," he said.

"Fred took the money and hit the road," said Jessie.

"But he had a point," Cody said.

"Granted, but then so do I," she said and the red-headed barman smiled at her.

"Granted," he agreed. "But I'd sure hate to lose the likes of that," and he nodded to a table where a group of Nigerian graduate students were hunkered over their engineering textbooks in the dim light.

"Why?" said Jessie. "They'll order one pitcher and sit there for four hours."

"They're funny, they're interesting, and they push the boundaries of this little valley. They're what this bar is about," he said.

"I thought a bar was about money," she said.

"A one-note song that grows tiresome," he said.

"So, what's it about, then?"

He ran his hands through his soft, thin hair, let his fingers linger a moment on the back of his neck while he looked around.

"This bar is one of the few places you get a little of everything in the valley. You get the university crowd, you get the Mexicans. Every now and then you get the crew from the rocket factory over in Tremonton. It's everything, Jessie. Common laborers, philosophy professors, ranchers. I mean, real estate agents have been known to frequent this place for hell's sake," he said and grinned at her.

"So what?" she said.

"Don't be so obtuse," he said. "How many places do you think there are like that in the entire Beehive State, let alone here in Willow Valley?"

"I'm not being obtuse. I'm being contrary," she said. "So what?"

"Homogeneity is death," he said. "It's like inbreeding. It leads to madness. And this is the antithesis of that. When people come in here, they see a wider world than they're used to. Blacks, whites, Hispanics, old people, young people. Some of them are Einsteins and some never learned to spell. And it's small enough and quiet enough that they end up knowing each other."

"That's not anything that you don't see in any church congregation," said Jessie.

"The church imposes its stamp of conformity on a congregation. A church group functions as a single entity. It's like an ant colony. Differences are submerged for the common good of the whole."

"Good grief, Ben, listen to yourself," said Jessie. "It's just a bar, for cryin' out loud."

"It's more than that," he said. "But if you go doing a bunch of advertising or bringing in a band or something to try to increase your business, you lose the funky atmosphere, you lose the real connections people make here. You know Ralph Bates, that one-armed guy, usually sits down there?"

Jessie nodded.

"Well, he can greet people in about four different languages, thanks to the foreign students coming in here."

"He's a drunk," said Jessie.

31

"But he's still a human being. And he's one with a wider perspective than he'd have had if this bar was only about a bottom line."

"I doubt it," said Jessie.

"Why do you want to trade it all in for a bunch of noise? You do that and you've got just another dive on your hands."

"I don't have a problem with that," said Jessie.

"Well, I do," said Cody and he turned away from her to busy himself with ministrations over a young couple in the corner booth near the juke box.

It seemed to Jessie like a good time to go home and she went out into the alley and toward the street, turning to glance over her shoulder at the lone spotlight illuminating the door. About two blocks from her grandfather's house, she smiled into the darkness. She had an idea, a heck of a good idea. Practically visionary. It made her dreams that night sweet.

The next afternoon she got on the phone with a monument company in town that didn't have what she wanted. She couldn't find one to supply her in Ogden or even Salt Lake City. And she had almost given up when someone suggested a manufacturer up in Pocatello who could probably help her. And so she called the Pocatello outfit and they said, yes, they had what she wanted, but no, they didn't deliver. Yes, they could ship, but it would take at least a week. Standing in the doorway of her little office behind the bar, she fumed, waiting as they put her on hold for the third time. She glared at the Basques who sat before her nursing a pitcher.

Jessie didn't like the Basques, and the Basques didn't like Jessie. The Basques had stumbled into Bridger in the early 1960s, on the lam from Elko, where they had dispatched a slot machine having a lucky night at their expense. They'd had no intention of staying in Bridger, but it was summer and sheepherders were in demand. The Basques knew a thing or two about sheep. So they tended flocks, grazing them on the slopes of Renegade Canyon a little north of town. That winter they would have headed out, but discovered there was decent money to be made selling marijuana on campus. Other odd bits of skulduggery came their way and winter led into spring and another summer's worth of shepherding. Another year rotated by. Gradually their plans to leave became as hazy and distant as the smog of Salt Lake City. Renegade Canyon beckoned them with its willow-lined streams, its bright slopes, the pungent smell of sage. The Basques lingered. Time dragged its heels across their weathering faces. Gray flecked their dark, wavy hair. They kept meaning to move on and they moved, but they didn't leave.

Jessie had hired the Basques a few times. In her real estate career she had managed a few rental properties where tenants demonstrated no respect for the concept of the regular monthly payment. Jessie had no patience for them and no respect for the slow turning of the wheels of justice. And so on two occasions she had hired the Basques to go in and remove the tenants for her. No muss, no fuss. No lawyers or sheriffs or thirty-day eviction notices. No time for the tenants to trash the place.

The occupants, awakened in the middle of the night to find themselves and their meager belongings dumped abruptly on the street, had not cared to cozy up to any wheels of justice, either, so Jessie got away with it.

The Basques spent most of their free time at the Tabernacle Bar. They had quite a reputation for their heavy-handed technique with women. They'd never, as far as Jessie knew, raped anyone, but they'd been known to grab a woman and slam her up against the wall for an impromptu grope now and then. One of them had tried that routine with Jessie on a smoky summer night a few years back. Jessie matter-of-factly kneed him in the groin and kicked him hard when he went down on his knees. All she got from them now were lewd grins. Sometimes they unnerved her. But as she huffed about, waiting on the phone and looking at them looking at her, she said, "You guys want to earn some money? Run up to Pocatello and pick something up for me?"

And they looked at each other and back at her and nodded. So she hung up the phone, gave them directions and money and off they went to fetch her a nice little replica of the Angel Moroni.

It was the Angel Moroni who in 1823 had introduced Joseph Smith to the golden plates that later became the Book of Mormon, the inspirational cornerstone of the church Smith founded. Mormon temples boasted a golden statue of the angel atop their highest pinnacle, and Jessie thought a scaled-down model of the icon mounted above the entrance to her bar could offer substantial inspiration to her customers.

The Basques left quickly, but they took their sweet time coming back.

A day went by. A week went by. Jessie got moved into her grandparents' home. She fretted now and then over Nephi's absence. She took over bookkeeping at the bar, got excited by the profit margins, got bored with the bookkeeping, and turned the books back over to Ben. She fought with her parents when they found out she'd mortgaged the peach orchard and the house. She came face to face with a sawed-off 12-gauge, first time for everything.

It happened like this:

It's evening, just beyond twilight, a glimmer of red shimmers at the crest of the mountains. Jessie walks into the Tabernacle. She smiles at Ben behind the bar.

"Thought you might could use a little help," she says.

Ben, stacking glasses on the shelves beside the cash register, nods at her.

A couple of farm boys lean over the juke box, dropping in quarters and laughing. Two professors sitting at the bar argue the merits of tenure.

Jessie dims the lights a little, is surprised and pleased when Max Logan comes through the door. He sits at the bar. She pours him a beer.

"You work here?" he says.

"I own here," she replies.

"You own a lot."

She smiles. They talk. The color of the sunset figures in their conversation, followed by the various qualities of skies and sunsets they have known. Max describes dawn over the Atlantic Ocean. Jessie mentions towering thunderheads spiked over Green River. Trees come up. Jessie doesn't know the hardwoods of the East, the oaks, the elms, the hickories, the walnuts. Max doesn't know the poplars, the aspens, the cottonwoods. Their hands rest on the gleaming cherrywood surface of the bar. Now the ocean laps at their conversation. Jessie has seen it only once, as a girl. Max has lived in it. Surfed on it. Sunned by it. Worshipped and cursed it. He misses it now, as their hands touch and then pull away.

And then the door slams open and Caroline Baugh comes through it with such an angry presence that the air flows away from her in nervous gusts.

"Where's Fred?" she says to Ben, her curly red hair bouncing at her shoulders as she crosses the room. Caroline is beautiful in her tight jeans and T-shirt, a fact not lost on the various men in the bar, or Jessie for that matter.

"Gone," says Ben, not looking at her.

"What do you mean, gone?" says Caroline.

Ben doesn't answer, continues loading beer bottles into the cooler.

"Oh, like hell he's gone," she says and makes for the office behind the bar. She thrusts the door open then turns around and says, "You tell me where he's gone to, Ben," all steady and hard.

Jessie answers. "He hasn't been here in a couple of weeks, Caroline. He sold the bar to me and he's gone."

Caroline's face colors brightly and she grows still. "He sold you the bar?" she says.

"Yes," says Jessie.

"He damn well can't do that," says Caroline. "I own half this place. He couldn't have signed it over without me."

"You want to see the papers?" says Jessie.

"Where is he?" says Caroline.

"I don't know."

Caroline leaves, not closing the door behind her. Jessie follows to shut it, but as the latch catches, Caroline pushes back through. She has a sawed-off 12-gauge in her hands, and she places the end of it under Jessie's chin.

"Where is he?" she says again.

"He's in Cheyenne," says Jessie.

"Where in Cheyenne?" says Caroline.

"I don't know."

Caroline thinks about this to the degree that a raging person is capable of thought. The motion of the bar has come to a standstill. Ben has a strange look in his eye, almost a glassy stare. The color has drained out of Max's face. He's standing, ready to lunge toward Caroline, but not stupid. The other people watch as though it's the bottom of the ninth World Series time and the game is up for grabs.

"Yes, you do," says Caroline, "and you're going to tell me."

Jessie has confronted fear a time or two in her life, but this is new, this yaw into panic, her muscles all rubbery and shaking. Then a part of her mind seems to separate from the action, now watching as though it were happening to someone else. She feels the fear, but she also sees herself feeling it and then she knows to look beyond it at something else.

She smiles, sort of. "You don't want to shoot me over an address, Caroline. Do you?" Her voice sounds breathy, like too much air is passing over her vocal cords.

Nobody notices how Ben comes to be standing beside Caroline, but suddenly he is. "Talk to me," he says, and the sound of his voice, lustrous and deep, has a mesmerizing quality. Caroline lowers the gun a little so that it points at Jessie's chest.

"If he sold the bar, he owes me a lot of money. I mean a lot of money," says Caroline.

Ben looks at Jessie. "And you're going to stand here playing chicken with her over a damn box number in Wyoming? Take it out in the alley, ladies." He goes back behind the bar and pours himself a cup of coffee.

Somehow the drama fades. Max feels the tension sliding out of him. Caroline appears to have lost confidence in the efficacy of her weapon. Jessie feels foolish. What in hell was she thinking?

She pulls a slip of paper from her shirt pocket, looks at it, then hands it over to Caroline, who lowers the gun and leaves.

Jessie stands still but looks at Ben, who is shaking his head.

"Didn't anybody ever teach you to pick your battles?" he says.

Jessie doesn't respond to this but goes into the office and sits down with a pen and paper.

Ben stands in the doorway, saying, "You want the cops?"

"Ahhh, no," she says and begins writing.

Dear Fred:

I hope you get this letter before your wife gets to you. That's why I'm sending it by express mail. When she left here she was in a big damn hurry and she knew where she was going.

I meant to keep your secret. I was all set to bicker till dawn with ol' Caroline, but I wasn't set to bicker with a shotgun and when she shoved it in my face I thought better you than me.

Sorry. Hope it all works out.

Jessie

P.S. She did not look or sound at all happy. I hope you've got fast reflexes and good insurance.

By the time she finished the letter, the bar had become itself again; a noisy, happy buzz underscored the sound of the juke box. Max watched Jessie, how she busied herself loading and unloading the dishwasher, how her hands trembled now and then. He stuck around till closing, helping her and Ben stack chairs on top of tables, taking out the garbage, mopping the floor. When she left, he went with her. They walked through the night to Jessie's house. She kept a fast pace, the gait of a woman walking something off.

Max swung along beside her, remembering his own brushes with violence, the time he'd beaten a Marine senseless over a casual insult. How rage was followed by an overriding sense of power, and in the wake of the Marine's bloody face, the onslaught of guilt.

"Let's sit out here a while," Jessie said when they reached the front porch.

What's the chaser to an evening like this? An hour or two of passion? Maybe an all-night talkfest where substantial pieces of deep feeling bleed into view? Truth or consequences?

Max didn't know, and Jessie wasn't telling. She shut off the porch light and they sat in the darkness for a long time. She on the stairs, he got comfortable in the wicker chair. They watched the moon. The air was still.

Later Jessie came and sat on his lap, nestling her head on his chest in that seductively childish way women sometimes use. He smelled the stale smell of cigarettes on her and, faintly, her perfume. The angular weight of her body warmed and settled him. He put his arms around her and it was clear that the dialogue would be physical. Dawn offered rumors of its arrival when they finally went inside.

At first glance the antidote to lust seems to be sex, but sometimes the cure is worse than the disease. Max, in the eye of the hurricane that was Jessie, had a bad moment when her arms tightened around him and he called out. And then she shuddered and sighed, and their passion seeped out of them, leaving a yawning space between them, two strangers thrown up against an unknown shore. Jessie left the bed and went to sit on the floor near the window where faint light muttered promises.

Max lay still, noticing how his heartbeat slowed and wondering whether the woman of the melancholy letters would ever let him go. The woman by the window had distracted him. He had used her to distract himself from the past, but the distraction lasted as long as his arousal. Nothing had changed. Scratch that. He still had all the old feelings. Now layered on top were the beginnings of something, filaments of new sensation webbing about his heart. If Max could have given himself instructions just then, he would have ordered himself to let go of the past and embrace the present. But his sleepy mind was all a muddle.

Jessie came back to the bed. She slipped under the sheet and lay with her hands behind her head. "What are you afraid of?" she asked him.

"I'm not the one who left the bed," he answered and pulled her next to him where, tangled together, they slept well into the day.

The sound of a key in the lock woke Jessie. It was early afternoon. Her body sticky with sweat, she inched her arm from underneath Max's head, threw on a robe, and went out to find her mother in the living room holding an empty box.

"Are you just getting up?" said Dorothy.

"Uh huh."

"I thought I'd come get some of your grandmother's clothes to take to Goodwill. I'm going over that way."

"Now's not a good time, Mom," said Jessie.

"It'll only take me a minute. I'll be out of here before you know it," Dorothy replied, bustling past her and toward the bedroom.

Jessie went into the kitchen and dropped into a chair. Soon her mother returned and they stared at each other for several seconds.

"Most people knock," said Jessie.

"I won't tell your father about this," her mother replied.

No, but he'll read it in the slump of your shoulders, the droop of your mouth, thought Jessie, and he'll pry it out of you. She watched her mother leave, carefully closing the side door from the kitchen to the driveway.

Jessie wanted two things from her mother: her respect and freedom from her influence. In order to get one, however, it appeared she must sacrifice the other. Thus one triumphant self sang praises to this latest confrontation, while the other stomped around angry and confused. What to do, what to do ... Jessie thought a pot of coffee might come in handy and put some water on to boil. In not too long the aroma filtered through the house, waking Max.

Amazingly evocative, the odor of fresh coffee. It prompted a forgetfulness in Max. Lust, long-gone woman, confusing feelings all faded as he stretched on the bed. Someone was making coffee and the world was good.

It turned out that brewing coffee wasn't the only one of Jessie's culinary talents. Although it was late in the day, she organized a fine breakfast, eggs and bacon nestled between warm toast and home fries on the bone china that her grandmother had used only for special occasions. She sat across from Max in the kitchen and they smiled at each other, shyly, but also as though they shared some secret. A pleasant unarticulated intimacy held them in its embrace. Max gave himself up to it, not asking himself all the usual questions (How can I get out of here? When can I come back?) as steam from the coffee swirled up before him.

A knock at the kitchen door broke the spell. This time it was Jessie's brother. Certain tensions broadcast themselves about the room as introductions were made. Max excused himself and went to take a shower.

Jessie invited Daniel to sit down.

"I've been calling your office all week. You're never there."

"I'm there when I need to be," said Jessie.

"Well, you're never home, either."

"What do you want, Daniel?"

Daniel stalled. This was not how he had imagined the conversation. He wanted to get up and go out and come in and start over. Finding a strange man with Jessie, taking a shower in his grandfather's house, spoke reams to him about how tough his job was going to be. Still, Daniel knew he had a worthwhile goal and he persevered. "Well, I just wanted to see you, hang out, see how you're doing."

"I'm doing fine," said Jessie.

Daniel squirmed a little in his chair. "Because some people in the family weren't too happy about the will and all that. I wondered if you'd been getting any pressure, like from Dad or Aunt Claire, or something."

"Just the usual," said Jessie.

"So is there anything I can do?" he said.

"I don't know," said Jessie. "What do you want to do?"

"I want, well, I wondered if I could get you to come to church with me on Sunday," he said and immediately wished he hadn't.

"No, thank you," she said. "You want some orange juice or something?"

He shook his head. She sat down and pulled a knee up, hugging it into her chest.

"Was this your idea or is there a family committee thing going on?" she said.

Sibling resentment flared up in him, but he pulled it back. "I was thinking at Grandpa's funeral that you looked lonesome and kind of on the outside of things. And I thought, well, I bet no one has invited her to church in a while. So I thought I would."

"And what did you think I'd say?" she asked him.

Daniel was silent. They could hear the water running in the bathroom.

"Where did you meet him?" Daniel asked.

"At the Tabernacle," Jessie lied.

"The tabernacle?"

"The Tabernacle Bar."

Daniel's eyes got big. "Jeez, Jessie. That place is a total dive. If you're going to hang out, couldn't you pick a more respectable bar, the Sherwood or something?"

"Danny, I own the bar."

"You own it?" Daniel's deep voice came out of his mouth as though it had traveled a ways.

"Yes."

"Tell me why you own it."

"I own it because it has the potential to make a lot of money."

"So does a Baskin-Robbins," said Daniel. "What's your point?"

"I don't necessarily think I need one, Danny," said Jessie. "This isn't the mission field, OK? I know the drill. I probably know it better than you do. So let it go."

"But a bar," he persisted. "Why?"

"Think of it as my affiliation of choice."

The silence that now stretched between them also included the silence from the bathroom, where water wasn't running anymore. Daniel sifted through his mind for some response, a word, a gesture, anything that might open her eyes. But nothing came to him, none of the inspiration that he had counted on in the past, no welling up of emotion, nothing. He was alone with his distant sister.

So he hauled out his big gun, his testimony of the gospel. "I want you to know that I know, with every fiber of my being, that Jesus Christ died for my sins and Joseph Smith is a prophet of God, and I truly believe through them is the only route to happiness and eternal life."

"Well, if it is, then I'm screwed," said Jessie.

"Who's screwed?" said a clean and happy Max rolling back into the kitchen.

Daniel recognized an exit line when he heard one. He delivered a neutral goodbye to Max, tried and failed to keep from glaring at Jessie, and left the two of them alone.

Six

Nephi stood on a grassy butte. Rolling terrain stretched away in all directions. There was no water; his mouth was dry. The sun had begun its morning ascent. Nephi stood until his legs felt rubbery, and then he knelt until the muscles of his thighs began to tremble. Then he spread-eagled himself on the ground, his arms and legs flung out like spokes of the wheel of his body. Horses sped around him, through him. The thud of hooves stampeded across his mind. He licked dust from his lips. It had a salt taste to it. He found he could not move. One of his legs throbbed with pain. The sun began to set. The wind rose with no trees to give it voice. With the cool air came a silence and then later, riding the silence, a gentler sound, one horse coming toward him at a slow walk. The weight in his arms fell away. He sat up.

Starlight, moonlight. He shivered. Something about the darkness frightened him. Something about it reached into his heart with twisting pangs, feelings he did not know and did not want to know.

A horse and rider stood before him. They glimmered a little in the darkness. Nephi grasped the leg of the rider. He looked up and saw the unsmiling youthful face of his mother—her black hair whispering down around her arms. She reached out and ran her fingers through his hair, trailed them across his cheek. Tears started in his eyes.

Her horse jerked her away. She circled back and called something to him that he couldn't hear, then sped away at a sudden gallop.

Nephi wanted to sleep. His tired body drooped as he watched the disappearing rider. All night, as a half moon rotated across the sky, as a coyote lamented, as a solitary bat radared through the air, Nephi stood. He could hear his heart murmuring in fluttering rhythms and wondered whether it might leave him.

When he opened his eyes, he stood before a huge boulder, half again as high as he was tall and split down the middle. His mother was climbing out of the tear in the rock. They stood before each other. And then she faded into a wisp of smoke, tailing up before him into a sky that was white and not blue.

When he finally came out of his drug-induced sleep, he saw a large nurse standing over him, his wrist in her hand. She watched the clock on the wall. He blinked a few times.

"My mother is dead," he said. He didn't know why he said it.

The nurse asked him how he felt.

Nephi let his mind travel over his body. "My leg hurts," he said.

"Do you remember what happened?" she asked.

"No," he said, though it wasn't quite true. Nephi remembered the sound of the rattlesnake; he felt the shock of the bite in his mind. But he also had a powerful image of horses tap-dancing across his chest, and so he didn't trust himself. He wanted the snake story confirmed by outside sources. He wanted a second opinion.

The nurse verified his memory and began talking tissue damage and swelling and recovery periods, while Nephi faded a little. He thought he might be detaching from his body; he thought he might be rising to the ceiling. He seemed to be simultaneously looking down on and up at the nurse. I should be concerned, he told himself. These are good drugs, he opined to the light fixture. Far away the nurse's voice was saying something about the girl.

Nephi felt himself descending. It was a slow process. Light refracted through him. The light seemed to be pulling the disparate parts together, winching him back down inside himself.

"The girl," he said when his double vision cleared.

"Melody," said the nurse.

"The girl?" Nephi said, aware now of large porous holes in his snake memory.

"She's been in a couple of times to see you. She said to tell you she brought your truck up and didn't wreck it." The nurse was now messing with Nephi's pillows, tucking bed linen around him, adjusting blankets, fussing in a way that might have annoyed him if he'd noticed. But Nephi was trying to contain his memories in the leaky colander of his consciousness and somehow the girl kept slipping through. He remembered leaning his head against the dashboard of his truck. He remembered shifting gears with his left hand, and that was about the best he could do.

"She said she'd be back to see how you were." The nurse was standing in the doorway now. "The doctor will be around in a couple of hours and he can tell you when you'll be going home."

Nephi dozed again, and as he drifted off, he thought about Jessie. He didn't think anything in particular about her. She moved into his head and took up residence in a smiling, noncommittal, hello-I-must-be-going kind of way. Before he checked into sleep, he wondered if he owned his insides or if Jessie were his insides or if there were insides as opposed to outsides and how in the hell were his horses.

After time had circled into Nephi's room, moving the dust around, inflicting undetectable yet absolute amounts of itself onto Nephi's still-pretty-youthful body, the snakebit rancher woke up again.

Eyeing him with shy insistence was a girl. Her arrival brought all the missing bits of recollection out into the open where Nephi could get a good look at them.

"I've been sleeping in your truck," was the first thing Melody Stardust said to him.

He didn't reply right away. He traveled over the contours of her young, clear face. He caught the sun glinting off the white-blond highlights of her braided hair. He lingered for a while in the blue of her deep-set eyes. Jessie thoughts decamped.

"Do you remember me?" said Melody.

"Vaguely," said Nephi and was aware that his chest felt weak.

They commenced explaining themselves to each other. Castle Valley arrival times, supplies on hand, emotional accouterments, retrospectives ... gory details neatly repackaged in the telling. Something in the cadence of their stories about themselves dulled the antiseptic edges of the hospital room. They were in the room, but elsewhere, a sensual elsewhere conjured by Nephi's resonating voice and the slim line of Melody's neck. Nephi had an artless charm. The space around him seemed inviting. He extended a diffident invitation to Melody— who saw more sick boy before her than threatening man.

With her prompting, he described Willow Valley, dusky stretch of land between two mountain ranges, and his own small corner of it. He talked about stream-laden canyons and fertile fields. The spare images that Edward Abbey had used to entice Melody into the desert dulled to dust in the face of Nephi's dreamy talk. She had a moment of indecision, what-ifs all skittering around in her mind. But Nephi drifted off to sleep just then and the sweep of his dark lashes against his cheek disarmed her. She put her hand over his calloused fingers. All the things she thought she might want seemed to remake themselves before her in the shape of the sleeping cowboy. When he woke again a little while later, she asked, "Did you mean it?"

"Mean what?" he said as he pulled himself to a sitting position.

"Oh, nothing," she said, crestfallen and shy.

"Mean what?" he said again, but she wouldn't answer and so

Nephi searched for what he knew of women, which sent him into a welter of Jessie memories, all angles compared to the softness of the girl before him and he realized he knew nothing.

"Let's get out of here," he said and swung his legs over the edge of the bed. The hospital gown was short and bunched near his thighs so that when he threw the blankets back, Melody saw, however briefly, his sleepy wrinkled penis, a first for her. She looked quickly away.

"I'll wait outside," she said and slipped from the room.

The Green River hospital wasn't ready to let Nephi go. He didn't care. Weak, leaning on the willing Ms. Stardust, he hobbled out of the hospital, got his butt in his truck, and north the two of them headed toward the dwindling ranch in the high valley, to the Tabernacle Bar. And Jessie.

He wondered where her various appetites had taken her in his absence, how sated she might be. He looked at Melody as the road ran away from them and felt some small misgiving. If he were an arsenal, Melody was his newest weapon. If Jessie were a battleground, Nephi had just sent a sniper to the peace talks. It was both more and less than that, he said to himself as he tired behind the wheel somewhere outside of Salt Lake City. It was time for a change. He pulled the pickup into a rest stop along the highway, found a drinking fountain, and splashed water over his face while she stretched beside the truck. They swapped places and Melody, once she got the vehicle on the highway, felt more confidence than she had a right to as she watched the road and the traffic and the sky and the clouds.

And Nephi.

They watched each other, as the air between them grew heavy with expectation. But there was a patience in it and in them. It was night when they rolled into the valley.

"We can find you a motel," said Nephi, who realized she ought to have some options. "Or you can use my spare bedroom."

Melody didn't want to be the one to decide. "Well," she prevaricated. "I'm a little short on cash."

Nephi directed her toward the ranch, what was left of it. And soon they had fallen into separate beds, Nephi exhausted, Melody wide-eyed with surprise and anticipation.

Each day he waited for her to leave and each day she didn't and one day they found themselves living an easy rhythm, not quite knowing how it had happened. She didn't know how to ride, but she was a willing student. She helped him where she could and got out of his way

44

where she couldn't. She demonstrated decent though uninspired cooking skills and she made him laugh. Nephi had never actually cleaned his house. He'd let the old newspapers, empty bottles, ragged-out clothes, the dust, the grit, the junk of his life settle into space as though part of the house's internal structure. Melody, used to the antiseptic cleanliness of life with Mother, set about cleaning it up. Thus went their days.

Their nights? Bend closer while we whisper the answer in your ear. Melody, Nephi discovers, is a virgin, a sweet, tanned, healthy, perfectly normal woman-child. Has never foundered in the riptide of passion. Never melded herself to the shape of a man's lust, never bled on the sheets of love.

Nephi wasn't especially anxious to have that introduction resting on his conscience. It's one thing to be young yourself, groping around in the back seat of deep emotion. You can't be held accountable because you can't see the future. But Nephi, adept at tunneling visions into his own tricky past and with eleven years on Melody, held himself back.

In the evenings he sometimes held Melody in his arms and watched, willing his breath to be still, while she cautiously explored the landscape of his man's body, slowly noticing the ways in which hers might fit. But he always disconnected himself from her before things had gone too far, slipped to his own room or sometimes up to the benches where he'd throw himself on the ground and gaze at the stars until the ache and quiver had subsided. An amazing patience held sway in the house.

It held sway until the impatient day Jessie Cannon bounded up the front steps and banged on the door before barging in.

Jessie, meet Melody. Melody, meet Jessie.

The two women looked at each other in Nephi's living room. And one of them thought, "Oh, shit," and the other one thought, "What does he see in her?"

Nephi stayed in a neutral corner and hoped for the best. It troubled him that he had no idea what the best might be in a case like this. When Jessie commenced interviewing Melody in her enthusiastic, we're-gonna-be-pals fashion, Nephi heard his horses calling and went out to the barn.

Jessie's raucous laughter ricocheted around the room when she learned how they met. Man, woman, snake: You couldn't concoct a more fated introduction than that. Melody's story unfolded bit by bit.

And as the young Californian told her tale, Jessie caught the basic theme. What she had before her was an idealistic young searcher, somebody after truth, someone who thought there might actually be explanations somewhere for the shape of the universe. Got just the thing for you, honey, Jessie said to herself.

Before Nephi returned, Jessie had talked Melody into a canyon outing. Just her and Melody and Nephi and, maybe, if he wasn't too busy and could be persuaded, Jessie's brother Daniel.

Nephi was incredulous when Melody told him their plans. "She says she thinks I'll really like this one hike," said Melody. "Yarrow Springs, I think she called it."

"Christ," sighed Nephi and went to the refrigerator where cans of beer lurked. Yarrow Springs. Yarrow fucking Springs. Nephi recalled the tiny canyon where a thin thread of creek trickled its narrow way. Nephi and Jessie had staked an emotional claim where the creek gurgled up out of the ground when they were teenagers. He no longer recalled the nature of it, but it was one of those places that belonged to them jointly. Fortified by a few beers, he got her on the phone.

"What the hell game are you playing, Jessie?"

"I don't know," said Jessie. "Spurned lover. Something like that."

"Tell me you're not sleeping with that guy in your condo."

"Come on, Nephi. This isn't about you and me. It's about Melody. Have you introduced her to a soul since she got here?"

He didn't say anything.

"Yeah, I didn't think so. Well, you may enjoy isolating yourself out there for months on end, but a woman needs some company now and then."

"You're trying to tell me Yarrow Springs isn't about you and me?" he finally said. "If you're jealous go break a few plates."

"You know," said Jessie. "I'm not jealous. But I am kind of annoyed that you almost died and I had to find out about it from a stranger."

"I'm not going," he said.

"Suit yourself," she said. "We'll go without you."

"Fine."

"Fine."

Seven

Melody sat between Jessie and Daniel in a '75 blue Ford pickup with oversized tires and plenty of chrome trim. She didn't know quite how it had happened. A morose and uncommunicative Nephi hunkered in his living room amid beer-can tailings, the dross of a sleepless night. He wouldn't say what was eating him and he wouldn't tell her what to do. When Jessie and Daniel arrived, he went into the bathroom and refused to come out. Melody hovered between them, uncertain and confused. The drawback of being an only child of a single mother is that you never learn the group dynamic, getting yanked around simultaneously by squads of people and learning how to hold your own. She was easily manipulated away from Nephi, out of the house, and into the truck.

Before too many miles had spun back away from them, she forgot about Nephi as Daniel whisked them into Bridger Canyon and Jessie played tour guide. Clouds rimming the western sky suggested a change in the weather, but the blue pickup was pointed east and its occupants paid it no mind.

At first Jessie did most of the talking, looping family stories around the scenery they passed. Those narrow caves in the rock face up there? Daniel got lost in them when he was ten, and it took several hours for searchers to find him. He'd come out of the cave drenched in bat shit. "And Mom hugged you anyway," laughed Jessie. "But Dad wouldn't let you get in the car until you'd been hosed off."

That dam holding Bridger River in check and creating a small lagoon? That was the premier make-out spot for Bridger's teens. Daniel's face flooded with color when Jessie reminded him of the winter night he'd got the family car stuck in the snow there. He and his date had had to hitchhike out and call a tow truck to retrieve the vehicle.

Then Daniel recalled the time Jessie—around fifteen—had run away from home, determined to live in the mountains off the land and never come out. "That lasted three days," said Daniel. "She snuck back home one night, crept in through her bedroom window, and came down to breakfast the next morning like nothing had happened. Mom didn't speak to you for a week over that one."

Melody began to get a sense of how it must have been to grow up not only with a sibling and a father, but with a swarm of cousins always near. She was invited to picture a noisy household, wild games of tag with neighborhood kids as twilight settled in the sky on summer nights, long hikes in these mountains. She pictured Christmas mornings with presents and relatives strewn throughout the house. She saw Halloweens where children turned into munchkin-sized hooligans. She pictured a dad and a mom riding benevolent herd on these two ruffians and their various friends and cousins as trees were climbed and fallen out of, forts built in the back yard and torn apart, piles of spent leaves in the fall, and snow caves in the winter. Her mind embellished the stories Jessie and Daniel gave her, and she concocted a kind of perfect family image that she was suddenly jealous to possess.

Her own childhood had passed quietly in comparison. She had tiptoed across the hardwood floors of her mother's apartment (no scuff marks, now, Melody). She had been allowed whatever hushed activities children may indulge without disturbing the spiritual aura her mother's clients paid good money for. She had been allowed to bring home a friend now and then from the expensive private school she attended, but any noise beyond giggles in the far bedroom had been forbidden ("Melody, please. Can't you see we're focused?").

Melody had taken up residence in books. She had inhabited them to the exclusion of the real world, the ultimate silent adventurer. Now, with a smog-free sky above her, the strength of Nephi's warmth backing her up, the happy chatter of these two strangers engulfing her, she felt, at last, the adventure of her own life beginning.

The picnic included a scrambling ascent up a rocky hill, a mile hike across a flowery meadow and then a slow descent into a small canyon. Melody gathered it all in, the powerful odor of dead cottonwoods, the freshness of sage crushed under her boot, the sound of water racing downhill, the chatter of magpies, the breeze messing with the leaves, the veiled heat of a summer day with the sky above them clouding over. They spread lunch out on a large flat rock.

Daniel, watching the fine hairs that straggled out of Melody's ponytail, was having a change of heart. He'd started out the day peeved at Jessie's insinuation that he might need help meeting women. He'd agreed to go because he thought he might have an opportunity to push his own agenda, namely getting her to see the world more from his point of view. But Melody—all innocence and charm—distracted him. His course veered slightly as he listened to her talk and as he saw the rapt way she listened to him.

Jessie veiled her self-satisfaction. Daniel, casting about for someone to convert, Melody searching for deeper meaning: They were a pop tune waiting to be played and Jessie felt as though she had just written the music and assembled the band. She left them alone and wandered down the path along the stream.

Which is more or less when Melody discovered that Daniel had an aura. It sounded, when she first thought it, like the goofy language of her mother's crowd, but it was unmistakable. The more she looked at him, the more he glowed with his square face and green eyes shining and his short brown hair all tousled. He was scrubbed and clean in his immaculate white T-shirt and pressed blue jeans, and he shimmered in the air before her.

Prompted by his questions, she talked about her world, the high-rise in Los Angeles, the private school, watching the comings and goings of famous people in her home. She told him how she'd lied about her mother's work at school, telling friends she was an accountant to the stars because how could you explain a thing like trance channeling?

"Yes," said Daniel. "What is trance channeling anyway?"

"The spirit of a nonliving being speaks through my mother," said Melody in a sing-song voice.

"Yikes," said Daniel. "The occult."

Melody didn't know exactly how to take that, so she ignored it and smiled off vaguely into the middle distance.

"So, do you believe in what your mother does?"

Melody was surprised by the question and surprised to discover she didn't have a ready answer. She realized she hadn't ever tried to figure out what she believed in regard to her mother's vocation, beyond finding it socially embarrassing. She thought about it now.

"I don't know if I believe in past lives," she said.

"Past lives?" said Daniel. "You mean like reincarnation?"

"Yes."

Daniel acted like he had something pressing to communicate. She looked at him, but he shook his head, "No, go on, tell me more."

"Well, I do think there is something to what my mother does, because people keep coming back to her, year after year. And it's not just flaky celebrities with a lot of money to spend, either. It's, like, politicians and businessmen and people you would really take seriously, you know? There must be a reason they keep coming back."

"What's it like, exactly, what she does?" Daniel asked.

Once again Melody had to think. She had watched her mother channel countless times. It was like trying to explain how her mother ate or walked.

"Well, she sits in a big comfortable chair and sort of relaxes. Her head falls forward and for a few seconds it's like she's asleep. Then her head comes up and she has a whole different posture, very straight and upright with rigid gestures. And that's nothing like what my mother does when she's just herself. She's more like a dancer. Then she starts talking in this nasal East Coast voice, like from Boston or someplace. She sounds very proper. Then you could ask her questions about your life and she would tell you what certain events mean. Like, say you're unhappy about your career or your marriage is going bad, she would explain it to you in terms of your past lives, why it's happening to you karmically and what you need to do to resolve the karma."

"So she sort of acts likes she's someone else and then gives advice?"

"Well," considered Melody. "You could think of it as acting, but, you know, when you watch her do it, it feels pretty real."

"She must be very charismatic," said Daniel. "Like Billy Graham."

"There's a little more to it than that," said Melody. "Because she does have some way of knowing about people, even people she's never met before."

"How about you?" said Daniel. "Does she know things about you?"

"No," said Melody. "She could never do me. She tried once and Seedra said—Seedra's the being she channels—Seedra said there was too much emotional interference from my mother and she couldn't communicate with me."

Melody was tired of talking about her mother. So she launched into her story of coming to Utah, the same story she had told Jessie the night before. Some audiences, however, are better than others. Daniel wanted to know what she had been searching for in the desert.

She turned wistful and dreamy. She didn't know exactly. Just the openness, just some space to be.

Daniel knew what she meant, but he also thought he knew beyond what she meant. She hadn't started asking herself certain questions, the big questions, but she would, he thought. And when she did, he planned to be around to make sure she got the right answers. She was impressionable, he could see it. She was open. He damped down the part of himself that wanted to rush right in and tell her what she was missing and how she could go about getting it.

Jessie tumbled back into view about then, pointing at the sky, which had amassed a boiling pot of dark clouds. They gathered up the remains of their lunch and left Yarrow Springs.

On the drive back to Bridger, the storm hit, steady sheets of summer rain that turned the hot pavement slippery and slowed canyon traffic. Before long more than twenty cars were stacked up behind a semi. Daniel, about four cars back in the column, didn't mind the snail's pace. He and Melody were discussing their musical tastes and popping cassettes in and out of the tape deck. Jessie snoozed.

When Melody noticed Daniel repeatedly checking his rear-view mirror, she asked him what was wrong.

"Just a Camaro," said Daniel. "She's really riding me. Must be in a heck of a hurry."

And as though it were underscoring Daniel's point, the Camaro chose that moment to pull out and pass them.

"Bad decision, bad decision," Daniel muttered. "There's not enough room before that curve."

And, in fact, there wasn't. The Camaro rode into it neck and neck with Daniel. They all saw the Peterbilt in the oncoming lane at the same time. Daniel hit his brakes to give the Camaro room, throwing an arm across Melody as Jessie jerked awake and slammed into the dash. The pickup swerved as the Camaro crowded in, squeezing between it and the tractor-trailer rig blind-siding by. Just as it looked like everyone might survive the encounter, the Camaro dipped its passenger side front wheel off the road onto the soft gravelly shoulder, which caught the car and tossed it end over end off the highway. Two bodies smashed through the windshield, hurtled through the air, and landed crumpled on the roadside.

Daniel slammed to a stop, and he and Jessie were racing to the bodies before Melody could take in what she'd seen. By the time she caught up with them, Jessie and Daniel kneeled by a woman, Jessie's ear down by the woman's mouth.

"She's not breathing! She's not breathing, Danny!" yelled Jessie.

"OK, she's got a pulse," Daniel said. "Tip her head back, Jessie. Come on, come on. You know how to do this."

Jessie opened the woman's mouth and breathed into it. Her fingers gently pinched the woman's nose.

"OK, good," said Daniel. "I'll check the other one. Melody? Come with me."

Other drivers had stopped now and people gathered around the bodies in the dirt. Daniel and Melody squeezed past them because no one seemed to be doing anything. And when they saw the broken body of the boy, they understood why. He lay in a pool of blood. His vacant eyes stared at nothing.

Daniel reached into his pocket and pulled out a small vial, then knelt down. He opened the container and spilled a few drops of its liquid onto the boy's head. Then he laid his hands on either side of the boy's face and he prayed and nobody, not even Melody, heard what he said.

His prayer lasted a few seconds. When he was done, he tore open the boy's shirt, measured with two fingers up from the sternum, and with straight arms began rhythmically pushing on his chest. "You know CPR?" he asked Melody. She shook her head. "Kneel down by his head," Daniel said between counts. "Tilt his head back. Close his nose and when I tell you to, breathe into his mouth."

She knelt beside him in the blood.

"Now," he said.

From behind Daniel, somebody said, "The kid's dead."

Daniel kept pushing. He kept count. He told Melody when to breathe. And although it seemed to them like an eternity before the paramedics arrived, although the sweat poured off Daniel, it probably wasn't more than ten minutes.

Nobody died.

Daniel and Jessie and Melody stood in a knot on the roadside when it was over, bloodied, dazed. Melody's eyes shone as she looked at Daniel. Jessie noticed for the first time the lump on her forehead where she had smacked the dashboard. Daniel, still stunned by the bolt of energy that shot through him when he had prayed over the boy, felt euphoric and lightheaded. Something of fragile beauty wove itself among them. They drove back to Bridger in silence.

Eight

On a hot, bright July afternoon, the angel Moroni, all two gold-toned feet of him, was at last secured to a bracket on the outside wall of the bar. The Basques stood underneath it, folding their ladder and stowing it in the back of a rust-orange pickup of indeterminate lineage. Jessie did not care for the fact that they had taken three weeks to get around to the job. She also cared not at all for the scuff marks and scratches around the base of the angel. And so the amount of cash she counted out for them on the surface of the bar was less than she had promised.

A difficult moment: Jessie stuck her chin out like she wanted somebody to take a poke at it. The Basques looked at the cash, their eyes a flat stare as they turned to each other and then to her. She got that weak-kneed fear response she so detested and glanced sideways at Ben, who watched the Basques with a strange stillness in his face. It was an eerie moment, as though they'd all just made a pact they were going to break later.

"Beer," she blurted out to break the spell. "Come on, sit down, I'm buying." For a few seconds they wavered, then, shrugging, the two sat and Ben put full glasses before them. They drank quickly, then scooped up the money and disappeared.

"Oh, man," Jessie said and slumped onto a bar stool.

"You want to watch your back," said Ben.

"And my front and my sides," she agreed. "I think I made a big mistake."

Ben didn't argue with her. He spent the next hour topping off his bar stock for a Friday night that he knew wouldn't quit. Jessie had been changing the easy cadence of his work nights. Despite the fact that tips supplied him with a good portion of his income, in Ben's book more of something was rarely better. But more was what he was getting reacquainted with. More customers, more money, more work, even more co-workers. Jessie had brought in a C&W band from Salt Lake City and done more advertising than he thought prudent. She'd hired some extra help for the weekend.

He didn't like it and he didn't think it would go well. But he believed in the learn-by-experience theory of education and hadn't voiced any objections. Let her figure it out herself, he said to himself. Then we'll see what's what.

By late afternoon people had begun to wander in. Jessie worked with him behind the bar. The energy in her was strained and jerky, like she couldn't get a grip on who she thought she was.

A couple of university professors sat in front of them, physicists wrapping up a day at the rocket range by slugging down 3.2's. "Hey, got a joke for you," one said to the other. "What does the Mormon prophet tell his wife every morning?" Jessie, threading new paper into the cash register, said, "Hey button it, smut mouth." They looked at her like she was one of their failed testers, then shrugged and moved off to a booth.

"What's with you?" said Ben. "You told me that joke yourself not two weeks ago."

"I hate those jerks. They come in here and bad-mouth a culture they don't know dick-one about."

"I see," Ben said as he dumped a load of ice in the cooler. "You can ridicule them because they're your people."

Jessie glared at him, like she had something meaningful to say, but thought better of it and went into the office.

It was the kind of night that bar owners love and dread—reams of people sucking down booze like large porous sponges. The dance floor heaved with sweaty bodies working up a thirst. Energy—the kind that can explode into trouble in a nanosecond—bouncing off the walls. Jessie hadn't hired enough help. One big guy at the door collected cover, a waiter, not built for intimidation, a waitress, built for other things. Ben could see that she was getting the message, chalking up bar-owning demerits on herself as she watched the evening unfold.

Sometime after midnight Ben paused to survey the simmering mess and found a pocket of aggravation. He got Jessie and jerked his head down toward the end of the bar. The Basques sat there, flanking a woman, barely a woman, who was drunk in the way of someone new to the experience, arms flopping, head rolling, sloppy, and quite interested in her sloppiness, quite amused by it.

"Did you card her?" Jessie asked.

"It's her birthday, big twenty-one."

"She come in here alone? Hasn't she got some friends or somebody we could hand her off to?"

"Not that I saw," said Ben. They watched for a while and then Ben went over to the threesome, reached out and put a hand on the arm of the Basque nearest him, who recoiled as though he'd been stung.

"What did you say?" Jessie asked when he came back to where she was ringing up a tab.

"Nothing they heard," said Ben.

The hectic pace came back down on them. With the band blaring, they turned robotic, filling pitchers, pulling frosty bottles from coolers, popping off caps, and flicking them in the garbage, ringing up tabs, cleaning up spills. And there was that unfortunate altercation between the drummer and lead singer in the middle of their last set. Maybe somebody played something wrong, missed a cue, whatever. The music stops, the drummer's whaling on the singer, the crowd's ready for blood, and no way to get through them to break it up.

But Ben does; he parts the lake of bodies and in a couple of seconds the drummer and singer are disengaged, though he has not laid a hand on them. Hangdog looks, scuffling feet, minor growling. That's a wrap, kids, and last call.

Jessie grabs a load of trash and takes it out to the dumpster at the back of the parking lot. Beyond a bright circle of blue-tinged light, figures move. She shades her eyes from the streetlamp glare and sees the Basques, the girl sandwiched between them, her blouse wide open, her jeans unzipped. She's gurgling out a minor protest. Ah, shit, thinks Jessie and looks around for something like a weapon. The Basques don't take their eyes off Jessie, but they don't let go of the girl. She keeps moving, putting a small swing in the garbage sack weighted with bottles, but it's much too heavy for her to use. Inside the trash bin she finds a rotting, crud-encrusted length of two-by-four and doesn't want to touch it. The Basques start moving toward their truck, and Jessie summons up a yell from her gut that blows away her own inertia. She grabs the two-by-four and goes swinging toward them, yelling all the obscenities she knows. They drop the girl and scramble out of her way. But Jessie has the advantage of sobriety and whacks one of them square across his back as they stagger for their truck. She lets them go.

Kneeling beside the girl, she rearranges her clothing, gets her decent, half carries her back into the bar. Patrons are getting the idea that last call might mean it's time to go. "Call a cab," Jessie says over her shoulder as she hauls the girl past Ben and into her office where she deposits her on a chair.

"Don't be coming in here and waving that around," she gestures at the girl's lean body, "if you can't control it." I sound like somebody's mother, she thinks. No I don't. I sound like a man. Let's blame the victim.

"It's not my fault," the girl insists. "I didn't do anything. I was just trying to have a good time."

"Well, rape's a hell of a way to celebrate a birthday," Jessie said. "Do you have the slightest idea how many men go trolling for drunk little college students trying to 'just have a good time'? You want to rely on the kindness of strangers, fine. But do it somewhere else. I don't like to watch."

It was three in the morning before Ben and Jessie slid into a booth, tired and sweating and sipping club sodas. "I might have advertised too much," said Jessie. "There might be such a thing as too many people."

"The fire marshal generally thinks so," said Ben.

"Yeah, I know. I know. And I need more muscle on a night like this, don't I?"

"Yes."

"You didn't warn me."

"Oh, I think I did."

"Well, thanks for nothing," Jessie said, and then she told Ben about the parking-lot mess. He listened, not looking at her, his elbows on the table, head drooping, eyelids almost closed. When she finished, his eyes came up to meet hers, and she had the uncomfortable feeling that he looked through her to something she couldn't see. Then he nodded.

"So what do you think?" she asked.

"I think you're some sort of weird vortex. Violent things happen around you."

She thought about that, found it a startling, almost compelling idea, but she said, "I must be hanging with a better class of people. The insults are improving."

Ben smiled as he slid out of the booth and walked to the door. "See you Monday," he said.

He eased onto his Harley, jumped the starter, ran out the alley, turned onto the street, and headed west toward the Thunder Mountains. They loomed black against the night sky as his headlight made a narrow tunnel down the darkness. Pieces of his famous equanimity had begun splintering. He got the idea that the darkness kept the pieces from peeling away in the wind he made as he raced down the road.

That Ben could function in the dark was a miracle in itself. The big old Montana-bred boy had spent his eighteenth winter in Korea, where nights blistered a rank fusillade of guns. He had buried most of his Korean memories, the stink of the rice fields, the hysteria of Chinese attacks, the casual barbarities the Koreans visited on each other. There was only one episode he felt any pride over. He had saved himself and two buddies from the pass below Kunu-ri. When their platoon sergeant in a ferocious panic had yelled, "Every man for himself," and dashed insanely onto a road all but impassable with wrecked, burning vehicles, Ben had pulled the two aside and they had slipped away up into the hills. Somehow escaping the detection of the Chinese, they made it to Sunchon. They were the only members of their platoon who survived, a thing that carried its share of guilt.

When he'd come home to Livingston, Montana, in July of '51, the retch of terror had slowly drained out of him. He'd spent the summer working on a road crew resurfacing Highway 89 and grateful to be on the rolling plains where rounded hills hid nothing more menacing than coyote and antelope. As time fiddled with the bitter memories, he came to want his nights back. It was a slow course of years before he retrieved them.

Racing down the highway that night, he had all but forgotten the boy whose hackles had risen as the sky had dimmed. In about forty minutes he'd run the motorcycle to ground, up a dirt road at the base of the hills leading where he wanted to go. He pushed the bike in behind a tangle of chokecherries, pulled a knapsack from one of the saddlebags, slung it on his back, and, by the light of a quarter moon, found the narrow trail. He moved slowly, his nostrils flaring as he smelled dry leaves, deer scat, the nip of pine boughs. The pores of his body absorbed the clean night air.

Away from the bar, thank God, away from the noise of people so shallow you couldn't dip a toothpick in them. Why in the name of all that's holy am I still there? he asked himself as he listened to the sound of his boots in the dirt. Time to go. Time to go. He kept an even pace up the steep slope, and the words were like marching orders. Hadn't he done what he'd come to do? Found a teacher he needed, dispensed a few lessons his own self? Ben thought he'd mastered the art of surrender. His own impatience belied it. He smiled to himself. Mastered anything there, son? Didn't think so.

Ben Cody had retrieved his soul from the general skepticism of the twentieth century by burrowing for it in the spare spaces of Zen Buddhism coupled with the practice of tai chi. He believed that he had a purpose, even though he didn't know its dimensions. Things he was meant to do informed his dreaming life with fantastical impressions. He sought meaning there, a tough job when your dreams were so convoluted. But he had gleaned from them two things. First, fate meant for him to stay in Willow Valley just as surely as it also meant for him to leave one day. It was all just a question of timing. He didn't know when he would be free to go, but he also understood that at some point he would be. He was anxious for that point to close in on him.

About an hour of working his way along the dark path, a fissure in an uprising of rock stopped him. He felt it more than saw it, reaching out to run his hand along the inside. He pulled a flashlight from his backpack and shone the light in. Always such a drag to find out later rather than sooner that you're sharing space with creatures who prefer solitude.

The crack in the rock, large enough for him to squeeze through, led into a tiny cave, egg-shaped, not more than six feet deep and three or four feet across. He pulled a blanket out of his pack, wrapped it around himself, lay down on the hard dirt, and went quickly into the dream he always dreamed here.

The dream starts much like reality. He's asleep in a cave. He wakes and becomes aware that seven men in dun-colored robes look down at him. He stands up, discovers he's naked, feels intense shame to see his penis erect, but they don't seem to notice. They leave the cave and he follows, coming out into light so bright he can barely make out the trail they have indicated he must follow. He goes with them, surrounded by them. The light brightens. His eyes are slits. Despite the brilliance, he feels cold and fearful. He doesn't want to go to the top of the mountain. They arrive on what seems to be a pinnacle of light. Petrified now, he knows they want him to jump into the nothingness. The mountain exists on a separate plane and below it the universe sprawls out, sinking to black. He doesn't want to jump. He stands trembling, unable to move or speak. The robed figures encircling him change. They aren't men at all; they are stone, nobs of sandstone molded by wind and time. Suddenly he is lying in the cave and a woman is stroking him and then mounting him and he shudders with release.

Wakes up. Hell of a wet dream.

That's a thirst Ben Cody has not slaked waking in a decade. By choice. He's up to something else, trading in his sex life for a different kind of power. He wraps the blanket tighter around him, and now dreamless sleep softens the contours of the hard ground on which he lies.

It was midday before Ben emerged, stiffly. He took the trail back a few hundred yards to a narrow path, overgrown with saplings, where he stooped and followed, coming to a creek gurgling its way off the mountain. He stripped off his shirt, dunked his head in the water, and stood, shaking droplets off as he massaged his scalp hard with his fingertips. Ahhh, awake now. Dreams diffused.

Back at the cave, he gathered his blanket into the pack and set off again, taking the trail higher, heading for the long-running ridge below Bullet Peak. He walked and focused on his breathing, air in and down the throat into the lungs, lungs expanding, holding, holding, then releasing air up the throat and out his nostrils, air moving into him once again. His concentration on breathing did not obliterate the world around him. He heard the eagle keening off the ridge; he felt the heat drawing out his own sweat, saw the stalks of wild onion and the yellow bloom of arrowroot, but his mind, occupied with the flow of air, made no comment on the images. And so they blossomed through him. He became part of the landscape, not distinct from it, not separated by a wall of words. Trancelike in this moving meditation, he followed the ridge until long shadows and wind pulled him from the reverie. He reached the rounded peak he had been striving for all afternoon, stood looking westward as his breathing slowed and settled. The evening sun threw out gallant, bright-hued banners before retreating from the sky.

In the cool air he shrugged off the pack and drank deeply of the luke warm water he carried with him. The water entering his empty stomach set off rumblings that he ignored. He took out his blanket and sat on it cross-legged, facing east. He rested his hands, palms up, on his thighs and began once again to watch his breathing. After several minutes he no longer saw the lights of Willow Valley spread out below him. He followed a convoluted imaginary pathway imprinted on the screen of his mind. He watched himself moving through a sort of tunnel, vaguely green, that seemed to loop and dip and fall back on itself. He felt himself twisting and turning, some part of him, though his body remained motionless. Tunneling, he imagined flashes of iridescing light, then a rounded chamber with light refracting all about him. He waited, trying to empty himself of expectations, trying not to force the images, but ride them. It was difficult. A confusion of visions doubled up on him as though he were staring into an Escher drawing, seeing at one moment the sheerest slip of moon hovering over a rib of mountain, only to be distracted by the mind chamber and its light.

Night sounds—the wind whistling through pockets of rock, a coyote trotting along the ridge, an elk clattering across the talus—Ben heard all of it, though he tried not to. As the numbness of his muscles penetrated, he came up and away from his mind. Seeking guidance from an inner being whose wisdom he imagined to be greater than his own, he had fallen instead into a crater of loneliness. Stunned by his failure, he wrapped the blanket around himself and curled into a fetal position on the brow of the mountain. He slept, but it seemed to him more that he was hounded by short dreams flashing through him and gone before they became coherent. When the sun at last warmed him awake, he was drained of feeling.

He stumbled down the path that took him off the mountain and back to his motorcycle. He sat astride it, wondering that the Harley infused him with strength. The feel of the handlebars ran some sort of energy up his arms. A great hungry gash of sensation simmered into his gut, and he cranked the engine, unleashing the bike on the road. A cop nailed him doing eighty. He didn't care. It was only with a belly full of eggs, biscuits, and gravy that Ben began to think again. He acknowledged that he hadn't been released from this particular watch, and he laughed at himself for wanting it so much. Laughed at himself for all his lofty thoughts of being through with desire. When he walked into the cubicle of his one-room apartment, exhaustion overcame him. He threw himself down on his narrow bed and did not move for a long while.

Nine

Once Melody Stardust turned her blue-bright eyes upon the visage of Daniel Cannon, she was unable to look away. Her phenomenal world needed stretching out to embrace the thing she had seen. Having learned at her mother's knee to ridicule the various dogmas of Christianity, having confused mysticism with her mother's occasional theatrical excesses, Melody saw in Daniel an opening to a world as foreign and intriguing as the red sandstone bulkheads rising skyward in the blistering blue of southern Utah. He was a kind of spiritual Door Number Three. She didn't know jack about Mormons, but she was willing to learn.

Having hitched a ride to the valley on the Nephi train, she had a few bad moments before leaping off, destination Daniel. But the slow tuning of her woman's body was nothing to her. The quiet ways of the Shoshone rancher paled against Daniel's aura. Awakened to the miraculous, Melody wanted a close-up and personal look at the power behind the blessing that had made a living child out of a dead one.

With Daniel's help, she found a small apartment and a job as receptionist in a medical clinic. During the first week of this new life, she missed Nephi, but not enough to slow down her heady rush to enlightenment.

Daniel embraced the task at hand. Like most young Mormons, he'd been sent out for two years to a far corner of the globe (Wisconsin, in his case) to introduce Latter-day Saint theology to those people Mormons refer to as gentiles. He'd been good at it because his own conviction was heartfelt. But the mission field was strictly business, no contact with women at all. Now as he sat sharing the meaning of eternal life with Melody, he could enjoy the considerable pleasure of putting an arm around her shoulders or taking her hand. A double passion pulsed across their synapses. It would have been difficult for Melody to separate the one from the other, and it never occurred to her to try. Daniel was aware of the difference, but found the fusion of sensations—when he pulled Melody to him, wrapped his arms around her, and whispered the secrets of the celestial kingdom in her ear—too overwhelming to resist. They spent all their waking spare time together and dreamed each other's dreams at night.

But if the miracle that connected Melody and Daniel seemed to provide a context wherein all their wishes might come true, it left Nephi staring at the empty bowl of his future, unable to avert his gaze. One afternoon he slipped into the Tabernacle Bar to get out of the sun, get away from the look of his life. Circling the block once to assure himself that Jessie was off cooking up schemes elsewhere, he parked and went inside. Ben set him out a beer without speaking and continued with the supply list he was making. But he didn't stray far from the rancher, and soon Nephi began to talk.

"I don't know, Ben," he said. "I can't seem to pull up off these bad feelings. It's like I'm on a runner, you know? Except it's not the booze. It's just nothing. Just a big nothing right in the middle of my life. I can't even smoke it away anymore."

Ben put down his list and leaned on the bar in profile to Nephi.

"What do you know about your mother's people?" he said.

Nephi's head jerked up. "My mother's people? You mean the Shoshone? I know they got screwed out of all the north basin country, Idaho, Montana, Wyoming, northern Utah."

"I was thinking more about her family. Your relatives."

"They're all pretty much dead," said Nephi. "Her dad got shot when she was fourteen. Booze killed her mom right before I was born. They lived outside of Pocatello. She had a sister, Sarah, I think. Last I heard she was living in Missoula, but that's like maybe nine or ten years ago. I don't know if Sarah was married. Maybe she's got kids. Then there were two brothers. She hated their guts. But I learned that stuff from Dad before he died. She never said anything about her family and we never saw them. It's like she didn't want me to know. Or maybe they didn't want to know her after she married a white guy. I don't know."

"People can't go forward, sometimes it means they need to go back," said Ben.

"What do you mean?" said Nephi.

Ben poured himself a cup of coffee before he answered. "You said you're stuck in some bad feelings, what kind of bad feelings?"

"Oh, hell. I don't know. I just don't give a shit about anything."

Ben took out a piece of paper, wrote something on it and slipped it across to Nephi. "That's a phone number of a guy I know, Shoshone elder, got a lot of connections. He'd probably be able to help you track down your mother's people."

"Why should I?" said Nephi.

"No reason at all," said Ben and backed off.

"My dad's side of the family's never done much for me," Nephi mused. "They were always kind of mad at him that he married an Indian. And he never got around to forgiving them for making it hard on her. Then after he dies, they came around a while, trying to get me to mend my ways. Get me active in the church again, but that was pointless. They laid off after, well, it eventually was obvious to everyone how futile it was. Which is fine with me. Who needs that noise?"

Ben listened with a kind of stillness. Nephi finished the beer and pushed the glass forward for another fillup. "I don't know," he said when he'd had a minute to think about it. "Family always seems like it's causing confrontation, a lot of pain and suffering. Kind of makes you take to strangers. At least they're polite, mostly. And they sure as hell don't know where your soft spots are. You can protect yourself."

"Well, there's family and then there's family," said Ben. "And what you don't know about your family can do you as much harm as what you do know. We all need to understand our own context."

"Why's that?" Nephi said.

"How about a plant metaphor?" Ben said. "Say you're trying to grow some tomatoes but they're not doing all that hot. 'What's wrong with these damn tomatoes?' you ask yourself. Well, maybe it's that they're not getting enough water, maybe they've got bad soil, too much clay, not enough sand, or vice versa. Or maybe they need a good dose of compost, some fertilizer. To know how to make the tomatoes better, you have to figure out what they're missing."

"So, I'm the tomato in your metaphor?" Nephi said.

"You're the tomato," Ben agreed.

"And my family is what?"

"The soil," said Ben.

"Huh," said Nephi. "You must be some frustrated writer or something."

"Something," Ben agreed.

"Metaphors are for books, not people," said Nephi, and after a while he left the bar. But he still had the phone number Ben had given him in his pocket, and he was aware of the tiny slip of paper the way you're aware of that bill you should have paid three weeks ago that's still sitting in a pile of stuff on your kitchen table and that maybe you ought to pay. Nephi let the number burn a hole in the back of his jeans. He transferred it from one pair to another, handing it from pocket to pocket when he changed clothes. Perhaps a week went by, and he told himself he couldn't care less about his mother's people. He didn't give a flying fuck about his mother. Just run off. What kind of worthless shit is that, leaving a kid and a man and disappearing?

But the piece of paper had the properties of a match, igniting a rage he had been squashing for two decades. The only time he had let himself be angry was in Vietnam, when the single thing that obliterated fear was mindless fury. The one way he'd figured out to put the war and all its pain behind him was to block feeling. But he couldn't anymore. Rage lurked at the fringes of everything he did.

If he dropped a bale of hay loading feed for his horses, he kicked the truck fender as hard as he could. If he slipped in horse shit, he racked the air with profanity. When the Dodgers lost a ball game, he threw his beer can at the television set. Once at two in the morning when the phone dragged him out of sleep and he was certain it must be Jessie and it wasn't but instead a damn wrong number, he punched the receiver through the drywall.

Jessie would have been surprised by and attracted to these outbursts if she'd been around to witness them.

One morning he called the phone number on the bedraggled piece of paper. When an ordinary voice on the other end answered, he realized he had nothing comprehensible to communicate.

Finally he said, "Ben Cody gave me your number and said I should call."

Silence on the other end for a few seconds and then a slow, easy chuckle came back across the line to Nephi. "That old son of a bitch still around, huh? He's a meddler. Well, you come see me if you want to." He gave Nephi directions to a garage on the west side of town. "I'm usually there till around six," he said, and then he hung up.

Nephi sat holding the telephone in his hands and staring at the wall. A single small ember of curiosity ignited.

Ten

Maxwell Logan possessed no time pieces. No watches, no clocks, nothing that ticked or hummed or buzzed or beeped or cuckooed or chimed. The day before he left Groton forever, he took his wristwatch and bedside alarm clock and the wall clock from over the sink in his apartment and the small round digital clock that adhered to the dashboard of his car, and he chucked them all into the muddy water of the Thames River. When he pointed the Corvette west, he set out to discover the feel of time slipstreaming across him, unbroken by the rhythm of the second hand.

Max had done his time. The last ten years of his life had been choreographed to the cadence of a submarine. Three months at sea, three months on shore, three months at sea, three months on shore. A metronomic pattern shaped his life. At sea the rhythm quickened. Six hours on, twelve hours off. Six on, twelve off. The passage of days warped and distorted into nothing. There were the hours ticking and the duty and the drills and the seconds and the minutes always pinging in his ears. Only sleep could stop the rhythm of the hours ticking by.

Max wasn't doing things that way anymore. Anymore, he navigated his way through time by feel. He'd given himself the gift of a summer wherein he had no responsibilities, space to uncoil from the demands of superior officers and inferior officers. He let himself have his way with time. He set sail upon the blissful sea of the present. The future meant nothing to him. He never roused himself from sleep until the vestiges of exhaustion had drained away. He ate when his stomach growled. He moved when his body tired of its sun-induced torpor. Max, who had started down the road to adulthood thinking there was some place to go and something to do, was evolving a new ethos as time loosened its grip on him. It was reductionist. He moved toward what made him feel good and away from what made him feel bad.

In the matter of Lainie, however, he faltered. Max had a string of intense relationships that bobbed from his past like buoys marking a stretch of rocky coast. But it was Lainie, the last one, who left him foundering. He couldn't get past her. Lainie had been like an addiction. Together they had been like a drug. He and Lainie had constituted a single entity in his mind. They had played a wild dark game, all passion and temper, a scalding thing for which there was no language but the body. She hadn't been easy. She had been chaotic, ravaged by emotions that swelled in her like seas and no telling when ecstasy would funnel into dread.

A high-maintenance girlfriend. It had occurred to Max that she might commit suicide. It had never occurred to him that she might embrace the world and abandon him. Nine months before he left the Navy, he came home to find the apartment door ajar, a note stuck to the doorjamb: "Baby, don't ask. It's all in the past, all our love. I won't be devoured and you won't meet me on neutral ground. Make your stand. Live your life," and that little scrawled "L" at the end, looping freely. She fancied herself a poet and wrote in a self-conscious kind of prose that he always felt on the verge of understanding. Lainie had been so wrong—this is what killed him—she had been so wrong. He would have met her on any ground she chose: neutral, contested, mined with deadly explosives. But he never got the chance to say so.

He had taken everything she'd left behind and set it on fire. Everything but the letters, and why he hadn't destroyed them first—the concrete evidence of their connection—he didn't want to think about.

He did all the things you do. He drank himself into countless stupors. He slept with pretty women and ugly women and old women and young women. He hung out at pool halls. He threw himself into a workout regimen that pumped his muscles and drained his brain. Once in a flurry of despair he'd taken himself to a psychologist whose silence terrified him even more than the sound of his own breathing in the dark.

Time, of course, had been his ally. The more time passed, the less he had to work on denial. Still, now and then, these rocketing memories of Lainie blasted him out of the present and into a past where her embrace constituted the circumference of his world. Max was a bit of a romantic.

Now Jessie. Not someone to share your soul with. She kept her soul to herself. She was all motion. If she did reflect, she did it on the run. What to do with a woman who lived by the clock? That's not what I signed on for, Max said to himself one morning when he would have liked to wrap himself around her. But she was not there, not at her house (he'd phoned). It bothered him that he didn't know where she was. It didn't bode well. On the other hand it didn't necessarily bode ill. Why get tied down to one when so many would be within his reach so soon? Well, because he wanted back the illusion of his past, the illusion of his heartbeat imprinted on someone else's psyche. Except that with Lainie it hadn't been illusion, had it? Maybe the compression of his real life into three-month blocks had created the illusion. The knowing that just as he and Lainie worked out their own rhythm of togetherness, he would be shoved back into a black tube in the ocean, had required both of them to create something out of nothing.

I'm doing it again, he muttered. I'm falling back into the sea of her memory. He hauled himself up off the bed and went to shower.

———

It should be said that the collective mind of Bridger did not care at all for the two-bit gold-toned fraud of an angel gesturing toward the Tabernacle Bar. Nobody likes having their profound convictions held up to ridicule.

The lack of respect, the effrontery, the shame of debasing a sacred image, all this and more was declaimed from various pulpits of the many Mormon congregations in Bridger. The city council, all devout Mormons, took it up in a secret (illegal) meeting, in which they came up with no concrete plan against the bar, but did consider sending a nasty letter to Jessie.

A debate about the angel also seethed on the Letters to the Editor page of the *Bridger Bee*. Wasn't the angel's placement a moral outrage? For that matter wasn't the bar itself a moral outrage? Couldn't the owner be hauled into court for infringing some sort of copyright or trademark law? Couldn't the owner be shot? Wasn't it time to crack down on bars and outlaw alcohol? Couldn't somebody do something?

Somebody did do something. Jessie, walking up the alley late one afternoon, looked up for her daily dose of inspiration and had to content herself with an empty expanse of wall where the angel should have been.

"Ben!" she yelled as she walked in. "Did you see this?"

"Uh huh."

"Well?"

He looked at her impassively.

"Those damn Basques."

"Not to contradict your theory," he said, "but three-quarters of the people in this town rank right up there as potential suspects."

"Yes, but theft is against their religion."

"So was the Mountain Meadows massacre," said Ben.

Jessie called up the monument company in Pocatello and had them set aside another angel for her. She made the drive herself, loaded the statue into the back of the Land Cruiser and headed south to Bridger, feeling in control. Got an angel and a man and a bar and some money and a battle with unseen foes. What else could life hold? And wasn't that Nephi's truck hauling past her on the highway just north of Swan Lake? Why, yes, it was. She watched in her rear-view mirror as his brake lights flashed and realized that she herself was braking. She came to a stop, highway clear, so she backed up, as did Nephi. They rolled down their windows and looked at each other.

"Where've you been?" asked Nephi.

"Pocatello," she said. "Where you going?"

"Pocatello," he replied. Jessie felt a spasm of missing him rattle her. She tossed her head back, hoping to clear it.

"I'm going up to see if I can find my aunt," said Nephi.

"I didn't know you had one," said Jessie.

There wasn't much else either of them could bear to say just then, and a semi barreling along in the southbound lane suggested they cut the conversation short. They headed away from each other, eyeing their respective mirrors, wondering.

Back in Bridger, Jessie learned that she'd have to drill holes in the statue in order to hinge it to the bracket. Nothing is ever simple. No wonder I hire people to sweat the small stuff, she thought as she yelled for Ben.

He looked at her problem and shrugged. "I don't do decor," he said.

A hardware store clerk introduced Jessie to the intricacies of the electric drill, and soon angel Moroni II settled into place above the door. Jessie proceeded to act smug. Take that, you slime, she said to the sheepherders. She didn't actually say this to their faces, because she hadn't seen them since the unfortunate coed-in-the-parking-lot incident. They must have found someplace else to sit and stare into the middle distance. No sweat for Ms. Cannon. She was glad not to have to look at them.

When the second angel disappeared, Jessie banked the anger. Save it for later when I'll need it, she thought. She considered going to the police. But the more she pondered this, the more she acknowledged her abiding distaste for all forms of authority. I am my own authority, she concluded. Someone is stealing from me, not from the cops or the city or the state. Therefore I will deal with it. Jessie didn't share these thoughts with anyone because she didn't want to be talked out of it. No. No. No. Just be a quiet vigilante.

First task: Drag your butt back up to Pocatello for yet another angel. Second task: Unmask the thieves. Third task: Devise a suitable punishment. What was suitable in the case of angel theft? Time enough to sort that out. As she stood in the alley, staring up at angel Moroni III, she saw beyond it to the tabernacle, to the domed apse at its east end. Standing on the hot pavement she flashed on a childhood memory, sitting on a hot Sunday morning inside the tabernacle, listening from the pews in the balcony to the drone of church leaders speaking their various truths. Sometimes her mother would let her slip from the pew and over to one of the wide windows where she could gaze out on a blue-sky day, examine the streets, the tiny people moving along them, and, perhaps, feel a slip of breeze coming in through the raised pane. A good view.

In fact, a great view. Slivers of happy adrenaline needled through her as she trotted out the alley and back to her grandfather's house (still not hers yet in her mind) and opened the door to the one room she had not entered since she had moved in, his study.

She sat behind his walnut desk, covered now with dust, a few papers on it where he'd left them. She tried a drawer and found it locked. Tried all the drawers and found them locked.

She had hung out with William Moroni in this room the last few months of his life. It was where he wanted to be. She didn't know why. She'd stop in after work three or four times a week, sometimes staying to cook him supper, and he'd be there, papers flying all around. They'd sit in the cozy room and argue politics, semantics, ethics, and still the papers would fly. He could do several things at once. He seemed not to comprehend that he was old and feeble. Whenever she asked him what in the heck he was doing, his hands would shoot out dismissively and he'd say something like "totaling up accounts" or "doing the books." But the papers were covered with words, not numbers, and she couldn't sort out his meaning.

Since the funeral she had pushed thoughts of her grandfather from her mind. She had refused to wonder at the why of her inheritance. I won't be drawn into that game, she had decided. Whatever Grandpa thought he was doing, it'll have to be a one-hand-clapping kind of deal because I won't go along for the ride. She had left everything in the house as it was, bringing only her clothes, leaving her furniture for Max at the condominium. She didn't personalize the house because she never paused long enough to think about it. She didn't buy art. She didn't collect knickknacks. With Jessie, function triumphed over form. You deduced her from her books (long, rambling works on physics, British thrillers, Anais Nin), her music (Kris Kristofferson, Willie Nelson, Patsy Cline, Roy Orbison). These things she had left behind, promising Max she'd get them out "sometime," but showing a curious reluctance to do so. She might as well have been housesitting, awaiting the return of her dead grandparents. She showed no interest in making their home her own.

Now, as Jessie sat in William Moroni's highback leather chair, memories of her grandfather slowed her down. He had the gift of listening, and when he turned his gray eyes on you, a certain stillness descended upon him that somehow invoked in you the urge to tell all. When more than listening was required, his facile intellect made debate with him a pleasure. He was never shrill, at least not until those last few months. Certain feelings welled in Jessie, but she wouldn't have them. She pushed herself out of his chair. Where would he keep the keys to his desk?

He liked being organized. He cared not a thing about cleanliness, but he was appalled by clutter. Jessie went to the small closet by the back door, which opened to reveal several sets of keys hanging neatly along a pegboard.

Part one of the Jessie assault on the Mormon tabernacle: She took all the keys—about two dozen—with her. Early afternoon nobody seemed to be about. She went to the east side door. A couple of towering sycamores hid her from the street, which was a good thing, because Jessie didn't think anyone who knew her would imagine for a second that she had legitimate business inside the house of worship.

None of the keys worked.

She couldn't believe he'd kept them all without labeling them. Scuffling back home, dragging her feet like a disappointed eight-year-old, she walked in through the kitchen, back down the hall to the closet to replace the keys. As she put them back on their hooks, she noticed a couple of smaller keys on a hook almost hidden from view behind a pair of gardening gloves. She grabbed them and went into the office. They opened the desk. She pulled out the middle drawer. Lying across the top of it was a letter. It was addressed to her.

Dear Jessie:
I'm guessing I've been dead about three months by the time you find this letter. You're probably looking for something unimportant—say

paper clips or a stapler. You'll find a lot more in these drawers than of-fice paraphernalia, Jessie. I suggest you pay attention.

Love, Grandpa.

PS. The stapler is in the bottom drawer. The paper clips are under this letter. If it's tape you want, sorry. I'm all out.

She sat down in his chair.

Dear Grandpa:

I'm looking for the keys to the tabernacle. You can keep whatever else you've got in this desk because, frankly, my dear, I don't give a damn.

Love, Jessie.

PS. I hope you're finding lots of people to manipulate in heaven. Some of us down here aren't buying into it.

Oh, he's clever, she muttered to herself as she pulled out drawers and looked in cubbyholes. She had about given up when she spied a small box in the back of the middle drawer. In it were several keys, all labeled. They seemed to belong to various churches around the city. One of them said, east door, T.

Midnight seemed a reasonable time to go trespassing. On her way out through the kitchen, Jessie grabbed a beer from the fridge.

The key worked fine, thank you, Grandpa, and Jessie slipped inside the silent, dark, cavernous building. Do not be confused. Jessie hadn't broken into a temple, those super holy, super secret buildings where Mormons with special permits go to commune with God. No, a tabernacle was a lesser edifice in the LDS building hierarchy, simply a meeting place where multiple congregations came together.

Jessie walked up the circular staircase that took her to a small room on the third floor, tucked behind the dim glisten of the organ pipes. She went to the window that faced north where she could see the well-lit front of the bar, spotlight on the angel. She twisted the top off the beer and settled on the wide window ledge. In forty minutes the bar would close. Then she'd see whatever there was to be seen.

In order to do that, however, it's helpful to stay awake, and Jessie, by about three in the morning, had nodded off. Spying is boring work. That's why people with large imaginations do it. Startled awake by her own lolling head, Jessie looked out on a graying sky. It was almost 5:30. Her angel still in place, she headed home.

Eleven

God—it appeared—had serious anger management issues. So thought Melody as selected readings from the Judeo-Christian Big Book became part of her daily fare. She had never taken the time to reflect upon the nature of God, and now, as Daniel introduced her to the Bible and the Book of Mormon, she found the nature of God quite startling. If God had been one of the Seven Dwarves, she thought guiltily to herself one afternoon, he would have been Grumpy. Throughout the Old Testament, retribution rained from the heavens: Adam and Eve booted out of the garden, the entire planet flooded, countless plagues, armies backed by God slaughtering armies of lesser deities. It was a bloody, unforgiving text.

At first glance the Book of Mormon wasn't much better. It reeked with the abominations of man, countered by vengeance from on high. When Melody pointed this out to Daniel, he explained to her that God blessed the innocent and punished the guilty. (They never got around to discussing a complicated coda to this principle—the persecution of the faithful—despite its being an important Latter-day Saint litany.) Instead, Daniel directed Melody's willing attention toward the positive attributes of the Almighty.

This was much easier when they ventured into the New Testament. Daniel particularly loved the New Testament, and when he and Melody took turns reading it to each other, his eyes shone with a bright and happy light. One Sunday morning when they sat on the steps of the chapel waiting for the bishop to come and open the door, Daniel read to Melody from the Gospel According to St. Luke. Infused with the warmth of the sun and their own nearness, they leaned into the passage eagerly: "And a woman having an issue of blood twelve years, which had spent all her living upon physicians, neither could be healed of any, Came behind him and touched the border of his garment and immediately her issue of blood stanched. And Jesus said, Who touched me? When all denied, Peter and they that were with him said, Master, the multitude throng thee and press thee, and sayest thou, Who touched me? And Jesus said, Somebody hath touched me for I perceive that virtue is gone out of me."

Daniel stopped reading and Melody, who had been watching the darting motion of a small butterfly and listening dreamily, turned to look at him. Tears glistened in his eyes. He handed Melody the book. She took it and laid it aside, then took his hand and kissed the inside of his palm and laid it against her cheek.

"I, I, I felt that ... when ..." but he couldn't finish the sentence. He didn't need to. She understood him. The doubts that had nicked away inside her in the early days of her study tumbled away down the long slope which she had climbed. If it was possible to be enraptured, then Melody was. The simple creed of the Galilean—love thy neighbor as thyself—shot straight into her heart and lodged there, alongside Daniel.

Later, when he explained Joseph Smith's vision and mission—to restore the gospel as Christ had intended it, to sweep away the false doctrines of lesser Christian orthodoxies—Melody discovered a vision of the universe that she could embrace.

With Daniel directing her steps, it wasn't difficult.

She didn't pause a heartbeat to wonder whether her breathlessness had something to do with the way he brushed her hair back from her face as he explained why Mormons don't smoke or drink coffee, tea, or alcohol, or what Mormon heaven is like. She let all the sensations blend together. Sunday school with Daniel, sacrament meeting with Daniel, Bible study with Daniel, Book of Mormon study with Daniel, walking in the early evening on the temple grounds with Daniel, dancing at a church social with Daniel. It all had the same rich, mystical quality.

Only two things marred her pleasure. Lurking out on the coast of California, her mother did not like Melody's lingering in the land of Latter-day Saints. She did not like that what had started out as a summer trip to the desert had become a job, an apartment, and a boyfriend. The letters between mother and daughter skittered over the surface of the subjects that mattered most. They concealed as much as they communicated. Melody never mentioned the Mormons, and Moondance never mentioned her misgivings. But each of them knew what was on the other's mind, and the dance of letters escalated their mutual tensions.

And then there was Daniel himself. Daniel wanted to get married, like, say, yesterday. He talked about the future as though their coupleness were a foregone conclusion. Talked about going to college and where they'd live and what kind of work she could do while he studied to become a doctor like his dad. She enjoyed being swept along in his life plans this way. There was something tender and reassuring about it. But when she was alone, it rankled. What about my life? she wondered. What about my plans? Since she didn't really have any, yet, she felt a little foolish. But since the part of her mind that harbored misgivings was fairly small, she didn't fret often or long.

———

You could dock several luxury yachts in the part of Nephi's mind that harbored misgivings. Driving up to Pocatello, he couldn't help wondering if he wasn't making a big mistake. Maybe there was a perfectly good reason his mother had kept him away from his Indian heritage. Why was he taking the advice of a bartender and some Shoshone elder—might be a total jerk for all he knew.

He thought about John Tyhee as he drove, big son of a gun, could have been fifty or sixty years old. Nephi had walked into his garage, light cascading through the wide open door, to see him bent over the engine block of a dirty El Camino. He straightened up, squinting into the light when he heard Nephi, who stuck out his hand and introduced himself.

"John Tyhee," the big man said and wiped his hand on a rag from his back pocket before grasping Nephi's. "There's coffee, if you want. Come on in my office."

Tyhee's office was two chairs in a small patch of grass behind the garage overlooking a vacant lot full of daisies and dandelions, broken bottles and old scraps of newspapers.

They regarded each other several moments before Nephi said the only thing he could think of: "Wanda Buoyer is my mother." And after he said it, for some reason he felt stupid. He didn't know what else to say as he looked at the straight-backed, beak-nosed, leathery-faced old guy.

John Tyhee looked at him, too, and then into the mug of coffee in his hand. When he spoke, his voice had a mellifluous quality, like he might be singing, like he'd taken elocution lessons. "I don't know your mother, but I know the name. It's Tukudeka, mountain sheep-eater, from northwest of the Fort Hall reservation people. Her people were the last to come onto that reservation. They subsisted in the mountains for a long time. Real independent. They wouldn't take the government handouts until they were falling-down starving. Nez Percé's Chief Joseph was a big influence on them."

Something weird constricted through Nephi. He didn't know

what to call it. It reminded him of Vietnam—a flat-out scared, run-away-now kind of feeling. But in this context it seemed to need another name.

"I'm only part Shoshone," said Nephi. "My father was white."

"Well, you've been keeping to yourself," said Tyhee. "I like to think I know all our people in this valley."

"I was raised white," said Nephi.

"What are your thoughts on that?" said Tyhee.

"I don't have any thoughts. I told Ben Cody I was feeling like shit, and he told me to take a look at my past, and I said I don't have one, and he said come see you."

"So you don't know anything about your people."

"The Shoshone? Just what I learned in school."

"You don't know anything. You got no guiding spirit, never had a dream. No wonder you feel bad."

"Actually," said Nephi slowly, "I did have this dream." He stopped talking because the feeling that now rang his doorbell was déjà vu, like he'd been sitting here having this conversation all his life. Tyhee waited for him to continue.

"I don't know why this reminds me, but I did have this dream last month when I was down in the Green River hospital recovering from a snake bite."

"You were snake bit?" said Tyhee.

"Yes," said Nephi.

"Tell me your dream."

Nephi recounted it, and, as he did, Tyhee leaned back in his chair, stretching his legs out straight and crossing his arms over his broad chest. When Nephi finished, Tyhee seemed to be staring at his boots. The sound of a cranky blue jay mingled with a background of traffic noises. Kids on bicycles swooped happily by. Tyhee's eyes flickered up to Nephi's face and then away toward the peaks of the Thunder Mountains. Then he sat forward in his chair, bracing his elbows on his knees. He looked at Nephi again and said, "Well, you might not want the past back, but it seems like the past wants you."

Nephi took up Tyhee's pose, leaning forward in his chair, hands clasped loosely between his knees. He looked at the grass between his feet.

"Do you know what the other tribes called our people?"

"No," said Nephi.

"They called us the snakes. We carved and painted serpents on

75

poles. They were a powerful symbol for us. Now your people, the Tukudeka, they split off from the rest of the Shoshone people when we took up horses. They said they had no use for horses in the mountains where they liked to hunt. They preferred mountain sheep to buffalo. Going without horses limited their mobility. But they didn't have the Bannock and the Crow come raiding and thieving on them, either."

The sun's heat brought the sweat up on Nephi's back as he listened. He couldn't bring himself to look up.

"I never heard of a Shoshone before," continued Tyhee, "who got a guiding spirit and a dream when he wasn't even looking for them. You don't even know what it means. Lots of people go looking their whole lives and they never get it. They have to borrow somebody else's. So. What do you want to do?"

"What do you mean?" said Nephi.

Tyhee stood up and started walking back toward the garage, speaking as he went. "I mean, yeah, I can help you find some of the stuff you're missing." Nephi followed him inside. "But when you go around pulling up rocks to see what's underneath them, you don't always like what you find. What do you want to do? You want to risk it?"

In the cool dim light of the garage Nephi wasn't sure he wanted to risk anything at all.

"I guess," he said.

Tyhee already had his head back under the hood of the El Camino. "Tell you what you do. Go on up to Pocatello and call this guy, Jimmy Little Soldier. He'll know how to get in touch with your mother's people. You find them and you find out as much about your family as you can. When you come back, let me know."

As Nephi turned to go, Tyhee said, "You drink booze?"

"I've been known to."

"Well, stop it."

—

Jimmy Little Soldier wasn't what Nephi expected. He dialed the number in Pocatello and got the smooth voice of a receptionist saying, "Burton, Raymond, Soldier, and Polk," and he said, pardon me, wrong number, hung up the phone, and dialed again. Same receptionist, same greeting.

"Ah, Jimmy Little Soldier," said Nephi.

"May I say who's calling, please?"

"Nephi Jones. Tell him John Tyhee told me to call."

"One moment."

76

Actually it was five minutes, Nephi standing in a phone booth on a busy street corner, wondering if someone came on the line would he even be able to hear them. But eventually a voice said, "What can I do for you?" So Nephi explained that he was trying to find Sarah Buoyer and the voice told him to hang on. He stood on the corner for another ten minutes before the voice got back on and said, "Sorry to keep you waiting. I don't know too many of those folks myself, had to get on the other line with a friend of mine who says your auntie is here in Pocatello. She works at the meat packing plant. You can find the phone number in the book. And listen, you remind Tyhee he still owes me some money." The voice on the end was gone quickly, leaving Nephi with a portal he wasn't sure he wanted to step through.

Ben woke up, slipped into raggedy sweats, and left his apartment. He walked about a mile to a small park, overgrown, not much used, stuck in a neighborhood of run-down houses and scruffy yards.

South Park Street bordered the overgrown mess, and he walked down a little path until he came to a quiet spot surrounded by cottonwood and pine, hidden from the street. Standing loose-limbed in the center of this secret place was a woman who may have been seventy or perhaps ninety. The seams of her face talked of decades' worth of living, but the message wasn't clear. There was a timelessness to her. And her body, clothed in white tunic and slacks, was not bent. She appeared strong.

She faced in profile to Ben, but when she heard him, she turned and smiled. Then she turned away, and they began a slow series of movements together, a dance of arms reaching and turning and legs stepping and kicking. Their movements were in such complete accord that Ben might have been her shadow. Arms going down and then up, seemingly weightless, turning slowly from the waist, torso straight but not rigid. The names of the shapes Ben made with his body moved through his mind: Stork Cools Its Wings, Green Dragon Darts Out from Water, Wave Hands Like Clouds, Snake Creeps Down, Turn and Hit the Tiger. The cool air of morning brushed him, and he felt the energy moving through him. He was aware of the woman, following her movements and yet moving in his own sure way. They spent forty minutes in this fashion, not speaking.

When they had stopped, the woman turned to him and smiled. "I'm happy to see you," she said.

"I've been extremely stupid," he replied.

She laughed at that, brightly, as though he were an appealing child. "Let's walk," she said and together they started down the path that led out to the street and back to the neighborhood nobody wanted to care for.

Ben described his trek up the mountain. When he was through, she said, "Observers of the Tao do not seek fulfillment. Not seeking fulfillment, they are not swayed by desire for change."

Ben said, "I've been trying to stay neutral, you know? But I'm struggling with it. I just want to get out of here sometimes. This place can be so deadening."

"Everything you push away clings to you. Stop pushing against your longing."

"You know, all these years, working in the bar, I thought it was good labor, good work. But it's some other damn thing, Felice. Thinking it keeps me humble is just crap. The fact that I'm thinking about humility means I'm miles and miles away from it."

"You think too much," she laughed at him a little. "It's charming, but it's also a waste of time."

They were now in front of a small house, immaculate in the surrounding dishevelment. The tiny yard had a garden of bright flowers tucked along the front of the house, which was painted white with gray trim. "Come inside and have some juice," she said.

They settled comfortably in chairs on her back porch overlooking an orderly vegetable garden not more than fifteen square feet. Heat had begun in earnest, and Ben was glad to be in the shade drinking apple juice and looking upon her tidy domain. He wondered again how old she was. But he knew asking was futile. Her bell-like laughter shimmered in the air whenever he brought it up. She had an ageless voice, neither young nor old. He tried to imagine the sound of her voice on the telephone. It couldn't be done. She owned no phone. Her name was Felice, and he envied and sought her wisdom and her power.

But at the moment, with the pungent aroma of growing things wafting back from her garden, he thought her serenity more valuable than anything else she possessed.

"I will tell you something you don't want to hear," she said. "You think I derive power from knowledge and from discipline. You think my strength comes from tai chi and that mastering tai chi, you will inherit these things. But it doesn't come from tai chi. I like to watch my hands in motion. I like the way my body feels. I infuse the tai chi with my energy, not vice versa. There are countless roads toward power: the yogi, the Zen monk, the Mormon housewife, even a banker, all make the same journey."

She drank a little juice and then tapped her chest. "But it starts in here," she said. "And then moves out. It doesn't come to you from the outside."

"I guess I have to stop grasping," he sighed.

"Have to?" she said heavily and laughed at him again. "You know," she said, "at one time in my life I preferred living in Manhattan. I didn't ask myself a lot of questions about it. I just lived there. Then came a time when I hated Manhattan with a passion, so I left. Back then I didn't like to be dirty. I didn't like the smell of my own sweat. I bathed twice a day and wore perfume. I didn't work in a garden, and I never got dirt under my fingernails. Now," she held up her calloused hands, "I'm not so fastidious. I'm not offended by my own odors. And I don't think too much about it."

"What are you telling me?" he said.

"I'm telling you there isn't any recipe for what you're doing. Fill out your skin. Live your life from the inside out, not the outside in. There's nothing more for you to 'get,' nothing better for you to be, no place for you to go. If you don't love the feel of tai chi, don't do it."

"I do love the feel of tai chi," he said fervently.

"Then don't worry so much."

Ben brought his mind to the sound of hot water filling the sinks below the bar, and he watched the steam from them rising around him. He felt the morning light tumble along the glasses that reflected sunbeams on the walls. The door was propped open, and a delivery man wheeled in cases of beer. He turned on the coffee machine and started a pot brewing.

Max came in.

The two men sized each other up, the way veterans do. Does the military glisten in the whites of their eyes? Some kind of aura? They didn't need to talk about it.

"Coffee?" said Ben.

"I was hoping for a beer," said Max.

"Not for another hour, yet."

"Coffee works," said Max. And when he had the mug of go-juice in front of him, he said, "So what can you tell me about Mormon country?"

"I don't know," said Ben. "What can I tell you?"

79

"General stuff, I suppose. Something. Couple of kids came to my door the other day and wanted to talk about eternity. I said, 'Eternity? Beg fucking pardon?' Then they wanted to know if I knew where I came from and I thought, hell, do I look that gone? So what's the deal?"

"Mormon missionaries," said Ben. "They do the rounds, trying to give you a comfy place in the Celestial Kingdom."

"Which is what, exactly?"

"Their version of heaven."

"Thoughtful of them," said Max. "So is it a cult or what?"

"I suppose that depends on how you define a cult," said Ben. "I think of Mormons as middle-of-the-road Christians. But I've been here a while so I'm used to it."

"Not a believer yourself?" Max asked him.

"In a way," said Ben, "I suppose I am. I believe in Mormons. Hell, I like them. They care. They're industrious. They want to do the right thing. They can get on your nerves. It's God and church twenty-four hours a day with them, which can get old. On the other hand, they don't go much for hell-fire and brimstone. In fact, the afterlife is a pretty good deal for them. They don't believe in hell, you see. They do believe in varying degrees of heaven, and the lowest level, the place where all the slime of the earth end up—murderers, child molesters, and whatnot—that place is so much more a paradise than the Earth itself, they like to say if a man could see it once, he'd kill himself to get there. And the heavenly levels just keep on getting better, the more righteous you are. When you reach the top, the place where all the best Mormons go, you become a god yourself, creating worlds, that sort of thing. Plus, that's the only place in the hereafter where anyone can have sex."

"Wow," said Max. "What a payoff for walking the straight and narrow."

"Very cool," said Ben.

"So what's the down side?"

Ben scratched his head a little. "I don't know that there is a down side, actually, except having to do what you're told. They've got a lot of rules. They don't drink tea or coffee or booze. They don't smoke cigarettes. They're pretty strict about sexuality. You can get your butt booted out of the church for fornicating with the wrong person. So it's all the standard Christian limitations, with a couple extras thrown in. On the other hand, they do like to have a good time. They're a pretty good party crowd for people who don't drink."

"What do they do in those temples?" asked Max. "I heard they have strange rituals."

"The rituals, I don't know about," said Ben. "They take oaths or something in there. One thing I do know, they're trying to baptize by proxy everybody who ever lived."

"Say again?" said Max.

"That's what all this genealogy they do is all about. They're trying to learn the names of everybody who ever lived all the way back to Adam, I guess. Because they believe that only people who have been baptized into the Mormon church can get into your higher levels of heaven. They don't want anybody left out on a technicality. So in the temple they have big pools where they do a lot of baptizing. Live people stand in for the dead ones."

"You mean everybody's going to end up in heaven?" said Max, warming right up to this heady idea.

"Not the highest levels, no. But they figure, get 'em all baptized and God can sort them out later."

"Wow."

"You said it."

"So what about Jessie?"

"What about her?"

"She told me she was a Mormon."

Ben chuckled. "Well, she is, born and bred. She took a philosophical detour a while back. But in some ways being born a Mormon is like being born Jewish. You might not go to the temple, but the heritage is imprinted on your psyche regardless of where you end up."

"Do they do confession, like the Catholics?" asked Max.

Ben scratched his head over that one. "I think they do forgiveness. But I don't know how it works, exactly. I don't think you're saved by grace like the fundamentalists. You have to do good. And somebody like Jessie, if her bishop got wind of her propensity for hopping in and out of bed with just anybody, they'd excommunicate her fornicating little butt right on out the door."

"Really? She doesn't seem too concerned about it," said Max.

"No," agreed Ben, "She doesn't. What you want to watch out for is, they will try to convert you. They think all the rest of the religions in the world are wrong, and it's their duty to make sure everybody gets a crack at the truth. That's why they have so many missionaries."

"Well, they do have good-looking women. That's one thing in their favor," said Max. "I was walking by a church up on campus last Sunday just as they were getting out ..." He let out a long appreciative whistle. "Lord, let me give thanks. You know, I like a heaven that everybody gets into. Especially since I don't think I'll be giving up beer anytime soon. Or sex for that matter. Hey, what about polygamy? Seems like I've heard something about that."

"Just out on the wild and wooly fringes," said Ben. "Mainstream Mormons quit that back at the turn of the century. No. It's against the law here, now. Which isn't to say it's not still done. But it's renegade Mormons."

"Renegade Mormons," repeated Max, liking the sound of it. At which point, Jessie walked in the door and into Max's arms who kissed her and said, "Ben says you have a propensity for hopping into bed with just anybody."

"Yeah," said Jessie, "well, Ben does have his little fantasies."

Twelve

The Mormon tabernacle became Jessie's sanctum. She hauled a blanket up to the small room, stashed it by day in a cupboard that was full of old hymn books, and took it out at night. Snuggled up on a chair, feet up on the window ledge, she looked out upon the darkness. She had never been able to count the gift of stillness among her attributes. Impulse tugged her through the welter of her days. Watching her was like watching the erratic flight of a butterfly—here and there and up and over to that flower and down and whoops! back that way and around and up and, hey, what's that over there? Introspection was not a by-product of this style of living. In fact, she had always thought introspection was for people who had no lives.

But when you're waiting for a crime to be perpetrated upon you, and you're damn sure you're not going to fall asleep, and the only thing you can do is sit and stare out a dark window into a dark alley, hoping some skulking figure will detach itself from the shadows so you can nail the SOB, there isn't much left but the playground of the mind.

The first night random thoughts tap-danced in her head. She found herself thinking about the lushness of sex with Max Logan, how hypnotized she felt by his attention to detail, thinking about this or that part of their lovemaking. Then it came to her that she needed to go grocery shopping; she was out of vegetables and getting bored with beans and rice as a steady diet. From that she jumped into thoughts about her mother, how her mother was a terrific cook, five food groups represented daily at her mother's table, and she wondered if she would ever live like that herself. Husband, kids, routine. And strange sensations swirled around her gut that at first she tried not to pay attention to and then she wondered what the feelings were and then she began to identify them. First one was fear. Fear? What's that doing down there? she said. Next one, even more surprising: regret. She fought that one a while. I have nothing, not a thing to regret. I've lived my life, not somebody else's, and I'm not sorry and I never will be sorry. Except an unmovable knot of something still lodged in her, regardless of denials.

Time to move on to other thoughts. Got to think about something else because this stuff is a bore. And then Nephi wanders into her mind and waves, and she smiles and recalls how they first met, that thing with the horse, and how Nephi's eyes were quiet and large and how he watched everything she did and said without comment. She thought how when they were around fourteen or so and stuck to each other like glue, she made it her responsibility to make him laugh. He had a good laugh, big and full, and whenever she heard it she felt like the world was worth inhabiting. Nephi's large brown eyes and his laughter were like anchors when she might have preferred to drift up into the clouds and not come down anymore.

And why, Jessie, would you like to drift into the clouds and not come down anymore? Don't want to go there, thanks. Don't want to visit that part of the past. Just want to visit the part of the past where Nephi loves me without regard for my status, my beliefs, my actions, or my looks. Just loves me. She recalled a time they were at an outdoor concert, sitting on the bank of a hill. She was in front of him. He had his legs stretched out around her, his arms wrapped around her waist, his face nestled in the curve of her neck. What were they? Maybe sixteen? Let's stop time here, thought Jessie. Let's just stay here in this moment where everything is wonderful and I love and feel loved and nothing else exists. She held the memory in her mind, turning it this way and that, as though it were encased in acrylic, two tiny people wrapped around each other and never moving from the embrace. But she couldn't keep her mind still, and soon she had moved on and it was to a scene she hadn't revisited in years, except of course, that it was lodged forever in her.

The trip to Elko.

No, I'm not looking at that, Jessie said to herself. I don't have to go there. It happened. It's over. No point in this revisiting, like it could make some sort of difference.

Suddenly she is in a Sunday school class. She is about eighteen or nineteen, in there with a bunch of other young adults and the topic is being morally clean. Jessie has ventured into the moral dirt, you could say. She has let Nephi's hands travel over her and let hers wander him. They have been on the journey together and have been amazed by the power in their own strong bodies. Jessie squirms in the folding metal chair because she knows she can't stop being with Nephi now that it has begun. The Sunday school teacher is saying that a woman's most important asset is her virtue. Those are the last words Jessie hears. She lifts out of her chair. A part of her beyond thought takes her out of the room and down a long hall and out the side door of the church into the haze of a low-slung December day.

Jessie hovers on the lip of this memory, willing herself to go farther into the feelings that crowd the nineteen-year-old shivering in the parking lot on a Sunday afternoon. *I am sick of the lies. I am sick of the masks. I am sick of myself listening quietly as though I believe it. When I know, when I have incontrovertible proof that it's all just a sham.*

It was the day she had walked out of the church in her heart and her soul, and had never gone back. It created terrible scenes between her and her parents—crying, screaming, slamming doors, the silent treatment. People tearing the hearts out of each other for the simple reason that Jessie would not say no to her physical body and refused to pretend that she would.

Awful memories. Let's get away from this stuff, Jessie said to herself in the dark small room of the Mormon tabernacle. Which was when she noticed that her mind had a lot of things it preferred not to dwell on. Like there were a bunch of rooms in her head she didn't want to go in.

What a strange thing, to be afraid to contemplate the past, to be afraid to look at the details that shaped your own life. It was like being afraid to look at your own naked body in the mirror. Jessie didn't like that at all.

Fear was bullshit. Never the thing to look at, always the thing to look beyond. She decided that as long as she was stuck waiting for something to happen, she would do a methodical journey through the course of her past. She would dredge up every memory she could, starting with her earliest childhood memories and moving steadily forward. She would look everything directly in the eye, fearing nothing.

Upon that thought, dawn said good morning to her. She hid away her blanket, sneaked out of the tabernacle, back to her home, and collapsed on the bed to sleep the sleep of someone preparing for battle.

Night two: Jessie discovered that you couldn't order your mind around in the way you did the rest of your body. What a strange organ, not at all subject to her will as, say, her feet. Tell your feet to walk and they don't start running on you. Tell your right arm to reach out so your hand can pick up a glass and your left hand doesn't shoot up and start scratching your head. Her limbs obeyed her. Her mind had other ideas. She told it to think back to the beginning, to bring up memories methodically, chronologically. First thing it does is jump into some rambling guilt thing about the fact that you never made it over to your parents' house today, as you had promised, to help your mother plan menus for an upcoming family reunion. And why hadn't you? Because after a night of sitting around waiting for somebody to steal from you, all you could manage was several hours of quiet snoring in a dark bedroom.

Hey, wait a second, the distant past is where this mind is headed, so let's get on with it. Jessie searched for her earliest memory and found a large table, a huge table with adults sitting around it and a noise like hammering and water running. And something blue, something blue in front of her that she wanted. And then Nephi crowded into the memory, and she wondered why she never knew he had an aunt and what he wanted to see her about. Back to the past, she ordered her mind, and off they went to a scene at Aunt Claire and Uncle Alden's house. She was drawing pictures with her cousin on a low table in the kitchen when they heard a terrific crash and then silence and then the sound of Aunt Claire's voice saying, "If you don't give it up, you will be barred forever from this home."

It was strange how, as she recalled this scene, a feeling of dread came up in her. As though she were still the five-year-old and she and her cousin Denny were even now not looking at each other, their shoulders hunched up around their ears and then Denny was pushing all the crayons off the table and pushing the paper away and then pushing his hands across the table sweeping, sweeping even though there was nothing there.

And the feeling of dread catapulted her straight over to Elko. She's twenty or so and driving to California where she'll catch a plane to Hawaii so she can be with Nephi. Dark bar, she's drinking tequila shooters, yanking on a one-armed bandit because she's never done it before. Feeling loose and silly, and a couple of guys come up on either side of her, and, before too much longer, she's in a car having sex with them. Just look at it, girl, don't yank your mind away. Get a good long look at it.

They hadn't forced her, hadn't coerced her. They'd been two horny guys, and she had jumped right into the middle of them without a single thought. Just gone and done it, naked groping around in a sweaty threesome that was noisy and funny until the instant it ended. And then it was ugly. Moral dirt. And they drove her to her motel and made sure she got into her room safe and sound. They both kissed her goodbye and wished her well and went off into the night, never to be seen again. And when morning broke on Jessie, she knew she couldn't go to Pearl Harbor because she was too disgusting to live. So she stayed in Elko and gambled and drank until Nephi and her frantic parents called out the state troopers to track her down.

When she told them she couldn't drag herself away from the blackjack table, they were so stunned by the immensity of her thoughtlessness that they treated her as badly as she figured she deserved to be treated. It went a long way toward making her feel better about herself.

But as she thought about it in the darkness of the Mormon tabernacle on night two of the angel vigil, she realized it didn't go all the way toward making her feel better about herself. And now, with this on the table, her list of crimes against Nephi mushroomed. And as each one poked up into her awareness, a new refrain began. What was I thinking? What in the sweet hell was I thinking? When I blew off the wedding, what was I thinking? When I came back to him after that one guy in Jackson Hole, what was I thinking? When I snatched Melody away from him, what was I thinking?

Complete emptiness in her head around this question. She could drum up all the memories she wanted to. She could feel the associated self-disgust. But when she asked why, the stillness of her thoughts, the dark hole of her thoughts on this question filled the cavern of the building where she hid.

She couldn't make sense of any of the stuff that had happened to her. It had all made sense at the time. She had wanted this one or that one. She hadn't wanted to be tied down. She had been afraid. She hadn't considered any of her actions, had just been out there doing, doing, doing, as though the motion of her life carried its meaning.

The recollecting stopped, and she rotated around the why, as though it were the Earth and she the moon, feeling its pull, but otherwise senseless. I need a net of meaning cast around my life to give it shape, to make it comprehensible, she said as dawn pushed her out of the tabernacle and off to bed, not a minute too soon.

She woke up much later to the phone ringing. And at first she didn't recognize the voice on the other end. A man's voice talking about a canyon and the heat and as she came into herself, the voice said, "I woke you, didn't I?"

And Jessie said, "Who is this?"

And the other voice said, "Max."

Round three of remorse. What in the sweet hell had she been thinking with regard to Max?

"I'll call you," she said and dragged herself up to sit on the edge of the bed. She cradled the telephone at her neck and punched in the office number of Uncle Alden. His voice came on the line annoyed and rushing.

"It's Jessie," she said. "I picked a bad time. I'll call you later."

"Call me at home," he said. "I'll be in a better mood."

She put the phone back down, showered, and walked out into the sweltering afternoon and down to the bar, where Ben presided over half a dozen people with nothing better to do than sit in the cool shadow of the day and drink.

She went into her small office, left the door ajar. Ben came and stood in the doorway. He didn't say anything, but she got the distinct impression that he was saying something. They held each other's gaze for several seconds. Jessie said, "What?"

"You tell me," said Ben.

She slouched back in her chair, "Oh, man. I feel like my head's going to explode. I've been thinking too much."

"Usually you come in here so wired, I get tired just looking at you. But you look like somebody pulled the plug on you and drained out all the energy."

"Who was it said the unexamined life is not worth living? The Marquis de Sade?"

Ben disappeared for a moment and Jessie leaned on the cluttered desk, propping her head on her hands.

"Dark night of the soul?" he said when he came back.

"Well, dark night of the mind, anyhow."

He came up behind her and started rubbing her shoulders with his short, thick fingers. His hands released the constrictions in her muscles. Something about his touch was relaxing and re-energizing. Her mind stilled itself under his ministrations. She let herself drift for several minutes, Ben kneading along her upper back, his fingers massaging her neck and shoulders. And then he stopped and, resting one hand on her shoulder, laid the other on her cheek, his palm cupping her face. This gesture started tears in Jessie's eyes.

After a moment he said, "What's going on with you?"

She shook off whatever tender feelings the sound of his voice evoked. "Oh, hell," she said and sniffed. "My head's just messing with me, you know?"

Ben didn't say anything, just ran his hands lightly through her short hair, patted her back, and then turned to leave her.

"Well, don't get lost in it," he said. "Keep checking back in with the rest of us."

She tried to assign some sort of meaning to her life. I was just trying to carve a place for myself that felt real, just trying to keep the bullshit from swallowing me, trying to find a place to be that didn't feel like lies. I was trying to keep them from stealing my life away.

Them? Them who?

She remembered the awkwardness of her teenage years, of choosing to rebel rather than conform, of being on the outside of teenage cliques and angry about it and hurt by it. Of wanting to be like everyone else and feeling like no one else at all. And after a while, she realized, she had embraced the fact of her differences, had made that her identity. How authentic was that, just reacting against everything?

But it wasn't just a knee-jerk thing, she told herself. Sitting in church and some twenty-year-old kid gets up and says he knows beyond a shadow of a doubt that Joseph Smith was a prophet of God with that shining, beatific look on his face and you know beyond a shadow of a doubt that he doesn't know dick. That it's going to be years and years and years before he knows, maybe if he's lucky, one tiny small burning ember of a thing beyond a shadow of a doubt. Kid's just toeing the line and that's how this whole edifice got built in the first place, on everybody else's say-so.

"I don't want them taking my life away from me," she muttered under her breath. "I'm not some damn parrot. I don't want people pointing at me and saying, 'See, she knows it's true. Therefore I also believe.' Maybe I'm some sort of blockhead. But I never knew anything beyond a shadow of a doubt in my life."

Ben poked his head in the door. "Are you talking to me?" he asked.

She shook her head and thought that for his age he was a pretty damned good looking guy.

She hovered around him the rest of the evening, helping serve people even though the bar was quiet, and he didn't need the assistance. She helped with the cleanup at night's end, and when they were done and Ben was emptying out the last of the coffee, which, as far as she could tell, was the only thing he ever drank, she went over and hugged him.

He let her, but she could feel him not respond, not lean into her or return it.

"I think I need someone to holler at me now and then," she said.

"Oh, yeah," he replied. "I'd have to agree."

He didn't give her time to embarrass herself further, but slipped out the door, cranked the Harley, and let her lock up by herself. She went out into the night, took a look at the tabernacle, the little window high up where her past was giving her a run for her money, and thought, I am not up for that tonight. On the other hand, she wasn't sleepy. A notch or two past midnight, what the hell. She cruised on by the old condo, where a light on was all the cue she needed, and she disappeared inside, looking for somebody to make it better.

Thirteen

A whispery quality to the way the wind slipped through Bridger Canyon and splayed its fingers out across the valley woke Jessie in the wee hours, fluttering at the curtain by the open window. Rapped around a pillow in a corner of the bed, Max's back to her, his breathing even, Jessie no longer recalled what had so disturbed her the previous night. What was there besides this? The sweetness of being near another human being. She reached over to where the fine hair along his neck curled toward his ear, and she ran her hand along it onto his shoulder, tracing the flow of muscle down his arm. He sighed in his sleep. She spooned herself against him, wrapped an arm around his waist, and breathed him into her. In a little-girl voice that only came out of her in the dead of night she said his name. And Max, surfacing from dreams, turned to face her, gathered her up, began to kiss her. With the tenderness of children, they caressed each other back to sleep.

At about that time a pickup, lights out, coasted into the alley. In front of the Tabernacle Bar it came to a stop. The driver got out, pulled an aluminum ladder from the back of the truck, set it up below the angel, climbed up, and by feel unscrewed the angel's base from the bracket. The statue was heavy and as it came loose from the mount toppled. The thief grappled to steady it but couldn't, and the angel bounced away from his hands, crashing through the plate glass of the bar window. He scrambled down the ladder and tossed it in the truck. Pulling the angel from the broken glass, he climbed into the cab and sped away.

Later Jessie's rage reverberated inside the empty bar in the form of a hoarse, frustrated growl, prompting an angry wave from Ben who was on the phone calling glass companies. She went to the storeroom for a broom and began sweeping up the mess. When she heard Ben get on the phone to the police, she almost stopped him, then reconsidered. When he was done, she got on the horn to Pocatello. One last angel in stock, unless she cared to order some more. No, thank you, but you better keep the one you've got because I'm coming to get it and this one will not disappear before I know the sorry son of a bitch who's ripping me off.

She piled into the Land Cruiser and headed north, a drive she had never enjoyed and which she did now with her tape deck blaring songs of revenge. Somebody would pay. Jessie swore vigilance, even if it meant being alone with nothing to steer her clear of the shoals of her mind. She picked up the angel. She turned back for Bridger. She wondered where Nephi might be. She wondered why she cared, since she had the fabulously accommodating Max. And then she wondered why she ought to limit herself to only one of them. Who made up the monogamy rules, anyway? Men. Except when it inconvenienced them. Then they made up the polygamy rules. Jessie let her anger run that riff for a while: men, the enemy. Whole damn planet's screwed because of the stupid patriarchal system. Put women in charge and you'd see a whole different playing field, by god. Well, nobody's in charge of me and if I want to have the two of them, then I damn well will. A small point being made at the back of her mind that she hadn't tolerated sharing Nephi with Melody, even while she happily dallied with Max, well, she thrust that thought as far away as she could.

It wouldn't hurt to call Nephi, let him know she was thinking about him. See what he was up to. But it turned out that it did hurt. When he answered the phone that evening, he just said no. No, sorry, can't do it no more Jessie. You're too out of control for me. I'm done being at your beck and call. Really. No. Sorry.

It was like a speech he'd rehearsed. She thought about it all night and she thought about it in the morning while she searched in the phone book for a welder, and she continued thinking about it as the welder came over to wed the angel's feet to the bracket for time if not eternity. When she was ready to let the issue of Nephi's rejection drop, her mind said, excuse me, but we aren't done pummeling this into the ground, yet, and so it kept up a steady background chatter as she paid the welder and went out to take a good look at his work. The thieves would have to expend a lot more effort if they wanted this angel.

While she stood there, her brother drove up with Melody at his side. They parked and came over to her, Daniel staring up at the angel and down at his sister.

She watched him convey several angry sentiments in the form of eyebrows coming together, deep furrows in the forehead, and lips working at the classic thin line. You could have drawn those lips, thought Jessie, with a single straight gash from a No. 5 pencil. Dear, dear, dear.

Melody waited for greetings from either party. None arrived. "What we came here for is to tell you that I'm getting baptized next week, and we wanted you to come," she said when she realized she might be the only party capable of speech.

"Getting baptized? Getting baptized?" Jessie said and noticed how Daniel's arm came up protectively around Melody's shoulders as she said it.

"Oh, yeah, I'd love to come," she said. Daniel glared at her more, if that was possible, and Melody looked from one to the other wondering what pieces of the conversation were getting past her.

"Also," she said a little timidly, then looked at Daniel, "should we tell her the rest?"

"Well, of course you should tell me the rest," said Jessie. "Don't be coy. Out with it."

Melody thrust out her left hand. On it glowed a largish diamond. "We're getting married!"

It was not the sort of announcement that should evoke, from the prospective sister-in-law, a wrenching in the gut. Jessie yanked on the only smile she could muster—a phony one—and hugged them both, muttering congratulations as though it were an epithet. Daniel had the presence of mind to recall some other place they had to be and off they went.

She banged into the Tabernacle and slugged down a beer and then another one and got up to get herself a third, but Ben intervened and took her glass away from her, saying, "Talk to me."

"I don't know, Ben. I don't know. I just don't know. You know what I'm saying? I'm sitting here and I don't have a damned clue."

"Well," he said. "It's a start."

Fourteen

Jessie sat with her uncle on her grandfather's front porch in the early evening, the sound of crickets sifting the air around them. She relayed the news of Melody's enlightenment, but her uncle had already heard.

"I feel like I ought to warn her what she's getting into," said Jessie. "I feel like I owe her that."

"You owe her something?"

"If it hadn't been for me, she'd be smoking dope and riding horses with Nephi right now instead of pondering eternity in the bosom of the church," said Jessie.

"And what exactly would you warn her about?" Alden asked.

She glared at him. "You know what I'm talking about. You live with it every day."

"No, Jessie, I don't know what you're talking about. You seem to think I exist in some sort of private hell, coping with the religious fanaticism of my wife and kids. But Claire and I made peace over our differences a long time ago. I have a lot of respect for her and for the church. I just disagree with its politics."

"And what about all the lies it's founded on? What about that? What about its grandiosity and its hypocrisy? What about the murders? How can you sit there and tell me you have no feelings about this when you were the one who showed me how systematically the church has erased from its records the truth of its origins? We're talking about an organization founded by a guy who probably lied about his visions, who lied about his writing, and who manipulated other people into doing his dirty work. We're talking about a guy who couldn't keep it right at home, so he invents polygamy to cover himself. I mean, he hands down the Word of Wisdom to his followers but himself goes around drinking booze, with an old stogie hanging out of his mouth. Then you've got these children, your children, growing up swallowing this moonshine about his being a prophet of God. And you're telling me you're OK with that?"

"I'm telling you I made my peace with it," he replied.

"Oh, yeah? And how did you do that?"

"I judge the church by its works in the present. The past is over and done. And, by the way, where is it written that a prophet is perfect? Consider this, Jessie. Suppose he did all the things you accuse him of AND all the things he claims he did. Suppose he was randy as hell AND still had visions?"

"No way. It's an all or nothing deal."

"And where did you come up with that rule?"

"Hey, that's the church's take on this stuff, not mine," she said. "They're the ones who insist it's all true or none of it is. Then they go around hiding historical documents that don't fit the image they want to project. Why do they hide stuff if they've got nothing to hide?"

"The past is over and done with," said Alden. "Is the church practicing polygamy now? No. Are its teachings good Christian doctrine? Yes. Is it damaging my wife and children in any way? No. Do they seem happy? Yes. Maybe it is founded on lies. You and I weren't there. We can't know and everything else is just hearsay. Anyway, I prefer to think of them as myths. The past is over and the present seems entirely reasonable to me."

"That's like arguing that it's OK to be a neo-Nazi because they aren't gassing Jews this year."

Alden sighed. He put his head in his hands. "That's a ludicrous comparison and you know it."

"And those lies you prefer to think of as myths? Some of them killed people. What about the Danites? What about Porter fucking Rockwell? I mean the guy was practically a paid assassin. And don't get me started on Brigham Young. Wasn't he the one who came up with that fine concept 'blood atonement'? Some sins are so heinous that even Christ's sacrifice can't save you? So, excuse us, but for your own good we're going to have to kill you. Trust us, you'll thank us later, once you're dead."

Jessie rocked the wicker chair back as she spoke until it was braced on its back legs, leaning against the wall. "But, hey, I wouldn't mind all that. I could tolerate all that, no problem except for the lengths the church goes to, to hide it all, and to make you feel guilty for being just like them. Why should I feel guilty for drinking when Joseph Smith ran a bar in Nauvoo? Why should I feel guilty about smoking when church leaders used to turn the insides of the temple into a giant fog of tobacco smoke?"

"You don't smoke," said Alden.

"It's the principle of the thing I'm addressing here. And I'm damned if I should see why I have to feel bad about my sexuality, when Brigham Young was knocking up women half his age all over the state, and picking and choosing which of his pals could indulge in the same privilege and, for that matter, shooting down in cold blood anybody who got in a little extra-curricular nookie without his permission.

"I hate all the holier-than-thou hypocrisy. I mean I really hate it. And it's not like it was only those early Mormons who couldn't follow the rules they prescribed for everybody else. It's all around you right now. People doing the righteous routine in church and then, hell, some of them don't even wait to get out of the church to get their rocks off."

"What are you talking about?" Alden said.

"I was eleven, OK? Eleven damn years old. What do I know about sex? And I go running into the church real early one Sunday morning to get one of the children's hymn books so we can practice these songs at home, and I pulled open the store room door and there's my Sunday school teacher, my damn Sunday school teacher, and the bishop with their clothes every which way in this giant clinch. I mean, Jesus, Alden, like couldn't they just have gotten a motel room or something?"

"You're kidding."

"Yeah, right. Big joke."

"What did you do?"

"What do you mean, what did I do? I didn't do anything. What would I have done?"

"Did you tell anybody?"

"No, I didn't tell anybody."

"Why not?"

"Because who was I going to tell? My mother? 'Hey, Mom, I just saw the bishop wrestling Sister Sorenson out of her Sunday best.' She would have slapped me."

"Did they do anything? Did they say anything to you?"

"Not a word. Not a single solitary word. Although she never taught my Sunday school class again. And I don't recall the bishop ever looking me in the eyes again. Not that I ever gave him the opportunity."

"Why didn't you tell me about it, or Aunt Claire? As I recall, in those days, you practically lived at our house."

"Because," Jessie said in exasperation, as though explaining something to a child. "I didn't understand what I had seen right away. I didn't really get what sex was then, although I figured it out pretty fast. But by then it was SEX, you know. It was this yucky thing. I wasn't going to bring it up."

Alden didn't say anything else for a while and neither did Jessie. She'd never told anyone the story before and thinking about it now made her feel weird inside as though nineteen years of shellacking over the memory had been stripped away.

Alden was shaking his head, shoulders slumped a little forward as though he had become tired of the world.

Jessie shrugged off the memory and said, "So you can see what I'm saying about Melody? About wanting to show her the other side of her shiny new coin?"

"But how do you think a conversation like that would go?" said Alden. "You say, 'Excuse me, honey, but everything my brother here has been telling you is a total crock.' Do you think she'll believe you? If you feel guilty because you introduced her to it, then feel guilty. But give it up. Once people get the fire for this religion, there's no turning them back. They've had a spiritual awakening, and nothing will sway them. The facts have nothing to do with it. And do you think Daniel will sit there idly while you go stomping all over her new-found convictions? No. Then the two of you will go to war over her soul, and I can't believe you've forgotten how ugly that can get."

"So I get out of the way even though I know the truth?"

"Tell me something, Jessie. That kid in the accident that Daniel saved. What do you think happened? Everybody there said it was a miracle, that Daniel brought him back to life with a blessing. What do you think?"

"I don't know, Alden. I just don't know. The kid was dead. Then the kid was alive. Maybe it was the CPR, you know? Maybe the blessing didn't have anything to do with it."

"I remember how the three of you looked when you walked in the door from that accident. You were all high. You, too, Jessie, don't try to deny it. At the time you were looking at Daniel like he was the king of heaven."

"Well, maybe he was the king of heaven. Maybe he did save the boy. But, if so, it's because of who he is, not because Joseph Smith founded something better than any of the other Christian denominations."

"That's my point. It's not keeping people from spiritual development. Miracles do happen, even to Mormons."

"I just get crazy thinking that I pushed her into it," said Jessie.

"So this is about you, not about her at all. You don't like the way it's making you feel. Why is that?"

She got up out of the chair and went to sit on the steps. "Yeah, I don't like it. But what's your point?"

"I'm suggesting you look at why Melody's decision matters so much to you."

"And?"

"Maybe her decision rocks your faith in the choices that you made. Maybe you wonder if she sees something you missed."

"No. Uh uh. That's not it at all. You're totally wrong on that line of thinking."

"I think I was wrong once before in my life. So I suppose there's a precedent for it," her dear sainted uncle said and laughed. "I gotta run." He came to her and put his arms around her in the famous Uncle Alden hug that no family member could resist. "Listen, I'm sorry you had to see your bishop and your Sunday school teacher in, what shall we call it? Flagrante delicto? I wish you could have grown up with more illusions intact. But maybe the naked truth is better in the long run. Who knows?"

"Who, indeed."

"There's a case to be made for doing something simply because you want to," he said. "Simply because there's something in here," he pointed at his chest, "telling you that's what you have to do, regardless of how it appears to others, or what the facts might be. Trust it. That's my philosophy. You trust your insides and let Melody trust hers."

"Yeah, just one big happy accepting family. Would you please go have this conversation with my parents?"

"Hey, you're a grownup."

The small, dark room in the Mormon tabernacle waited for Jessie. She didn't want to go. No point going up there when you know you'll be ambushed by your own head. On the other hand, being the victim of vandalism and theft overrode the reluctant self trying to wimp out on her. Jessie—with that feeling she recalled so well from childhood, when her mother wanted her to complete an odious task, the dishes, or taking out the garbage, or cleaning the mess out from underneath her bed—stuck her lower lip out and felt sorry for herself being forced to do something she would much rather not. Dragging up the curving staircase and down the long balcony behind the pews, up the three stairs over to the narrow door, opened and shut and inside sitting on the broad windowsill, looking out at the placid valley . . . Jessie what is happening to your life?

I'm reduced to pouting because I don't want the past, she explained to herself. Don't want to go there, thanks. But she could only focus on the pout for so long before the thing that she had successfully not thought about for so many years crowded its way front and center. What did it mean to be eleven years old and a witness to adultery?

When you are eleven, you are eager and bright, open to the world and curious, with a brand new bunch of reasoning capabilities that you try out on everything. On the cusp of childhood and adolescence, teetering between one and the other, you have no dark thoughts and no fears. You take the world at face value. You see your bishop as a wise, kind man, someone your parents look up to. Your Sunday school teacher makes you laugh, and she knows how to tell a story. She makes Bible characters come alive, backs up their stories with twentieth-century sentiments. She fills in the gaps, so you imagine Joseph with his coat of many colors to be a lot like this one kid in your school who brags and makes the other kids mad. Jonah doesn't like anything, even being successful, and yells back at God. Jesus hangs out with ordinary folks like you and me. Unlike most adults, he prefers the company of children and you like that about him. In fact, you prefer stories of Jesus to anything else except Nancy Drew mysteries. Your Sunday school teacher is beautiful and young and you want to grow up and be like her with her stylish dresses and her perfect hair and her confidence and her wisdom.

And one sunny Sunday morning the shape of the world shifts on a chance encounter that lasts a few seconds. The look of surprise on their faces, the scramble to order disordered clothing as you close the door and run back outside and run and run, scuffing your black patent leather shoes, tripping and falling, skinning your knee and ruining the white tights your mother has just bought you. You run through the neighborhood, the neat brick homes with their emerald lawns and bright flowers, the trees all bending west, trained that way by the wind. You run to the school yard and climb on a swing and ride it up to the sky and back to the earth, pumping hard with your stubby eleven-year-old legs.

The first thing you think of is that the stories are true, the muttered stories of how babies get made that have repulsed you and your girlfriends ... oh, how dreadful. They're true. This is the focus of your thoughts on a Sunday morning, and for the first time in your life you play truant. You do not go home and you do not go back to church. You stay at the school yard most of the day. And when you tire of the swings and the monkey bars, you climb a tree (black patent leather shoes now ruined, tights tattered) and stay high up in its sighing branches. It is late in the afternoon when you walk in through the front door of the house and your mother, half annoyed, half relieved, makes an angry fuss over the state of your Sunday best. You are scolded for missing church, even the bishop has asked about you, and you can see that your mother is embarrassed by this. When you run into the bathroom and throw up, your mother calms down and puts you to bed and you acquiesce (which worries your mother even more).

As the weeks go by, certain other things become clear. You have never understood what the word "adultery" means, something about being grownup, you had thought. Now you know. In the hierarchy of sins—you've heard this explained so many times—the only thing worse than adultery is murder. Your Sunday school teacher has disappeared from church, moved away, you are told. But the bishop is there, sitting at the front of the church every Sunday, addressing people in the same manner as before from the pulpit. Now you have a word to associate with the bishop, the word for the second-worst sin in the world.

You stop looking at men's faces in church and start noticing that central mysterious point on their bodies. You stop hearing anything. That lasts for months, that white noise of your own mind blocking out the sounds around you. And then, one day when you are twelve, when you discover one morning your pants stained with blood, your mother explains to you that you are a woman now. Your ears open up again.

Except that now you don't believe anything you hear.

So lost in this memory had Jessie become, she didn't notice the truck that pulled into the alley below her. It was only with the faint slam of the door that she flashed back into the present.

Below her the two occupants staggered over to the doorway of the bar and proceeded to unzip, flip out their units, and piss away a few moments of the night.

"Damn Basques," she muttered and raced through the dark building, down the stairs, and outside. By the time she hit the street, the truck had disappeared. All that remained was the tang of urine in the air. Gone, and a good thing, too, she realized. Because what would she have done? Scolded them? It came to her that knowing who was harassing her and having the wherewithal to respond were two different things.

It was time for weapons.

Ben refused to help her, despite his revulsion at the Basques' calling card. No amount of cajoling could convince him to help her buy a gun. "No guns," he said. "No clubs, no knives, no nothing. Nothing matters that much."

"But Ben, it's like we're under siege, here. Theft, vandalism, we have a right to defend ourselves."

She had been yelling this at him from her chair in the office and was surprised when he came in, grabbed the arms of the chair, and leaned over her. "Jessie, we are not anything. You, however, are thriving on a series of small crises of your own design. I don't care how you deal with it, but if you bring any weapons in, I'm gone."

"Big goddamn war hero, huh?" she said and then regretted it. But Ben just walked away. She called Max.

Max refused to help her buy a gun. "Sorry, Angel. I don't do guns," he said.

"What in the sweet hell is wrong with you? This is America. Everybody does guns."

"Listen, I had my finger on the trigger of one of Uncle Sam's larger weapons for eight years. Tell me something I don't know."

Jessie protested, but Max interrupted her. "I'll buy you flowers, candy, alcohol, sexy lingerie. Hell, Jessie, I'll help you pick out household appliances, curtains for your bedroom, dishes, art, wallpaper, if you want me to. But I'm not going on any gun-buying expeditions."

Nephi just hung up on her when he heard the sound of her voice.

Ben came back into the office and sat on the edge of the desk. "Jessie," he said, "guns blow holes in people. Then their insides come out. You never had to listen to someone drowning in their own blood. You never had to watch someone's face disappear in front of your eyes. Is that the kind of thing you want to see just because somebody runs off with a statue?"

"I don't want to kill them," she said. "I just want them to stop bugging me."

"Then stopped being bugged."

"Oh, yeah, Mr. Zen-head? Listen, I've got the right ..."

But Ben just walked out on her, right out through the bar door like he might not come back.

Fifteen

Another lonely night in the tabernacle, and another and another and another. Contemplation shot huge holes in Jessie Cannon's life theories. Up until now she had painted her past as a drama of independence and courage. She had refused to go to college, not because she was uninterested but because college had been expected. Everybody in her family went. She had gone instead to a real estate office to answer phones. She had refused to marry, had refused even to date the various young Mormons her aunts and her mother had tried over the years to pair her up with. She had even refused Nephi, horrified at the thought of doors closing on her, choices being curtailed. She thought that by marrying Nephi she might come to owe him something. The implicit obligation unnerved her. She ran in the other direction.

She had built her sense of worth on the shock value of her choices. I didn't do anything because I would like it, she said to herself in the dark. I did things because *they* wouldn't. The structure of her life, cantilevered out now over this broad canyon of speculation, appeared flimsy and chaotic. It's like I got born in a spider web, she said to herself, and I've spent my life trying to get unraveled from it. But no, that implied a specific goal, and Jessie had to acknowledge her own thoughtlessness. Just blown about by the wind of my own anger, she said to herself. She had no allegiance to ideas or to people. She knew one direction: away.

What struck her in the unwelcome glare of all this thinking (too damn much thinking) was how everything came back to rest on a single point in time. You could trace all the threads of her rebellion—which is to say most everything she did—to that moment in the church. Other people get epiphanies in church, she mused. I got sex education. Jessie was on the brink of her own epiphany that night in the tabernacle. Hovering just outside her awareness, this thought: Do I want someone else's adultery to be the defining moment of my life? But a truck pulling up and coming to a stop in front of the bar, no lights on, interrupted her before she got to it.

She grabbed the baseball bat she'd been hauling around with her and high-tailed it down the stairs, out the door, over the lawn, across the street, and into the alley as quietly as she could make her shaky feet and wildly beating heart go.

There was only one person in the alley. He had a ladder out and was climbing it. She stopped in the middle of the road, stared, and then backtracked around the corner. She recognized the blue Ford pickup with the oversized tires. She recognized the body going up the ladder. It took her a few seconds to catch her breath. Some surprises in life are a whole lot bigger than other ones.

A baseball bat was not the appropriate weapon. She slipped farther down the street and around the block, picked up the receiver of a pay phone, dialed 911, and got the police on the line. This thief deserved public humiliation.

She didn't stick around for the denouement. She went home. The thing was done. She would not have to spend her nights alone and wandering mental byways. "I win," she said to herself. Odd, though, how the triumph of her vigilance did not yield self-congratulations, which she had expected, but rather a blankness, which she had not. Suddenly she wanted a bath, hot and steamy and soothing. She started hot water in the tub. Her phone rang. She looked at the clock. It was 3 a.m. She picked up the phone and her brother's angry voice sputtered in her ear.

"I beg your pardon?" Jessie said into the phone. "You're ripping me off and you want me to come down there and bail you out? You must be kidding."

"I'm not going to call Dad about this," said Daniel. "His head would explode."

"Well, call Melody, then. Call Uncle Alden. Call your bishop or home teachers or somebody. I don't know. But I'm not getting you out of jail." She hung up on him and went back to her bath, sinking into the tubful of hot water and wondering at the head noise. Oughta be happy, but I feel guilty. He's breaking the law, so why do I feel like I'm the one in trouble?

She felt that way because she wasn't stupid, and in the course of about twenty-four hours she was in big trouble, her phone ringing off the hook with calls from outraged family members. Aunt Chloe: Was she out of her mind? Uncle Frank grabbing the phone away from Chloe: What had she expected, that people would just roll over and play dead like they didn't care? Cousin Raylene: I saw your mother this morning and she is sick, *sick* over this. Uncle David: I'll be defending

Daniel against the charges and I advise you to get a better lawyer because I'll just walk all over Marianne on this one, you bet your sweet life I will. Cousin Hyrum: Don't think it's over, just because you caught up with Daniel. There's a lot of other people in town ready to take up where he left off. Cousin Denny: Can't you, like, just let it drop, just back off?

Jessie tried to shrug it off. Sheesh! Don't these people have lives? But she noticed among the various phone calls that her parents were maintaining a conspicuous silence. And that rang all kinds of warning bells in her head.

The uproar made page one news in the *Bee,* with officious reporters calling her up to get a comment she refused to give. She was about the only person in town who wasn't commenting. Lots of family members, townsfolk, and bar patrons were more than happy to comment at length. And when the Associated Press picked up the story, and it made the Salt Lake City papers, her father finally checked in. He employed one of his tones from the past, one she had never been fond of: the wounded parent voice. It was time, he said, for a family conference.

The dreaded family conference, thought Jessie, her father's favorite ruse. He invited consensus decision-making, but when they had all expressed their preferences he ruled in his own favor. It was his prerogative as the priesthood-wielding Mormon male. Her mother had stopped having preferences years ago. She would not let herself be drawn. She listened and agreed. Jessie had stopped attending family conferences when she moved out of the house.

Family conference with a wounded parent, she thought. Could be dangerous. Better not back him into a corner. But on second thought that ship might already have sailed. On the drive to the house, she took consolation from the fact that the bar had become more popular with the news coverage. People from Salt Lake had even driven up to see what all the fuss was about and to check out her angel. People began standing underneath it and having their pictures taken.

But the profit angle didn't do much for her as she sat in her parents' living room, her mother not looking at her, her father looking at her with more intensity than she liked, her brother staring alternately at his hands and his father, with occasional side glances her way.

"Do you mean to sit here in this house and tell me you will not drop the charges?" said her father.

"You know, Dad, this is a conversation I should be having with

Danny. But no, I'm not going to drop the charges. What he did is illegal."

"What about what you did?" said her mother.

"I didn't break any laws," said Jessie.

"No, just a few hearts," her mother said and looked away.

Jessie let that slide. "Look, you can't go around breaking laws just because you don't like someone else's point of view."

"Jessie, I won't have my kids dragging private family business into a public courtroom."

"And how will you stop it, Dad, exactly?"

Her father stared at her, stared her down in a fashion that had worked well for him until she was around sixteen, but she didn't think he had noticed the decline in its efficacy.

"I'm asking you to show respect for the things that we hold sacred in this family. I'm asking you to remember that in this house we consider Joseph Smith a prophet of the most high God. The angel Moroni is not a personage deserving of mockery. If you can't find it in you to respect our beliefs, perhaps you don't really care to be a member of this family."

Perhaps he was right, she thought. Perhaps it was so. She looked at her mother and couldn't decipher the meaning in her mother's eyes. And because something in her was feeling hard and mean, she said, "If you want to pay homage to that two-bit con man, fine." She was facing her mother as she said this and didn't see her father get up and cross the room or the flash of his palm until it was coming away from her face.

The sound of the blow stunned them all. Jessie's eyes went wide; Daniel sprang forward as if to intercede but on whose behalf it wasn't clear. Her mother got up slowly from her chair and left the room.

Jessie blinked the smart away as the outline of her father's hand reddened on her cheek.

"You are killing your mother," he said and left.

She and Daniel looked at each other.

"Do you get some kind of pleasure from these scenes?" he said.

"Yeah, it's a real thrill for me," she said. It seemed like a good time to go. She left the big house with its curving driveway and orderly yard. The world turned on and on. She was another small piece of its flotsam, wandering out into the night, getting into her vehicle, pushing in the clutch, turning the key, shifting into reverse, backing down the driveway, and heading out into the rest of the world. Jessie wondered where she might go if she could go anywhere and what she might do if she could do anything. No answer came to her.

She stopped at a phone booth and called Nephi, but Nephi did not answer his phone. She drove to the condo, but the parking space where Max's sleek machine should be was empty. She drove home, to her grandfather's home, where she had squatter's rights. She parked the Land Cruiser but couldn't bear to go inside. More silent disapproval lurked there, something that emanated off the walls with their pictures of temples, crocheted samplers in the kitchen extolling biblical virtues, pictures of various family members being married, baptized, sent off on missions—the old wall of glory.

She walked away from the house eastward, up the long street, and into the wind that might have chilled her if she'd noticed. She walked, disconnected from sensations, wondering why, with the whole big wide interesting world to choose from, she couldn't think of a good place to go. She walked and walked. It was a moonless night. Perhaps the dim light from a small hill beckoned her. She found herself standing in front of the Mormon temple where it overlooked a quiet neighborhood with a benign if somewhat pricey electric glow. When Jessie was a child, you could roam the grounds of the temple. She had thought it was a big park. Times had changed, an iron fence surrounded it now. She put her hands on the cool metal and leaned her face against one of the tall, thin tines.

The temple looked inviting. It looked like it knew its business. The elegant lines of its stone towers gave off a serenity, a grace. Jessie had never been a good enough Mormon to be permitted inside. She stared at it now until it lost its sharp outlines and swam glowing in front of her. A certain dampness at the corner of her eyes turned the already soft outlines watery. Goddamnit, anyhow.

She walked back to the house, let herself in, and without turning on any lights made her way down into the basement where she stretched out on an old, overstuffed sofa, pulling a faded afghan around her and wondering about the image that kept inserting itself before her eyes. She was small, she had no idea what age. Old enough to be printing large, irregular letters in a notebook, making capital B's over and over again. She was concentrating on making the curves smooth and uniform, yellow pencil gripped in her left hand. She could hear her parents talking in another room. They were not using their happy voices. They were using their tight, stern voices, getting quieter and quieter. She got up from her small table and went into the hallway.

The voices came from her parents' room. The door was open. She went toward the sound, and when she looked into the room, her father was gripping her mother's shoulders and shaking her. Their faces were both quite red. She must have made a noise standing there, although she had not been conscious of it, because her father and mother turned to her. Her father's hands dropped to his sides. He had left the room, brushing past her as though she were the potted plant in the front hall. And her mother had taken Jessie onto her lap and rocked and talked quietly on the bed. The memory carried Jessie into a haven of dreams.

Sixteen

Sarah Buoyer sat across from Nephi in the dim cafe on the outskirts of Pocatello drinking iced tea. Nephi looked for a resemblance between her and the pictures of his mother, but other than their dark eyes he couldn't detect any. His mother had high cheekbones in a long, narrow face; his aunt's face was rounded and full. Not the beauty that his mother was, she had an air, something in the way she held her shoulders, in the way her black hair swept back from her face to be clasped loosely at the nape of her neck, that he found compelling. It had taken Nephi some time to work up his courage to call her. He hadn't been able to do it on his first run up to Pocatello. Even on this drive he'd almost stopped the truck and gone back. On the phone his aunt hadn't sounded enthusiastic about meeting him. The ground under his feet felt soft and unreliable.

"What do you want to know?" asked Sarah.

Her voice sounded neutral and something in it made Nephi defensive. He tried not to show it. "Just anything about my mother. What she was like when she was little. What kind of person she was." Nephi didn't notice that he was referring to his mother in the past tense, something he had never done before.

"Wanda was mostly angry," said Sarah. She didn't look at Nephi as she spoke; she stared at the window. He couldn't tell if her reflection in the glass held her attention or if she watched the traffic outside. She spoke slowly, as if words had to form little pools in her mind before she'd let any of them flow out.

"She was six years younger than me. I remember, when she was born, they couldn't get her to stop screaming. My mother had a difficult labor. They had a hard time stopping the bleeding, and she didn't really pay much attention to the baby. She was in a lot of pain. She was trying hard not to die. My father couldn't stand to be near Wanda. There was something, like he resented her giving my mother so much trouble. So they gave me the baby to feed and clean. It was a hard time. We didn't have a lot of food that winter. I think we ate a lot of bread and potatoes. Wanda would scream all night. I would try to feed her formula in a bottle, and if she would be quiet for fifteen minutes or half an hour, I was lucky. Then the house would be calm. Then Wanda would start to scream again, and sometimes my father would send me out with her to the shed in the back of the house so my mother could sleep.

"We had a little spot I made with blankets and hay, like a nest, and we'd go in there and sleep and sometimes Wanda would settle down for even two or three hours before she would wake up and start again. I don't remember how long it went on. It seems like that's all I remember from being six years old. But I know that it couldn't really have lasted more than a month or two. Because then two of my aunties came and took Wanda away, and she stayed with them until she was about three years old. Then she came back to us.

"She was more quiet then. But our house wasn't quiet anymore. My father was drinking. And by this time Ephraim and Leon—my brothers—were teenagers and they were drinking, too. So it was loud and angry in that house. Wanda would stay in a corner and play with small rocks; she would move them around. That's what she liked, little colored stones. We had more money then. Mom worked in the reservation store. And my father had horses; sometimes he'd sell them, and sometimes he broke horses for ranchers around Pocatello. We were well off for reservation people. We weren't starving.

"My father was older. He remembered being brought to the reservation. The first year he says his parents died of grief."

"How did your father die?" interrupted Nephi. It hadn't quite penetrated that he was talking about his own grandfather.

"He was murdered," said Sarah. She might as well have said he died of old age for all the emphasis she put on it. "Three whites tried to steal his horses, and he wouldn't get out of their way. They trampled him down and beat him to death."

Sarah stopped talking and Nephi didn't look at her. Flies buzzed around them, making dashes at the small drops of iced tea on the yellow Formica. Street traffic filled his head with sound.

"Wanda saw it," she continued. "She saw who did it. She told the reservation police, and they told the police in Pocatello. But no one believed her. There was no trial. That's when my mother started drinking."

"What about your brothers?" said Nephi.

"They left pretty soon after that. They went down to Reno. I hear from them now and then. They run a car wash. They're doing pretty good, got a good business."

"Did you ever see my mother after she left us?"

"When did she leave you?"

"1960."

Sarah was quiet for a few minutes. "Last time I heard from Wanda was 1961. She said she was fine, not to worry about her. That she was going to make everything right. I thought the way she was talking that she was drinking, so I told her I didn't want to talk to her like that and she hung up and she never called again."

"How did she meet my father?" asked Nephi.

Sarah smiled. "Oh, your dad was one handsome guy, just up from Salt Lake City trying to preach the gospel to us heathens. Wanda thought he was so beautiful, she couldn't stay away from him. She was only sixteen at the time. She hung on every word that came out of his mouth. He came back here after his mission was over and took her away. Married her quickly. I only saw her once after she married him. Right after you were born. You were such a good baby." Sarah laughed when she said this, "Not like your mother at all." She drank some more of her iced tea and looked out the window again. "I stayed with her in Bridger while your dad went off on some trip to Salt Lake City. I remember how you didn't hardly cry at anything. Even when you were hungry, you'd just pull at a corner of your blanket and suck on it."

She looked at him now, carefully, as though she were seeing him for the first time since they'd sat down at the restaurant. "You've got her hair and her eyes. But the rest of you is like your dad."

"How come she never talked about you? Why didn't she ever bring me up here?" asked Nephi.

"Her marrying a white about killed my mother. She couldn't stand the sight of whites after my father got killed. It was to respect her that my aunts and cousins stayed away from Wanda. And Wanda was so angry. She was too proud to come back here. I think I was the only one to ever visit her. I didn't tell anybody about that trip."

Sarah had both of her hands around her glass. They were muscled hands, like his own. He could see she worked them, and he focused on her hands because he was ashamed to be sitting in front of her and asking her questions about a world he had been excluded from.

She had to go back to work. They left the cafe and stood awkwardly in the parking lot. She patted his arm, gave him a brief smile. He thanked her and turned toward his truck.

"Nephi," she called to him as he unlocked the Chevy. "You call me anytime. That'd be fine."

Nephi climbed into his truck for the two-hour drive home. He was thinking about his mother watching his grandfather murdered. He could see this image clearly. It takes work to beat a man to death. A man doesn't want to die and will struggle and protect himself. Nephi had seen two infantrymen once, clubbing a Viet Cong with their rifle butts. They had been thorough, but they hadn't been able to beat the life completely out of him, had given up, and left him on the ground, blood streaming out of his mouth and ears, eyes dulled, still blinking.

The highway crept away below him. The black rock and scrub pine, the blue-gray sage of southern Idaho, stark in the August heat, said broken things to him, heartbreaking things. His truck slowed and cars piled up behind him until at last he swung off the highway on a side road and stopped. Tukudeka. He fingered the word with his mind, turning it over and over. Sheep-eaters. They had been used to the high solitude of the Bitterroots. Starvation had brought them down to this ragged burned landscape. His great-grandparents dead of grief, his grandfather murdered. He sat there feeling amazed that his mother hadn't drowned him when she'd seen the color of his skin. He wondered whatever had compelled her to marry his father. He remembered a slip of a quote from somewhere. A house divided against itself cannot stand. Nephi wondered at the split in him, what he was, where he belonged, how he fit in the world.

His parents tried to make the choice for him, shielding him from a river of his past. Now he'd ripped away the shield, on the advice of strangers. John Tyhee, Ben Cody, neither of them was anything to him. No one's anything to me, he said to himself. He could hear Sarah's voice, moving across the details of tragedy. Sarah, he hadn't noticed it at the time, but Sarah had revealed no emotion when she spoke. Nephi had revealed none himself. She had spoken and he had listened and they might have been discussing spark plugs that needed changing or the way a field of grain looks after it has been pelted by hail. Now feelings tramped out of his heart and made heavy boot prints on his insides. He brought his truck back out on the highway, but he wasn't conscious of the process that kept it heading south.

He didn't bother stopping at the bar when he got back to Bridger. He went to the state-run liquor store and purchased a gallon of Jim Beam, which he took back to his failing ranch in the south end of the valley. He got out a picture of his parents when they were still young. He'd never thought much about that. He poured himself a big tumbler of whiskey. Never thought how terribly, painfully young his mother had been when she married. Seventeen, for God's sake, seventeen. He put the picture and the tumbler down on a low table in front of the sofa and went to a box on the mantel above his fireplace. From the box he extracted a baggie full of green weed, a small, flat pipe, and a box of matches. He went to his stereo and from a collection of records, he pulled Jimi Hendrix and laid the disk on the turntable. Stretched out on the sofa, he bolted half the contents of the tumbler, then stuffed weed into the bowl of the pipe and lit it, sucking the smoke down into his lungs and holding it there for several seconds before expelling it into the room as the bristling chords of "Are You Experienced" banged against the walls. Paraphernalia assembled, Nephi commenced a long slow descent.

———

Ben Cody focused his attention on the musculo-skeletal interaction of his fingers. He had one hand on the beer tap, the other holding a pitcher, and he imagined he could feel the electrical impulses that told his muscles what to do, a radiant energy pulsing down his arms and into his digits. When he thought of his phalanges, the image of the smooth muscles caressing the white bone made him feel as though his hands were being massaged. He had screened out most everything around him—the nasal whine of some pathetic singer on the juke box, the hum of human voices, mostly male, air thick with smoke and the smell of beer, the faces of people he might have greeted. Ben poured. He rang up numbers on the cash register. He handled crumpled money. He threw empty bottles carelessly into the big trash can. He set glasses washing in the dishwasher. He answered odd questions from patrons hunkered at the bar.

The words "last call" came out of his mouth at 1 a.m. He hardly noticed that he'd uttered them. Customers had to be urged through the heavy door. It was 1:30 before the last of them disappeared, and then Ben heard something that reconnected him to the world beyond his body.

"Where in the hell you think you're going with that horse?" someone was yelling. "Hey, take it easy!"

He looked up as Nephi lurched inside, trailing a statuesque beauty of the equine variety right inside and up to the bar. Nephi sat. The roan mare, tilted diamond grazing her long, lustrous face, twitched nary an eye and ran her luscious lips over the surface of the bar. The salt and malt leavings set her velvet nostrils aquiver.

"Man, oh, man," Ben said and dropped the bar rag. He went around and ran a hand down the horse's muscled shoulder.

"Rode hard, put away wet," Nephi said and snorted through his nose, something that might have been a giggle misplaced or the sucking in of other emotion.

"You can't put her away here, my friend," said Ben, disentangling the reins from Nephi's loose fist and walking the big creature back through the door. The metal of her shoes rang a hollow sound on the wood floor. Nephi followed them outside.

"Do me a big goddamned favor," he said as he stood swaying in front of Ben. "And don't do me no more favors." He reached out to take the reins from the bartender, but something about the shape of the planet disagreed with the messages flashing between his sensory organs and his somewhat overstimulated cerebellum. He fell down instead.

"OK, then," Ben said and, dropping the horse's reins, went back inside the bar and locked the door behind him.

Nephi walked his hands up the horse's leg. She let him do this. She was remarkably fond of him for reasons dating back many years. He pulled himself upright, grabbed a fistful of mane, and leaned forward to capture the dangling reins. He shifted his weight and managed to get a foot in the stirrup, swung his body up onto her back, and then leaned forward embracing her long, lovely neck and whispered, "Oh, Baby, Baby," while she stood waiting for him to tell her which way they might go next.

Seventeen

Nephi woke up to a dry mouth, a thick tongue, a head that felt as fragile as bone china, and church bells shattering his equanimity. As though he had any equanimity. As though occasional shreds of calm had ever blown in through the gaping windows of his life. He didn't want to open his eyes. He knew he was not safe in his bed because his bed was much softer than whatever was now digging into his hip and shoulder. He knew he was not on his own land because the smell was wrong. And there was too much noise, traffic noise, people talking noise, the clumpfing sound of something near his head. He squinted through one eye. A large hoof and red foreleg appeared. Lord, may she not step on my head, he prayed.

Praying was bad psychologically. It cranked open the vast reservoir of Nephi's memories. Screw you, Lord. May you spend eternity with televangelists and their frumpy wives. Thus Nephi blasphemed the powers that be while contemplating slivers of irrigation-green grass through his squinting right eye. There was also the gnarled brown-gray bark of a cottonwood tree before him. Left eye opens with reluctance, sleep grunge hampering his vision.

Nephi made out that he was in some sort of park. Baby dropped her head down and brushed his cheek. She took a bit of his shirt in her teeth and pulled on it. He pushed her head away, then felt around for the dangling reins. How lucky. How lucky she hadn't wandered into the hinterlands, which she was capable of doing. People in fitness regalia trotted past him on a nearby path. They looked at him and his horse and then looked away, as though embarrassed for him, as though they'd caught him in an unnatural act. Weird, said Nephi, to himself and checked to make sure he still had his clothes on. He sat up. His head was not happy that he did so.

Southside Park, how had he got here? There was no knowing. The last twelve hours blurred to simple images. Nephi recalled watching, hawklike, his wheeling living room as marijuana and whiskey collided in his head and offered contradictory dissertations on the nature of walls and ceiling. He remembered a long spell of being fascinated with the saddle cinch buckle, pondering the beauty of the cast metal, wondering how such an ingenious device had ever been invented. He remembered a moment of communion with Baby, his tiny human eyes gazing into the great dark orb of hers, her long lashes sweeping down and then up as she blinked at him, air huffing out of her enormous—they seemed enormous at the time—nostrils. How beautiful and sincere she was. He remembered being inside the Tabernacle Bar, but this must be an hallucination because surely if he had been, if he had seen Ben, he would have the wounds of battle as a testament. And although he ached from having spent the night on the ground, nothing felt broken. He still had all his teeth.

Nephi stood and the ground canted dangerously for a few seconds. Still half in the bag, son. Time to go home. He didn't get on the horse, just walked her through the park, coming around a clump of trees upon a trail he'd never seen. It looked like a short cut to the road so he followed it. And in a few seconds stumbled upon Ben and some old woman contorting their bodies in slow motion.

"Cody, you sorry son of a bitch."

Nephi thought he said this with a certain authority, but neither Ben nor the woman paid him any attention. No sweat, he had been ignored before. It was no news to him. But he felt patient. He felt OK with it. He parked his lanky frame against a tree and let Baby explain her deep restlessness to him. Once he muttered back, "Hey, get in line, Darlin'. Take a damn number."

Ben and the woman looked like birds, like herons in the morning in the marsh west of town, awkward in their grace, and slow. Nephi thought he had seen the woman before, but he didn't know why.

Watching them distracted him from the billowing anger-and-vengeance medley he had been composing. His appetite for destruction waned somewhat in the presence of, presence of, whatever it was he was in the presence of. He sank lower against the tree trunk, and soon it seemed prudent to sit down. As he got comfortable and began thinking that he'd awakened too early and it might be nap time, Ben desisted his unusual contortions and turned to face him.

"You feeling OK?" he said.

Advantage, Ben, thought Nephi. What am I doing sitting on my sorry ass when I've come to whup this bugger? He stood and it took him a few seconds to get vertically calibrated.

"You gotta stop messing with people's heads, Cody," he said. "People don't need it."

The woman watched him. She had a something-or-other about her, thought Nephi, real strong something-or-other. She peered at him as though he were the most delightful thing she'd seen all day. Old gal doesn't get out much. He wrapped Baby's reins around a low branch and moved toward them.

"Talk to me," said Ben.

"I don't think I will, you know? I don't think I will," and Nephi threw a punch in the direction of Ben's chin. Ben's chin seemed not to be where it had been. Nephi staggered right, spun around, then barreled straight at Ben to knock him to the ground. But Ben deflected him, sending Nephi and all his momentum harmlessly by. Nephi tried the same move again, going lower this time like a human battering ram. He grabbed Ben around the waist, thinking to hurl him down, but his force turned to nothing. He might as well have thrown himself against a brick wall. He let go and staggered back a few steps.

"Talk to me," Ben said again.

Nephi tried a sideways kick toward Ben's stomach, but Ben caught his foot in one hand and all his forward motion came thrusting back at him and he was on the ground, thick-headed and tired. He didn't get up, and Ben and the woman were soon kneeling on either side of him.

"Talk to me," Ben said again.

"Oh, enough!" cried Felice. "Listen, young man, you and your horse need to be fed. Can you get up? Ben, help him up. That's fine, just fine. Now come along with me."

"I don't need anything," said Nephi, and he closed his eyes. How tiresome to be rescued by the person you've come to assault.

"But look at Baby," said Felice. "She at least, needs water."

That he could not deny. Feeling too pathetic to live, Nephi acquiesced. At Felice's spotless home a bucket of water followed by instant oats put Felice right up there in the mare's estimation. Nephi allowed himself to be fed a cup of chamomile peppermint tea ("This'll knock those toxins right out of you") and a big plate of eggs and potatoes.

The three of them sat in her kitchen where sunlight squared on the wall and floor. Because neither she nor Ben appeared to have anything to say, Nephi felt obliged to fill in the quiet.

"My mother might've left," he said, addressing the patches of light, "but she was trying to protect me. I should never have listened to you. What's the point of going backwards? There's reasons some things don't get said. There's good goddamn reasons people bury the past."

"That's always an option," agreed Felice.

116

"Yeah, but it's not mine anymore."

"Don't be silly," she replied. "Of course it's still an option. You didn't learn a thing you didn't already know. In your heart, anyway, you've always borne the emotional burden even if you didn't have all the details. It's ridiculous to suggest you can't continue blocking all that noise. It'll just take more effort than you're used to expending."

Nephi looked at her. "Excuse me, but you don't know a damn thing about it."

"About Wanda Buoyer Jones? Well, I imagine I know a couple of things about her, one or two small things."

Nephi was not prepared for this. He stood up and backed away from the table. "I don't care, OK? I don't care. There's nothing I can do about any of it. She's gone. My dad's dead. That's all over and done. Let 'em all just stay dead. I don't want to know anything more about it." He hurried out the back door, untied Baby from the fence rail, swung up onto her back, and urged her into a trot out onto the street. It wasn't until he had put several blocks between him and them that it occurred to him to wonder how the old woman had known the mare's name.

—

"So what was that all about?" Ben asked.

Felice got up to clear Nephi's plate and cup from the table. She shrugged. "He doesn't have to do anything he doesn't want to, Ben."

"I meant, I didn't know that you knew his mother."

"Wanda? It's a small town. It was a smaller town when she was here. What I want to know is what you were doing, bouncing him around in the park that way? You could easily have avoided contact with him at all."

"He caught me off guard," Ben hedged. "I just had all this energy and it was like if I thought it, I could do it."

"Ye shall say unto the mountain, remove hence to yonder place and it shall remove ..." said Felice. "Is that it?"

"Quoting the Bible?" he said.

"Well, sure, why not?" she said.

"But you know what I'm talking about."

"There's nothing unusual about it," she waved a hand dismissively, "once you understand the principle of atonement. And any spiritual discipline will eventually get you there. But there's a danger attached to power."

"Pride," said Ben.

"Oh, pride is the least of your problems. The problem you face is that you think connecting with the source is some sort of barometer of wisdom. In fact, you're still just you; you've still got an enormous capacity for stupid behavior. Now, don't take it personally. This is where many of the so-called prophets have failed, equating power with wisdom. That's why stillness and patience matter most at this stage. Waiting is also an action."

"Does that mean you never use it?" he asked.

"I direct my energy with my attention," said Felice. "When I work in the garden, the power goes there, in tai chi, the power goes there, or in our conversations."

"You're using the power of the universe to garden?" Ben said.

Felice heard the challenge in his voice and sighed a little. "Come with me." They stood on her back porch, and she pointed to the southern sky. "See that small cloud? Watch it."

Ben kept his eyes on it for about a minute as it seemed to grow smaller and smaller and into a thin gauze, and then disappear altogether.

"Look over to the west now," she said, "above Bullet Peak."

Ben's eyes followed hers, and he watched as a cloud slowly built itself out of the blue bright sky.

"I can fling it about thoughtlessly if I want to, but so what?"

"Are you showing off for me, Felice?"

"Yes," she said. "I guess I am."

Ben kept his eyes on the small cloud that hovered above the mountain. "Could you throw up a whole bank of clouds, Felice? Could you make it rain?"

"Ye shall say unto the mountain, remove hence," she repeated.

"Have you ever done it?"

Felice laughed deeply. "Of course not. I keep my garden and do my exercises and I stay healthy and happy. Christ had wisdom, as did Buddha. My vision is limited, clouded. I have a certain skill, but I lack wisdom. I understand the breadth of my ignorance."

Ben's mind suddenly racheted through the wealth of possibilities unlimited power would present and felt a crackling wild euphoria. Felice sat down in the porch chair, suddenly tired. "Time for you to go, Ben, I think," she said.

Eighteen

Jessie stopped answering the phone. Picking up did not pay off. She had nothing to say and couldn't think of anything she wanted to hear. She went through a few days of listening to the phone ringing and then just unplugged the thing from the wall. Ah, the silence, the liberation, the secret thrill of the disconnect, to no longer have a bell in the house anyone in the world could ring. Severing the audio tie, however, carried an unfortunate side effect. It arrived one hot August morning while she sat on the porch in ratty T-shirt and boxers drinking orange juice and gazing off into her own personal Never-Never-Land, a fantasy thing she was concocting, a place where other people's expectations evaporated every morning in the sunlight. As she added various tantalizing details to the budding utopia, the unfortunate no-phone side effect cruised down the street in a big white Pontiac: Aunt Claire and her mother, unannounced arrivals.

She watched them pull into the driveway and pondered whether relatives belonged in her brave new world. A large "no" vote came in from all districts. How're we going to work this thing? she wondered as they got out of the car and came toward her. She cranked up her standard blocking maneuver.

"So am I kicked out of the family or what?" she said.

Claire and Dorothy composed themselves on the porch bench. "I want to apologize for what your father did the other night," her mother began in an unhappy voice. "He was so angry, but ..." she trailed off.

"I don't think you get to apologize for him," said Jessie. "He did it. Let him apologize. You have nothing to be sorry about."

Something about the way her mother squared her shoulders as Jessie spoke made her sad suddenly for all of them, for the strange triangle of pains inflicted. She bristled against the tender emotion. "Dad can smack me all he wants, but nothing will be different, OK? None of the details have changed, not a single thing is better. Danny is still the person who started this and I'm still the injured party."

Claire interrupted her. "We came to talk about Danny," she said. "We wanted to discuss other options beside prosecuting him."

"Why are you doing this?" said Jessie.

"We could ask you the same thing," snapped her aunt.

"This is Danny's problem, not yours," said Jessie.

"It affects the family," said her mother. "If something happens to one of us, it happens to all of us. We're connected. We're together forever."

"Some of us are more connected than others of us," muttered Jessie.

"If you want to distance yourself," said Claire, "that's your choice. But you have to remember that you're the one who's moved away from us, not vice versa."

"I don't want acrimony," said her mother hastily. "I want harmony. How can we work this out?"

"Mom," said Jessie, "we did this dance the other night in the livingroom, remember? It's not your deal or Dad's deal. It's between Danny and me. If Danny wants to negotiate with me, let Danny come talk to me. But it seems to me that you've always taught us that we're responsible for the consequences of our behavior. Danny broke a couple laws and got caught. This is what happens when you do that."

"Well, we need to do something because your father will not stand for this much longer," said Dorothy.

"My father will not stand for it?" snapped Jessie. "And what are his options? Listen, you tell my father that hitting people is illegal."

"Jessie, can't you see who you're hurting here? It's not Danny. It's not your Dad. Oh, they're mad, all right, but they'll get over it. Look at your mother. What do you think this is doing to her?"

You are killing your mother, that's what her father had said. Jessie wondered what her mother's suffering was a euphemism for.

"I don't know," she said slowly. "What is it doing to you?"

"The only thing I ever wanted was a loving family," Dorothy replied. "That's the only thing, a family living in harmony with the principles of the gospel. This, this," she couldn't find the right definition, "it's breaking my heart," her voice dwindled away.

Claire glared at Jessie as she put an arm around her sister-in-law. Jessie knew what was required just then, and she delivered, going over to her mother, kneeling down in an uncharacteristic conciliatory act, taking one of her mother's hands and pressing it, but finding not a single word worth uttering that wasn't either a damned lie or a damned truth. She couldn't take the one and she didn't think her mother could take the other.

They went away, leaving Jessie to work out the emotional math if she cared to. She didn't care to. Some elusive feeling tracked little cat prints all over the rest of her morning.

What do they want from me anyway?

Another voice said, well, what do you want from them? It was not a question she was prepared to entertain. She went down to the bar. On her way a rust orange pickup slowed beside her and the Basques glared at her through the windshield. She flipped them off. They returned the gesture and added one of their own.

Nineteen

At the Tabernacle Bar, Jessie found Ben and Max with their heads together over cups of coffee, and the way they looked at her when she pushed open the door confirmed their guilt: gossip hounds caught in the act.

"What?" she said as she sat beside Max.

"We were just talking about you," said Max.

"I *know* that," she said. "What were you saying?"

"I was catching Max up on the soap opera of your life," Ben said.

"At least I have a life," she said.

"We were wondering if you really are going to drag your brother's butt into court," said Max.

"And what's the consensus?"

"Frankly," said Ben, "we're stymied. Max here wonders if you're bluffing. I think you're having second thoughts, but it might be just wishful thinking on my part."

"Why should it matter to you, either way?" asked Jessie.

"If your brother is found guilty, it's the kind of thing that'll follow him around a long time," said Ben.

"Well, he should have thought of that before he started screwing around with my angel. You know what really gripes me about this? Nobody seems to see my point of view here. I mean, I'm the one who's been victimized. Why is everybody mad at me?"

"You set yourself up," said Ben. "Nobody's shooting arrows at your sacred cows. Why should anybody care about your feelings?"

"I have a right to express myself," said Jessie.

"Let me tell you something," said Ben. "I've seen people who live like you do—in opposition to something else. It's not a very satisfying lifestyle. You're pushing against a brick wall, like you could actually move it. But if it disappeared tomorrow, you'd fall flat on your face. Your family is engaged in a positive pursuit. You, on the other hand, are merely reacting to it. You say you've got a life. As a purpose for living, I'd say it's way down there on the evolutionary scale."

"Unlike bartending," she snapped.

"Kids, kids," said Max. "How important can it be? You know what I say? Screw 'em if they can't take a joke. Come on, Jessie, I'm taking you for a drive."

Overbearing males, she thought, but she thought it in a good way and followed him out the door.

They drove in Max's sleek machine up Bridger Canyon. He guided the car at an enormous speed along the twisting two-lane. They didn't talk much, letting the rhythm of the road do its work. When they swept around a curve just above the dam, Jessie called out, "Oh, let's stop here, something I want to show you," and Max muscled the Corvette to a crawl in a splutter of gravel as they turned onto an old Forest Service road. He parked. They got out and Jessie led him to a narrow trail that began in a thicket of willow. It went through craggy cottonwood and chokecherry, then straggled through pine trees growing out of the rocky terrain. Eventually they broke out onto open hillside, and the trail guided them up high through dying summer grasses. They could see below them the meandering stream of asphalt defining the floor of the narrow canyon and, as they got higher, the highway traffic hum grew faint.

They passed through a stand of gnarled juniper where Jessie stopped to rest. Max pulled up beside her and parked on a small boulder beneath a twisting, ragged tree. Jessie broke off a couple of needles, bent them in her fingers, and sniffed. It was a powerful aroma, almost like the smell of oranges. She sniffed again and sighed.

Max took off his shirt and the shaded air blew gently across his sweaty back.

"You know," said Jessie, "some of these trees live a long time. There's one up here somewhere the Forest Service says is three thousand years old. Parts of it are dead, but other parts still shoot out new growth every year. Pretty amazing, huh?"

Max tried to measure the meaning of three thousand years. "So," he said, "a thousand years older than Christianity."

Jessie didn't know why this seemed so pleasant a thought. "Wasn't it the Druids who worshipped trees?" she asked.

"I don't know," said Max. "Religion hasn't ever interested me. Churches always looked scary, big buildings, serious people. Sin. Hell. You ever notice how preachers look a lot like jailers?"

"I've never seen a jailer," said Jessie. "So I wouldn't know."

"Well, they either look like jailers or twelve-year-olds," said Max. "Where are we going?"

She pointed above them to the south. "That saddle between those two peaks," she said. "That's where we're going."

Max squinted up in the direction she had indicated and whistled. It looked like the last few hundred feet went straight up over rock. "Up there?"

"From down here it looks kind of daunting," she agreed, "but it's a pretty easy scramble."

They started off again and the trail turned back on itself several times before delivering them up into a small sloping meadow dotted with quaking aspen. The air was still, not even a hint of a flutter from the delicate leaves of the tall, narrow trees that cast a filigree of shade on the meadow. In the heat tiny white butterflies executed stunning aerobatic maneuvers among the thin-stemmed harebells.

Max left the trail and waded in among the wildflowers, breathing the profusion of odors, the sweet blossoms, the musky dark scent of dying stalks, the freshness of aspen bark. He could feel the pulse in his head keeping time to some kind of music in the ground beneath him, and he turned to Jessie and beckoned her.

She came to him. He reached toward her and started to pull up the edge of her T-shirt. "What are you doing?" she said.

"I'm helping you off with your shirt," he said.

"Why?"

"Because I want to feel your skin."

They spread their clothes on the ground as a blanket. Jessie lay down on them and Max stretched out next to her, and certain sensations passed between them in the high heart of the Rocky Mountains where the sun rained all its blessings without regard for creed, color, gender, or lineage.

Later, clothed, hot, bedraggled from the steep climb, they stood on the saddle between the peaks and, sucking as much oxygen from the thin air as their overtaxed lungs could get, faced south where a sea of mountains stretched away before them.

"My God," said Max. He sat down abruptly on the rocky ground.

Jessie, legs apart, knees locked to keep her upright, crossed her arms, hugged herself, and felt the peaks resonating away from her, serrated ridges separated by narrow treed valleys, all more beautiful and somehow fraught with more meaning than anything the small circumference of her own life could throw up. The Rockies gave her the only context she embraced. She dropped down beside Max. They sat together and knew that from the sea of summer days washing them, they had pulled a pearl, a shared pearl that bound them to each other with silvery filaments, sensed but unseen. It was a long while before either of them wanted to go down to the rest of the world.

Descent, however, was inevitable. Why can't we stay up here forever in the heady atmosphere? wondered Jessie as they prepared to go. But as they moved down and down, as the muscles in her legs began to tremble against the insistent pull of gravity, she answered her own question. We have short attention spans. If we lingered, we'd grow tired of the vista. Soon we'd find it dull, and if we couldn't get away from it, we'd start to resent it. As she held herself upright on the steep trail, the details of her life climbed to meet her. She wondered if she might go to Melody's baptism, imagined emotional chaos if she did. Reason enough to go. Hey, I'm invited, she thought. In fact, I'm responsible. They ought to be thanking me. She stepped around the thorny issue of her brother. Maybe there was some sort of self-help book she could read, an etiquette for sibling rivalry when the siblings end up in court. It was his fault, Your Honor, he started it.

She thought about the way she was treated at family gatherings, the faintly demeaning attitude her cousins sometimes took with her. Like someone with a physical handicap, this treatment enraged her. There's nothing wrong with me, she wanted to yell. She remembered a conversation with Chloe's daughter LuAnne, who had actually asked her where she felt her life had gone wrong. Jessie had replied that it was probably the early years of glue-sniffing, and her cousin had refused to be amused.

But when Jessie was weak, tired, grumpy, lonely, hungry, confused, or otherwise under the weather, she tended to take the family view. What's wrong with me? What in the hell is wrong with me? Tottering down a path away from the various ecstasies of the afternoon, thirsty, exhausted, muscles all wobbly, doubting now the verity of the feelings Max evoked in her, she heard the chant beginning.

Max, turning once to keep a willow branch from brushing back into her, noticed the frown on her face, but he took it to be fatigue and kept to his own mental turnings. Wandering the corridors of his own past, Max searched to recall when he'd last felt as good as he had on this afternoon. At first he convinced himself that life had never delivered so much pleasure in so many excellent sensory details in a single day.

But the thought was a setup, a sneaky segue into memories of Lainie. Mean trick of the mind. Did he really want to go back to that place, where he and Lainie were the only planets in his firmament? No. He wanted to let her memory go. He didn't want to comparison shop. But he couldn't help feeling that if Lainie were hiking now beside him, they'd be chattering like squirrels, and if their words stopped winding around each other, they'd be holding hands. Here was Jessie, lost in her own thoughts, walking sometimes beside him, sometimes behind him, sometimes taking the lead, but never touching him, and he could read people well enough to know that if he reached out and took her hand she would be startled and annoyed.

He thought about his expectations, how his expectations built edifices that no one could inhabit. Jessie couldn't be Lainie.

He dredged up negative Lainie memories, hoping to dispel the past. Lainie's big fear had been to lose him. She'd clung to him, and hadn't he been stifled by her clinging? Hadn't a part of him been grateful to retreat every three months, to steal a few precious moments here and there away from her, where his own separate thoughts and feelings had room to expand and move about? Where he could be Max in the singular?

Lainie had been a mirror, had adopted his opinions and attitudes, had preferred whatever he preferred. For the first few years this thoughtful gift of throwing herself away for his sake had knocked him out. But in the long haul hadn't it become annoying? To always be agreed with and catered to struck him now as a sad thing. It was as though there were no weight to Lainie's being, nothing to lean against, just this insubstantial giving-way before him. He realized suddenly that this was why she had left, that she must have been suffocated by her own acquiescence, had blamed him for it, and run away.

For the first time in a long time, Max realized, he wasn't getting mush-headed over the past. He felt some sanity drifting his way, some balance. He watched Jessie moving down the trail in front of him, conjured the strong, muscled feel of her body, her opinionated ramblings, the fight in her, her unwillingness to bend toward him.

Jessie was not a talker. He couldn't anticipate her thoughts, had no way to gauge the value she placed on him. The uncertainty of it bothered him, but there was also an expansiveness in it. I think too much, he told himself. I just got to let it go and let the thing play out. Don't need to analyze it. Just move toward the pleasure and away from the pain.

In their mutually distracted states they arrived at Max's car near dusk. Jessie wanted to go home and Max dropped her. There was a little something he needed to take care of.

Back at the condo, the much-handled letters trembled in their envelope sleeves. Alarmed, but ultimately not the least bit surprised, they composed themselves. By the time Max yanked them from the shelf in the closet where they had thought their worst fate would be the slow accumulation of dust, they had become stoic. Letters aren't forever.

He drove over to the picnic area at Southside Park. He got out of the car, the letters in one hand, a bottle of B&B in the other. Starting a fire in a squat round grill by a picnic table, Max made a small ceremony of taking each letter from its envelope, balling it into a loose wad, feeding it to the fire, and waiting for all traces of it to disappear before sending the next one in. He swigged the expensive liqueur from the bottle as trills of liberty mingled with a distant fading sadness that no longer hurt. He felt halfway righteous as he watched the yellow fire illuminate and then devour Lainie's words. The burning of the letters took quite a long while. As the last one trailed its smoky leavings into the night sky, a pine cone fell out of the tree above Max and bonked him on the head. He laughed out loud, took a good long piss that doused the last fading embers, and went on home.

Twenty

The shadow world nickered eagerly as the barn door of night flung itself wide, that otherness of souls harboring all the dreamscapes, all the dark selves ranged out across the sleeping vale with wild superlative dramas, the willfulness of dreams, the sting of dreams, the ecstasy of dreams, the terror of dreams.

Or something like that.

Max, released from old bonds, had a new dream that night. He was in the ocean, not a rakish, frigid, beastly ocean, but something more benign—a warm, shallow aqua bay, where he swam naked along the bottom, breathing easily. He had mastered the art of filtering oxygen from the water and swam like a fish, his body undulating, happy to be at home in the buoyant fluid atmosphere with rays of sunlight refracting through the shallow water. Max played, darting here and there with schools of small multicolored fish. He wound himself through an intricate maze of coral. He shot up almost to the surface and slued about happily beneath that porous, swelling membrane where the top of the ocean pushes at the bottom of the sky. He somersaulted deeper, startling a big skate on the sandy bottom and trailing behind as it skimmed away.

And then Max tired. He came to rest, stretched out on his side, propping his head up on his hand. He held still. Various creatures of the sea moved toward him, orange sea stars lifting their light-sensitive limbs as though to see him better, purple sea urchins clambering along his arm. He looked at his feet, which were covered with barnacles, and he laughed, his laughter bubbling up to the surface, as he watched their tiny feather limbs reaching through miniature volcano-shaped casings to comb the water. Hermit crabs scuttle-dragging their shell homes approached him. Bright-hued anemones adorned his belly. He was not in the least alarmed, not even when he felt the odd sensation of cupped feet walking up his back and then saw the narrow graceful arm of a small octopus coming over his shoulder. He felt the creatures drawing some essence out of him as they anchored to his supple skin. I have too much of it, he told himself, and they need some.

The gentle motion of the water rocked him a little. He wondered if something on the other side of the dancing membrane called his name. He sighed in his sleep. He thought not.

Nephi, weighted down in a more oxygenated world, was wrapped around a pillow, clinging to it as his body formed a quarter moon on the bed in the boxed sky of his room. But the essence of Nephi had business in the garage, where he had propped up the hood of his truck and was staring intently at the battery.

The battery needed serious work. It wasn't an ordinary truck battery. Tiny knobbed boards, something like computer parts, studded its surface. They needed adjustment. He hadn't realized the battery was so complicated. He wondered, as he stared at the complex mess before him, how he had been talked into purchasing it. Then he remembered. This special battery would alter the truck's energy field, relocate its center of gravity. With this battery, the truck would fly. Take it right up off the highway any old time you please, son. You just have to get the dang thing working.

He looked in his tool box and found a small soldering iron and a thin coiled rope of silver. But when he turned back to the battery, he realized that his hands would almost certainly brush against the positive and negative poles. I can't do it, he told himself. It'll kill me if I try.

He really wanted the truck to fly. I'll be careful, he said. I'll be very careful. And so, hands shaking a little, he leaned in gingerly with the hot iron, cautious, working slowly. Something in the way the strand of silver melted onto the boards spoke to him. It spoke volumes about fluidity and adaptability. It spoke reams on hot motion and cold fusion. Some treatise on connection came next, on staying connected, on links in a system, everything linked or nothing could fly. Everything linked or nothing could fly. Nephi forgot about his hands just then and completed the connection between the battery's opposing poles. A bolt of lightning shot through him, electrified blue, stopping his heart dead in its beating tracks. He screamed and jerked awake. Drenched in sweat, he stumbled into the shower and stood under a stream of gushing water for a long, long time.

Melody stood in a pool of blue light staring at her hands. The blue light skimmed over her skin, glinting and glistening. The blue light seemed to emanate from the huge diamond on her finger. She walked down a shimmering corridor toward a different kind of light, a white light. As she walked, she realized that her mother was beside her and that her mother had become small. She was speaking. Melody had to lean down to hear her. "You have to give the ring back, Melody. They only loaned it to you. It's not yours. You have to give it back."

Melody didn't want to give up the blue light. She kept walking down the corridor. Her mother struggled to keep up. "Melody, if you don't give the ring back, you have to stay here," she said. "You can't ever come home."

Melody stopped and looked at her mother. The longer she looked, the larger her mother became, until it appeared that she filled most of the space in the corridor. "I don't want to go home," said Melody.

"We have to go home," said her mother. "It's getting too small here. There isn't any room."

"I'm going there," said Melody and pointed to the rays of white light splaying out from the end of the long, bright hall.

"They eat their young," said her mother.

Melody laughed and laughed. "No, they don't eat at all. They don't eat at all. I saw them. They set the stars on fire. And I can, too." She kept walking and her mother stopped. As she got farther away, her mother called faintly to her. She turned to look. Her mother beckoned. She raised her hand to wave back, and suddenly the blue diamond flew off her finger and spun down the corridor, disappearing into a black wormhole of the night. The blue light faded and Melody's eyes opened on the faint gray of dawn.

Jessie, who in the heat of the night had hauled a mattress and blanket out to the front porch, twitched a little, like a dog dreaming. She was dancing in a big, empty hall. Perhaps it was a gymnasium with painted lines on a slick wood floor. Alone she whirled, laughing, as music—fiddles, slide guitars, the rhythmic pulsing of an upright bass—rained from the high ceiling down onto her. Nothing anchored the lightfooted dancer to the floor. She came back to it now and then to hear the hollow beat of her boots on the wood. She had let go of some dark flame inside, had allowed the happy music to embrace her. Then in a leaping turn she saw that she was not alone after all.

Of course not. It always came when she forgot to watch. Lumbering toward her, a heavy, reddish, scaly thing. Dragon? Lizard? It gobbled up the music falling from above. Big shark's teeth shredding the meat of the dancing dream. Jessie drifted down to the floor as she watched the ugly thing. It had been invading her dreams since she was quite small.

For years it had been a simple pursuit dream. She ran. It bungled along behind her, chewing on her shadow, sending spikes of terror across all her tender synapses. But lately a new pattern had emerged. She no longer ran from it. She just stood there. And the thing with teeth would come upon her and begin devouring, tearing great rifts out of her side, ripping into the meaty portion of her thigh. It didn't hurt, but it did look hideous, muscle and bone exposed, blood splattering everywhere. She watched, unblinking, as the creature ate her. After several dripping mouthfuls, it always stopped. Then it moved away, looking over its shoulder at her, wide snub legs dragging its fat belly off, pinprick eyes glaring at her as though she had spoiled something. As she stared after it, a cranky noise distracted her. She woke, opened her eyes, and saw on the porch railing the long iridescent tail of a magpie, squawking at the morning, hopping up and down.

Daniel, embraced by a gentler frond of the night, slept dreamless, deeply, in blessed silence, knowing nothing but his own shallow breathing, his own steady heartbeats.

Twenty-one

Melody Stardust sat in the foyer of the church with a Bible and a Book of Mormon in her hands. They were beautiful volumes, leather-bound, with her name inscribed in gold in the lower right hand of each cover. She held them with a kind of wonder, with a kind of humility, stunned by the depth of the feeling that the sacred texts evoked. Sensations she hadn't anticipated spilled into her from some deep, unknown place. She could hardly contain them as she waited to see the bishop, waited for her pre-baptismal interview.

She opened the Bible, first to Psalms, where she found these words: "Show thy marvelous loving-kindness, Oh, thou that savest, by thy right hand them which put their trust in thee from those that rise up against them. Keep me as the apple of thy eye, hide me under the shadow of thy wings."

She turned to the New Testament, and the book opened at Matthew, where she read, "Ask and it shall be given you; seek, and ye shall find; knock, and it shall be opened unto you."

Melody had discovered an amazing trick. She would hold a thought—a question—in her mind and then let the scriptures fall open where they would. Somewhere on the page would be the response she needed, almost as though it were a personal message to her.

She turned to the Book of Mormon and, holding in her mind a curiosity about the sensations she felt, let the book open. Her eyes wandered down a section of 3 Nephi, and this is what she read: "And no tongue can speak, neither can there be written by any man, neither can the hearts of men conceive so great and marvelous things as we both saw and heard Jesus speak; and no one can conceive of the joy which filled our souls at the time we heard him pray for us unto the Father."

To Melody it seemed she had somehow been transported beyond the world she inhabited, that for a moment she wasn't sitting in the church foyer waiting for the bishop, but rather surrounded in a world of light where she felt the presence of others who shared her conviction. Nothing in her life had prepared her for the experience. Nothing remotely compared.

It was at this moment of reverie that the bishop came out of his office and found Melody, rapture glowing upon her. As she became aware of him, the glow evanesced. She walked toward him and held out her hand. He took it in both of his, and they went into his office where he proceeded to assure himself that Melody understood the principles of the Church of Jesus Christ of Latter-day Saints. Daniel had been an excellent teacher. The bishop, satisfied, certified her worthiness for baptism.

Daniel was waiting for her when the bishop let her go. She went into his arms and he held her tightly. She looked at his face and saw in it the vestiges of worry.

"What's the matter?" she asked.

"Oh, just Jessie. Still Jessie," he said and sighed. "It's really destroying my mother. I can't get a grip on it at all. I don't know what to do."

"Have you prayed about it?" Melody asked.

"Daily," he said.

"And?"

"If God's answering my prayers, I'm too dense to get the message."

"Well, remember what it says in Matthew about seek and ye shall find, ask and it shall be given," said Melody, delighted that scripture now figured into her conversations. It felt so good to understand what the source for wisdom was.

Daniel, who'd memorized that particular scripture when he was probably six years old, gritted his teeth and said nothing as they left the church and walked down the road that led back to the street Melody lived on. The truth was, he was a little scared, because if he did have to go to court and if somehow Jessie's lawyers could convince a jury that he had stolen her angel, not once, but three times (to say nothing of the busted window), he could, conceivably, be in big trouble. And jail was not in Daniel's five-year plan.

His lawyer-uncle and his father assured him that it was unlikely it would get that far. They were talking a plea bargain to vandalism in exchange for her dropping the other charges. But in his heart Daniel knew Jessie wouldn't drop anything. He knew she'd push it the way she pushed everything.

"Explain to me again, exactly how the baptism will go," Melody said, more to take his mind off his sister than anything else.

Daniel ran through it for her, how she'd be dressed in a white gown and he'd be dressed in white, too, and they'd meet in the baptismal font at the church. The water would be warm and it would be a little more than hip deep. After he blessed her, he'd grip her arms and dunk her completely under the water. She had to be sure to be completely immersed, otherwise they would have to do it again. Then she would go and change into dry clothes and later the bishop would confirm her a member of the church. He warmed to his topic as he listened to himself recite the details of the familiar ceremony.

"It'll be so wonderful, Melody. You will feel so blessed. When you're baptized, all your sins are forgiven. It's like being given a clean slate. You're as pure as a newborn after you've been baptized."

———

The morning of the day Melody was baptized dawned surprisingly cloudy, one of Utah's summer rarities. Melody thought it a positive omen, just because it was different. What would be really special, she thought, what would be uncanny, would be a good thunderstorm. That would almost seem like a miracle, a voice from on high. She caught herself wondering if the desire might be evil. Was she tempting God? Wasn't it miracle enough that she had found the truth, all through the unlikely avenue of a book by Edward Abbey and a wayward snake? No sense asking for more. One niggling thought, what to tell her mother. She hadn't told her mother about this step, had not wanted the interference. I'll tell her later. As she dressed, she ignored the pale blue envelope on the corner of her small desk, which contained the most recent letter from her mother:

Dear Melody:

I was so happy to receive your letter and know you're enjoying yourself. But I feel strongly that I must remind you to avoid the Mormons. I'd hate to see you saddled with the guilt and shame of the Christian dogmas. Only fundamentalists are worse in their determination to ignore the truths of the universe. And you certainly know how I feel about them.

I know it's important for you to create your own reality, declare your independence, and begin working on your own issues, but these things could easily be done right here in California where the climate is more loving and accepting, and your opportunities are so much broader.

When I think of you in Utah, a kind of darkness shadows my mind. I am uneasy. Please reassure me that my concerns are unfounded.

Melody hadn't answered the letter. She didn't have the confrontational skill it would require. The only way she knew how to stick up for herself was to keep her mouth shut. It was a start, anyway.

The gathering to witness the baptism wasn't large. It consisted of Daniel's family and a few of Melody's new friends from work and from church. Both she and Daniel were just stepping into the baptismal font when the door at the back of the small chamber opened and Jessie slipped into a chair.

No muscle on Daniel's faced moved. Melody smiled in Jessie's direction, her heart full of love for everything around her. The small group of people fidgeted.

Or maybe that was just Jessie's imagination.

The ceremony was brief. Daniel blessed Melody, immersed her in the water, and then pulled her upright. The two of them gazed into each other's eyes, love and respect mingling. He wanted to hug her but knew that in their clingy garments, they would feel almost naked to each other. Despite his red-blooded American maleness and the enthusiasm with which he anticipated shedding his virginity, he didn't want to spoil the moment for Melody. So he squeezed her hand and let her go and waded away from her, up the steps leading back to his own small dressing room. She did the same. As the gathering waited for them, cousin Denny sang a favorite Mormon hymn: "Come, Come, Ye Saints."

At the back of the room, no one acknowledged Jessie. The people sitting next to her steadfastly looked ahead. You'd think I was the devil, come to spoil the party. You are the devil come to spoil the party, a part of her retorted.

When Denny finished singing, silence bonked around the room like a ball bearing, a glaring sound, insistent, annoying. Jessie noticed that even Uncle Alden's back was ramrod straight. She wondered what he was thinking. Could he be smiling on the inside? Then she wondered what she was thinking. Am I nuts? I don't even like Melody.

At that point the couple returned, sat down, and somebody else got up to give a talk on the beauty of baptism. It was an instructive experience for Jessie, who hadn't been to a church meeting of any kind in at least a decade. There was no false piety here. The speaker, someone she didn't know but who looked and sounded like a bishop, absolutely believed the words he was saying and said them with a relaxed and pleasant conviction, as opposed to the aggravating insistence of some bellowing televangelist. Jessie had forgotten how easy it was to get caught up in the spirit of a meeting. Everyone sincere and caring. But not me, not me, she insisted to herself. I do not care.

The bishop spoke about the love of God for his children. "I want you to imagine," he said to the group, "yourself at your most loving and generous. Imagine the strength of your feelings for your own children or for your husband or wife, or for your parents. Hold that feeling in your heart for a few minutes, get a good sense of it." He paused. "Now I want you to imagine that feeling increased a thousandfold. And still it does not begin to compare to the love God has for each one of us here. Each one of us," he repeated then paused again, and Jessie got the idea he was looking especially at her. She stared flatly back at him. His is speaking for himself, she thought. He is not speaking for me.

Not at all.

He didn't say much more and she, resisting, didn't hear it. Then somebody said a prayer about love and forgiveness and eternal joy, and the meeting ended. People surrounded Melody. Much talking, much standing about and chatting. And Jessie was surprised to find herself included.

Aunt Claire came over and asked how she'd been. Cousins Frank Jr., Raylene, and a very pregnant Lisa greeted her. The only people who seemed to ignore her were her parents and even this notion had to be abandoned as her father confronted her when she turned to go.

"Jessie." He said her name as though it were a verb, as though she were being commanded to do something.

She looked up at him, "Dad." She used his tone.

"What a pleasant surprise to see you here," he began.

"I was invited," she said.

"We're having a gathering for Melody at the house," he said.

It seemed to Jessie that he might be extending an invitation. "I guess we're pretending now that we didn't fight?"

"Let's not do this," he said in a low voice. "Let's let Melody and Daniel have this day to enjoy in harmony."

"I will if you will," she said and went to Melody who had reached such a level of euphoria that she threw her arms around Jessie and hugged her tightly. Jessie was surprised at the warmth of the embrace, surprised at herself to be moved by it.

"You know I owe all this to you," said Melody. "You were the one who introduced me to Daniel."

Jessie tried hard not to think of Nephi as she smiled.

A lavish dinner awaited the tribe at John and Dorothy's, and cars began loading up with family and friends. Jessie cut out. There was only so much conviviality she could stand, especially with Daniel casting baleful glances her way, strange looks, part forgiveness, part rage. She could tell he was really struggling to be a good boy. She went to the bar.

Ben motioned her over to him. "There's somebody needs you," and he pointed to a booth where a small but imposing-looking woman dressed in a silk jumpsuit sat nursing a soda.

"Moondance Stardust," said Ben.

"Excuse me?" said Jessie.

"Moondance Stardust," the woman interrupted. "I take it that you are Jessie Cannon and will know where I can find my daughter."

Jessie slid into the booth across from her. The woman before her, silver-haired with the kind of busy coif that required several layers of lacquer, had donned as many bright baubles as her various appendages could support, silver rings with unusual designs, a snake, a yin-yang symbol, some sort of cross, a large amethyst, silver bands with Northwest Indian patterns on both her wrists, moon and stars dangling from her earlobes. Makeup in discrete layers upon her face, bright lips, dusky eyelids, rouged cheeks. Jessie looked at the person who had spawned Melody and thought how incongruous. Melody preferred the scrubbed look and rarely decorated herself with jewelry. I guess all we really want to be is whatever our mothers aren't, she thought.

"So Melody's your daughter? Did she know you were coming?"

"No," said Moondance. "I thought I'd surprise her. But she wasn't at her apartment. I left a note on her door."

"As a matter of fact," said Jessie, "she's at my folks' house right now, having dinner. I can take you over if you want. You want to call and let them know you're coming?"

"I'd really been counting on surprising her," said Moondance.

"Oh, it'll be a surprise, all right," said Jessie. "I'm guessing she hasn't stayed in touch?"

"Children," sighed Moondance. "You feed, clothe, and house them, then off they go and they forget your name. She wrote me a letter last month, but it said so little that when she didn't answer my next letter, I started to worry. I thought I'd better come see what was going on for myself."

"What exactly are you worried might happen to her?" asked Jessie.

"I'm surprised you'd ask," Moondance said. "She's only nineteen. She's dating someone, some local boy, god knows who. I'm worried she might be unduly influenced by the, ah, local culture."

"Would you like a beer?" Jessie said. "I think we need a couple beers over here. Hey, Ben. Two please."

"I'd prefer a vodka gimlet," said Moondance.

"And so would I," agreed Jessie. "But you're in Utah, now. Bars can only serve beer."

"Good heavens, how barbaric."

"Amen," said Jessie. When the frosted mugs arrived, she said, "You know, your instincts are good, but you're timing's a little off. Melody was baptized this afternoon."

"Baptized?" Moondance said it in a way that others might have said "fallen off the planet" or "sucked into a black hole."

Jessie had both hands around the base of her glass, and she looked into it as though she saw something tantalizing in the bubbles sashaying up from the bottom.

Moondance quieted for a few moments, staring off above Jessie's head. Then she said, "Well, we'll just have to get her unbaptized. Take me to her."

"Right now?"

"Right now."

Moondance had always been the consummate party crasher. It was how she got her start in Hollywood. She had a knack for slipping in and mingling, seeming to be someone that somebody had brought. But this affair was much different. Here Moondance functioned more like the party SWAT team, rushing in to blow the festivities away.

One minute Melody was happily balancing a plate of food in one hand and a soda in the other, and chatting with Dorothy about plans for the wedding when she looked up to discover her own mother advancing on her in that tight-lipped way that meant trouble.

Mother and daughter confronted each other, words that might be said presenting themselves to each mind and being discarded.

"Everyone," said Jessie, "this is Melody's mother, Moondance, just in from Los Angeles."

John Cannon moved in to cover snickers over her name from the younger cousins. He said welcoming things to the tiny woman whose face had taken on colors one associates with screaming infants. Introductions happened, neatly, like dominoes stacked and falling. John was only through about two-thirds of the family before the appropriate words presented themselves to Moondance.

"Melody, come with me. I will not have you connected with this ... this cult."

Jessie shook her head. Somebody with worse manners than me, she thought. Where did people develop these parenting skills? Boot camp?

Moondance turned her back on the group, as though they were so many unusual insects, and walked toward the door. Melody didn't move.

"Melody!" she said in that voice that had indicated in Melody's youth that her mother would brook no disobedience.

"In the first place," said Melody, who was making instantaneous strides in the self-expression department, "it's not a cult. It's a perfectly respectable Christian denomination with eight million members and a living prophet. In the second place, I am not coming with you. I am engaged to marry Daniel and nothing you can say will stop me."

"In that case," said her mother, "goodbye forever."

She left the house, and Jessie followed her out the door. Behind them came Daniel.

"Mrs. Stardust? Wait! Let me talk to you!"

She turned and faced him and Jessie went on toward her car to give them a little privacy.

"Mrs. Stardust, I love your daughter. I would never do anything to hurt her. I know you love her, too. Why don't you just stay, spend a little time with us, get to know us. You might like us. We're not what you seem to think. My father is a surgeon. My mother is a devoted homemaker. I'm going to college, pre-med. We all love Melody. We imagine you're just as wonderful as your daughter. After all, you're the one who raised her."

Oh, slick, thought Jessie. Mr. Charm School. He can really dish it out when he wants to. She wondered if now would be a good time to mention pending court actions. No, they seemed to have their hands full.

"Look, you young punk," said Moondance, although the last thing the clean-shaven Daniel could be considered was a punk. "That talk may have snookered my daughter, but I don't buy it. You people have not heard the last of me. I want my daughter back, and I intend to get her back."

She stalked off to Jessie's Land Cruiser and got in with as much dignity as rage could lend. Jessie and Daniel looked at each other and Jessie shrugged. Daniel turned his back on her and went inside.

Jessie got in. "Excuse me, but didn't you just say goodbye forever to your daughter?"

"I don't feel any pressing need to explain myself to you," Moondance replied. "Take me to my car."

"I beg your pardon," said Jessie. "I don't feel any pressing reason to do you any favors. Get out."

"What?"

"I said get out of my car."

"Oh, for heaven's sake," fumed the aging Californian. "Don't be ridiculous."

"Ridiculous?" said Jessie. "Calling my brother Daniel a punk is ridiculous. Referring to my parents as cultists is ridiculous. The pink spiked heals you're wearing are ridiculous. The name, Moondance, well, but I digress. Get out of my car."

"But I have no idea where I am."

"You've got that right. And you know something? It's your problem, not mine. Now, my parents, they'd probably be happy to give you a ride to your car, sick cultists that they are. That punk Daniel'd probably carry you to the damn thing. Me, personally, I don't care. I guess if you really want a ride you'll have to throw yourself on their mercy."

Moondance had her pride. She got out of the vehicle and headed down the driveway to the street. Jessie went back to the house.

"I'm sorry, Melody," she said. "I had no idea your mother would be so annoying."

"Where is she?" John asked.

"Walking back to her car. She was having a little attitude problem."

"Where is her car?" Dorothy asked.

"Down by the bar, I guess. That's where I found her."

"And you're making her walk back?" said Dorothy. "Oh, John, she can't be allowed to walk in those shoes. She'll hurt herself. We've got to give her a ride."

The suggestion triggered Daniel and Melody's first dispute. Melody wanted to go; Daniel, all wounded ego, thought the old bat deserved a hike. The womenfolk won out, and pretty soon John and Dorothy and Melody and Daniel had loaded into the family Caddy and gone to the rescue.

Jessie went over to Alden and said, "Why don't we go watch?"

"OK," he said.

"Oh, Al," said Claire. "Let's just let it go. Let's not turn the thing into some sort of spectacle."

"What do you bet she refuses a ride?" said Alden.

"I don't know," said Jessie. "Those shoes of hers definitely weren't meant for walking."

"Come on," said Alden, "I'll drive."

So Jessie and Alden and a reluctant but curious Claire piled into Alden's minivan and off they went. It didn't take them more than a few seconds to catch up with the Caddy, which was crawling along to keep pace with Moondance whose clack-clacking gait couldn't have been more than three miles per hour, tops. Daniel and Melody, heads hanging out the window, tried to talk Moondance into the car. She ignored them. Alden's minivan pulled up behind the Caddy, and they proceeded this way for a couple of blocks on the narrow road, other drivers honking and glaring as they went by.

"I think she's cracking," said Jessie. "Another block, and those feet of hers are going to just flat give out."

"I don't know," said Alden. "She looks pretty determined to me."

At that moment the Cadillac stopped and Dorothy got out. She trotted up to Moondance and fell into step beside her.

"Oh, nice touch," said Jessie. "I say she's in the car before we get to Fourth North."

"Bet you dinner at the restaurant of my choice," said Alden.

"You're on," said Jessie and no sooner had those words spilled out than Moondance stopped. She and Dorothy spoke for several more seconds, and then the two of them got into the back seat of the Caddy and it sped away.

"Never bet on a woman in heels to go the distance," said Jessie. "Those shoes are some sort of sexual come-on signal designed by men to hobble us."

"Jessie!" said Claire.

"Sorry, but am I right or am I right?"

"They are pretty uncomfortable," agreed her aunt. "Still, I always feel so attractive when I wear them. They give such a slimming look."

"Oh, yeah," snorted Jessie. "Hurts like hell, but at least I look anorexic."

"Now where do you suppose they're off to," said Alden. "I thought you told me her car was parked by the bar."

The Cadillac had turned east on Fourth instead of west. "Uh oh. It looks like Dad's taking her on The Drive," said Jessie.

"The Drive?" said Claire.

"Don't tell me you don't remember The Drive," said Jessie. "I complained about it enough. It's this problem-solving technique Dad dreamed up when I was a teenager and Mom and I were fighting, big time. He'd make both of us get in the car. He'd drive somewhere, anywhere, and we couldn't get out of the car until we'd figured out a way to reach an agreement or compromise. I got so I hated it so much I just stopped talking and went ahead and did whatever I wanted. Getting grounded afterward was more pleasant than those car rides. I can just imagine it, now. Dad's probably telling Moondance and Melody to apologize to each other. He's probably explaining the psychological roots of the mother-daughter conflict. If I were Moondance, I'd just take off a shoe and beat him until he stopped."

Twenty-two

"Tukudeka," said John Tyhee. He drew the word out, exhaling the last syllable as though it were cigarette smoke coming up out of his lungs. He and Nephi stood on a hill east of town, watching as lights flicked on in homes on the neat, wide streets below them. "So your grandpa was murdered by whites and your grandma drank herself to death and your mother ran off and your father smashed himself up in a canyon and your girlfriend keeps dumping you for other men."

It didn't sound good, Nephi had to admit. It didn't sound like the stuff of dreams at all. He felt some flickering angry thing. He kept his mouth shut and looked ahead of him, wishing the old man would blow away into the dark, wishing he didn't know any of it or that he knew it about somebody else.

"Where do you feel it?" Tyhee asked him.

"What do you mean?" said Nephi.

"I mean where does it hurt?"

"It doesn't hurt," said Nephi.

"It hurts," said Tyhee, turning to face him. "Only question is, where is it hurting?" He spread his hand across the center of Nephi's chest. "Maybe it hurts here," he said and pushed Nephi hard, so that he staggered backward. "Maybe it hurts in your gut." He made a fist and swung toward Nephi's stomach, but Nephi side-stepped out of the way. Tyhee dropped his fist. "Maybe it hurts up here," he said and tapped the side of his head.

"Why are you doing this?" said Nephi.

Tyhee ignored him and started down the hill. Nephi watched him. He didn't want to follow, but he didn't know what else to do. As twilight got narrow and compressed into nothing across the western sky, he trotted down the short slope and sat down in the long grass by Tyhee.

"How many ways to get up that hill from here?" said Tyhee.

Nephi didn't answer. Stars suggested their arrival to him and he watched the sky.

"Same as anything else," said Tyhee. "You start where you are and work your way. Trouble is, you've got to know where you are, where you came from, and where you want to go. You want to get past the pain, you have to go right through it. You can't go around it. You can't avoid it. Move toward whatever you're afraid of."

"Or not," said Nephi.

"You think your mixed blood is some unique problem. Listen, we all straddle the worlds. I got a wife, hates me, won't have nothing to do with me. I got a son at Point of the Mountain doing time for assault and a granddaughter hooking in Salt Lake City. I've got a daughter who's a churchgoing Mormon and another son preparing for a sun dance. What's me in all that?" Tyhee waited a while before answering his own question. "I choose."

"Hey, I didn't choose any of this," said Nephi and felt anger doing somersaults inside.

"No, but you're choosing now. Self-medicate or wake up and feel. Go over the hill."

"Why should I?"

"When you clean out your stables, you're working with horse shit. This is a lot like that. You've got to muck around in it a while, before it gets anything like clean," said Tyhee. "But then, after a while, the feelings stop getting worse and they turn around and they start getting better."

"These damned metaphors," said Nephi.

"What do you mean?" said Tyhee.

"You and Ben. You guys talk in metaphors. Look, I am not a tomato and my life isn't horse shit."

"What would you call it?"

"I'd call it empty," said Nephi and then the truth of that emptiness yanked a howling cry out of him, and he was shaking with emotions he'd not been feeling for years, but which he had always waited to feel.

Tyhee was silent and near. In a while Nephi's storm ran its course. The sounds of night and the patterns of the stars held the two men together, breathing evenly in the dark air, which was warm and tangy with summer.

"You're looking for some place to belong," said Tyhee. "You're looking for something to believe in. I can help you, but you have to stay sober."

"I don't think I can," said Nephi.

"Nobody does at first," said Tyhee. "It gets easier. How do you feel right now?"

"OK, I guess," Nephi said. "Drained. Not so heavy."

"Good. Let's call it a night."

———

Opposing feelings breached the surface, sucked in big gusts of air, and dove for the bottom in the small ocean of the Stardust family. Melody sat in her mother's red Saab and wished for better words, stronger words, more convincing words. She had conjured up nothing that made her mother see the overwhelming beauty of the choices she had made. She built up fragile sentences full of her new ideas like "spirit" and "God's love" and "miracle." And each of the tentative, brave, searching sentiments keeled over and played dead as they vibrated across the distance that confined the two women inside the car parked on Main Street at the edge of town.

"You should have told me," Moondance said.

"So you could come out here to stop me?" said Melody.

"I hate to see you make such a big mistake. Throw your life away on some boy you've barely known a few months."

"It's my life," said Melody.

Moondance had no response to this. She knew it was true, yet she rebelled against it. "You are my daughter!" she wanted to say. "You will do what I say," she wanted to insist as she had so often before. Certain visions regarding her daughter's future had long embedded themselves in Moondance's rich fantasy world. She didn't want to let go of them as she looked at the girl now. "I'm your mother," she said out loud, and the sentence limped into the middle distance between them before falling down. "There's so much you don't know, so many things you need to learn." This sentence had no staying power, either. Moondance tried something more imperious. "You have no idea what a choice like this means, the repercussions, the price you'll have to pay."

Melody yanked out a stream of thought she'd never given voice to before. The vehemence in it startled both of them. "I am not a pawn, OK? I'm not a piece on a chess board that you can move around to make you feel good about yourself. I don't tell you anything about me, because you don't care about me, the person who's really in here," she said and thumped her chest with her fist.

"The only thing that matters to you is how I make you look. Do I reflect well on you? Can you brag about me to your friends? Am I being 'good,' whatever your definition of that is on any given day. Why should I tell you how I feel or what I believe or what my hopes and dreams are when the minute they don't fit your expectations, you start telling me how wrong I am? You don't hear me. You don't even want to hear me. You've got some make-believe daughter in your head. You want that one. You don't want the one who's sitting here."

"That's not true," protested Moondance.

"Does it matter to you how happy I am? Can you even see it? No. You're probably thinking how embarrassing it will be to have to explain to your friends in California that your daughter just joined the Mormon church."

The remark stung Moondance because it was so true. She had tried to imagine herself concocting some version of the truth that wouldn't shame her in front of the people who mattered to her. And in no version of the truth did Moondance or Melody appear as she would have liked.

"Melody, you're so young. That's what I'm worried about. You think the things you're feeling so deeply will last forever. You think you'll always feel the things you feel and believe right now. I'm telling you, that's not always the case. I'm begging you not to commit to something that might not be good for you over the long haul. I'm trying to help you keep your options open. And each step you take into that church shuts down your options."

"You don't know anything about it," said Melody. "You don't have any right to criticize me."

"I know enough," said Moondance. "If it's such a fine upstanding organization, how come they won't let the rest of us see what they're doing in those temples of theirs? Secrets breed distrust, Melody."

"People who don't understand can profane sacred rituals," said Melody, even though she herself didn't yet know what went on in temples.

"Melody, am I going to have to hire someone to counteract this brainwashing and bring you back home to me?"

"Right. Have a nice life, Mom," Melody got out of the car and started across the street. Moondance jumped out of the driver's side and called to her daughter over the hood of the car. "Wait, Melody! Please!"

And because the pleading sound in her mother's voice echoed so sadly, so unlike her, Melody stopped and, instead of stepping up onto the curb, turned back suddenly into the street, into the front grill of an oncoming car. It caught her and pushed her up into the air where she hit the windshield and was slung off the side into oncoming traffic, where a passing truck slammed on its brakes but couldn't refrain from crushing her precious skull.

146

Twenty-three

Let us examine various qualities of light. Say a sudden flash, as when the sun glints off a mirror and blinds you, or the beam from a tiny pen-sized light that drills a neat hole in a black square of room, or the cool glow from a long fluorescent tube that pulls at the blue of your skin, say a bloated moon that makes a long shadow of your body against the pale ground or the incandescence of a naked bulb that illuminates something harsh, something difficult to look at. Illuminations accompanied by an expanse of shadows, the indissoluble marriage of light and dark. You can stand on the cusp of dawn where vision fails. You cannot see into the brilliant glare of morning. If you pivot toward the shadow side, your dilated pupils fail you. Balance there in a kind of shock.

Daniel brought himself to the rim of unknowing by staring repeatedly into the light and the dark, the moment before and the moment after. He lay on his bed with his eyes on the ceiling, examining the flurry of opposing convictions. He could see Melody in his head, and he knew she wasn't dead. He knew it the way that he sensed his hands, motionless now but able at any moment to reach and touch. She is not dead, he would say to himself and then the facts of the previous forty-eight hours would reassert themselves. She is dead, the words in his mind affirmed, and he felt nothing. He felt nothing because it was untrue. She is not dead. Despite evidence to the contrary, she cannot be dead.

They had not let Daniel see the evidence to the contrary. When he had come racing into the emergency room at the hospital, they had not let him see her. Crushed skull, crushed legs. Behind two big swinging metal doors lay the dream of his life, and neither the doctors nor his father would let him see what had become of it. Daniel had swung around, as though to throw off some binding thing and seen Moondance in a corner, his mother to one side of her. She leaned forward in the chair, holding her body the way someone does in the grip of a frigid wind. He could not go to her. He stumbled outside, unaware that his father followed him. In the darkness he felt the rich scent of cut flowers on the warm air. He heard a confusion of voices in the parking lot. He wanted to walk but his leg muscles stiffened and balked.

His father had spoken to him, words that at first he didn't hear and then didn't comprehend. He heard them again as he lay on his bed. "She felt no pain, Daniel. The truck came out of nowhere. She didn't even see it. It took her instantly. I know it's small consolation, son. But she didn't suffer."

Small consolation that she had felt no pain. In the dark room he realized he was feeling no pain himself. He was feeling nothing because he had managed to keep himself from believing that the smiling eyes of Melody and the wide, full lips of Melody and the short fingers and fine-boned wrists of Melody and the long sweet neck of Melody or Melody's little way of tilting her head and looking at him while he spoke, all these attributes that had the power of provoking rapture in him, had ceased to be.

And at that moment, contemplating Melody in his dark room, his denial crumpled. The image of a smiling Melody fractured into bitter shards, replaced in his imagination by what she must have looked like beneath the wheels of the truck. He sucked air into his lungs. His chest began to heave, his heart slamming as the shattering fact slipped through the prison he'd tried to encase it in.

The fact of his loss. The fact of his loss. Daniel swung his legs to the floor and stood up. His muscles had no interest in sustaining him and he sank to his knees, leaning forward until his forehead rested against the carpet. He wrapped his arms around his head and a low moan escaped him.

Outside his room his father sat in the hallway, knees pulled up to his chest, hands resting palm up on the floor. John heard the stuttered, heavy breathing of his son's grief. He had been anxious for signs of it. He got up and went back to his bedroom where Dorothy sat in a small circle of yellow lamplight, her Bible in her hands. She had fallen asleep, chin on her chest, reading glasses slumped forward on her nose.

John took the book from her and gently removed the glasses. She woke and pulled him close, hugging him hard around the neck.

"He's starting to feel it," said John.

She slipped from the bed and went to her son's room. Daniel, huddled on the floor, didn't move. She knelt beside him, put her hand on his arm.

"Danny," she said, "Danny, it's only sad for us, you know. For Melody, her death was a gift, a beautiful gift. Can you see that?"

Daniel didn't move. She stroked his hair back from his temple. "Danny, the Lord loved her so much, he didn't need to test her. She had just been baptized, son. She died sinless. There can be no greater blessing than that. She'll be waiting for you in the Celestial Kingdom. In a way her death is a miracle, a miracle we can celebrate. She's safe now, son. She's home."

Daniel didn't respond. She could not hear him breathing. He might have been a hologram. Was it his skin she felt under her hand or a paper-thin husk of something? She gave him back his solitude, went along down the dark hall to her husband. Despite her brave Christian sentiments, she felt herself engulfed by the midnight terror of parents, the deep knowing that she could not fling herself between searing pain and the delicate being she and John had lovingly built. They clung to each other until daylight took away the stars.

―――

In the hours after Melody died, Moondance ordered the chaos of her misery thusly: The Mormons had crushed the only gem she possessed. Twin thorns embedded deep in her, the irreparable loss of her child and a newborn seething hatred. She took her daughter's body back to California, refusing the Cannons the memorial they wanted. She told them to stay away.

―――

Language delivers a deadly word into the vocabulary of toddlers. Why is the sky blue, Mama? Why are we going to church, Mama? Why is the sun so far away? Why is it dark, Mama? Why are there flowers? Why is it so cold? A single answer won't satisfy the child's voracious curiosity. Three-year-olds backtrack causality relentlessly and to the despair of their darling mamas. "Because, Honey," their mamas finally say with a sigh, "just because." The existential "why" in the inquisitive repertoire never dies. It just goes underground, rumbling out each time the world stuns us senseless.

Why did Melody die? But why did she get hit by a truck? But why was she in the street? But why was she arguing with her mother? Jessie followed the thread of whys down a winding path that led incontrovertibly to her own door. The more she tried to manipulate it away from herself, the more entangled she became. At last she settled into a follow-up game. "If only," she said to the dark thread. "If only I hadn't been such a bitch. If only I had minded my own business. If only I hadn't introduced Melody to Daniel. If only, if only, if only."

Sitting in her cramped office in the bar, she took a break from the guilt to call the district attorney's office, telling them she was dropping charges against her brother. The relief she expected from this move did not materialize. Instead she felt worse, tapping a pencil against her desk, staring at a big dark thing on the edge of her guilt. The guilt had a strange, tranquilizing effect. There was a comprehensibility to it, a safety in it. The blotchy thing that awaited outside the guilt, though, that was something else, something else entirely. A black hole of meaninglessness that insinuated itself upon her consciousness the more she tried not to look at it.

When Ben came in and said, "Talk to me," she said, "Can you think of anything that matters?"

"Give me a context," he replied.

"Anything about the human experience that matters?"

"You mean besides birth and sex and death?" he said.

"What does any of it mean?" she said.

"Jessie, you aren't a human meaning, you're a human being. Being is what matters."

"It doesn't feel like it does."

"Come with me," he said. They went outside and he took her over to the garden in front of the tabernacle where white blossoms of alyssum spilled out around petunias and the deep purple of heliotrope. He stuck his nose down among the flowers and made Jessie do the same. "This matters," he said. He took her to the base of a pine tree and put her hands on the rough bark. "This matters." He dragged her away from the tree onto the grass where they could see the mountains ranging west across the sky. "Those matter," he said. He pulled her against him suddenly and she felt his muscled length as he pressed himself against her. "This matters."

She pushed away from him. "Sensory input," she said. "So what?"

"There is no greater misfortune than wanting more," he said.

"Where do you come up with this horseshit, Ben?"

"Jessie, what else are we? We're one big mass of sensory receptors. We smell, we see, we touch, we hear, we taste, and then we do one other thing, God help us all. We feel. We pay attention and we feel. We are the earth's way of thinking about itself, of appreciating itself. And that's the beginning and that's the end."

"Well, I don't want to."

"Well, then, let me pour you a drink."

Jessie needed no assistance in pursuit of anesthesia. She left Ben and went home. She snagged a bottle of brandy from the kitchen cabinet and wandered outside into the backyard where the disorder of her summerlong neglect reigned. Healthy weeds choked out the delicate blooms of day lilies and dianthus. Even the sturdy marigolds straggled like beggars under the fierce heat. She could hear Ben's voice in the garden and went back inside scowling. Up the hallway, down the hallway, into the bedroom, out of the bedroom, back down the hallway, she stands outside the study door, curses, kicks it open. All right, old man. Let's get it on.

Snorting brandy in gusty mouthfuls, Jessie settled into Patriarch William Moroni Cannon's chair. She put her feet up on the desk and opened the file drawer. Rows of folders organized alphabetically filled it. She pulled out the first of the "A" files and flipped it open. Inside was the transcription of a blessing her grandfather had given one Mitchel Andreason, dated 1952.

She closed her eyes and set the folder down on the desk. It had never really occurred to her before to think about the nature of her grandfather's church calling. He had been a patriarch, responsible for blessing the members of the church, a kind of Latter-day Saint psychic, channeling information from God to his chosen people, individually. Members had come to her grandfather and he gave them a glimpse of the possibilities of their future if they remained steadfast in their faith.

Jessie had never received a patriarchal blessing. You had to demonstrate a certain level of compliance in order to get in the door and compliance had never been her forte.

She picked the file up again. Mitchell Andreason's blessing was printed in carbon on onion-skin paper. Attached to it was a letter from him to her grandfather, dated 1970.

Dear Brother Cannon: I don't know if you remember me or not. You gave me my blessing in 1952, when I was just about to go on my mission. Many things have happened to me in the eighteen years since the blessing, and I just wanted to let you know that your words have been both a comfort and a confirmation to me about the life I have chosen. In the blessing you said I would comfort the many, despite the pain in my own heart. I didn't know what those words meant at all, but in the last five years I have found myself counseling grieving parents after recovering from the death of my own son. You said that after a period of great darkness I would know joy. This has happened to me. In the last year I have relearned the art of living and have been able to see things of beauty

beauty without feeling a simultaneous sense of loss. Your words provided both reassurance and revelation. I have never forgotten them.

———

Jessie held a mouthful of lukewarm brandy against her palate, grimaced, and returned the file to the drawer. She pulled another one out. Stephanie Monson: 1961, age 22. With the onion-skin carbon of the blessing was another letter.

———

Dear Brother Cannon: Words cannot express how much my patriarchal blessing has meant to me over the years. When my marriage collapsed in adultery and divorce, I thought everything I had been promised in the blessing—a loving husband, harmonious home life, strength, and wisdom—were lies. My heart was closed to the truths of the gospel for a long time. Then one day when I was cleaning out the last bits of things my husband had left behind, I came across my blessing. I was about to throw it away as well when these words seemed to come up off the page for me to see: "Remember, there is no room for bitterness in a heart that wants to be open to love. Don't allow painful circumstances to harden your tender feelings. Stay as open as a child, ready to learn and ready to give."

Those words were the beginning of a long road back for me, back to the Lord and eventually to a loving husband with whom I have been able to learn and to grow. I don't know that I have developed wisdom, but the painful experiences of my first marriage have given me a kinder and more forgiving outlook. I realize there is no room in my life for judging others. That is a task for God.

———

Every file that Jessie took from the drawer held a blessing and a letter, each of them variations of a theme. Her grandfather had given them hope in times of turmoil or had accurately predicted their futures or had warned them about experiences that might hurt them. He had strengthened their faith or reminded them of their responsibilities or somehow changed their lives for the better. She read the files and drank the brandy, her head swimming in a strange alcoholic concoction of hope and dread. She pulled one last file from the drawer: Daniel Cannon, 1979. She skipped through the introductory parts and went right to the meaty middle and this is what she read:

———

Daniel, there will be times in your life when you will think the Lord has forsaken you. There will be times you will forget your heritage and curse your lot in life. Do not be dismayed. The Lord has not forgotten

152

you. Turn to him in your greatest hour of need, and he will shower you with blessings you cannot begin to fathom. There will be but a little pain, a little sorrow, and then the warmth of God's love will shine on your life.

Do not wander from the path in your agony. Hold firmly to the rod. With it comes salvation and a joy beyond joys.

———

Jessie carried the thin pages in one hand and the bottle in another, went out to the kitchen, and called her uncle.

"Have you ever read any of these patriarchal blessings that Grandpa gave?" she asked him.

Alden had not.

"I never really understood what this whole blessing deal was all about," she continued. "But it's like he was clairvoyant, a sort of Mormon Edgar Cayce. He told people what their future would hold and what they should do about it. You should see some of the stuff in these files."

"Aren't those files private?" Alden said.

"Uncle Alden, this is what he was up to when he left me the house. He wanted me to read this stuff, but he wasn't going to force it on me," she said. "It's like he knew damn well I'd never bother with this if anybody put it in my hands. He set me up. God, he was a crafty old man."

"You're sounding a little wild," said Alden.

"Yeah? Well, I'm feeling pretty weird. I mean it kind of rocks my world. Jesus, Uncle Alden. What if they're right and we're wrong?"

She could hear Alden sighing on the other end of the phone. "I've always tried to find the middle ground, Jessie. You don't have to align yourself inside or outside. Your grandfather had an incredible wealth of spiritual power. He chose the Mormon route. The question is, does that make the route more true?"

"Well, after reading the substance of these blessings, I have to wonder," said Jessie.

"In that case, why isn't the route less true, since you and I and a host of others didn't choose it?"

"Because," said Jessie. "You and I do not have any spiritual power. Because you and I are just mucking around down here making big mistakes."

"Black-and-white thinking," said Alden. "We're either saints or sinners and no middle ground. I don't hold with that Jessie. World views differ. You think truth is something that comes on a placque you can nail to your wall?"

"I don't know. *I don't know,*" she replied. "I've got to get out of here for a while. I've got to go."

She went to the basement and gathered up her backpack, sleeping bag, and tent and brought them upstairs. She stuffed various jeans, shirts, and socks into the pack. Time to get out of Dodge for a while.

She called Ben and told him she'd be hiking the north fork of Blackstone Creek if anyone cared, probably be gone three or four days. She drove to the grocery store and picked up a supply of food for the journey. On the way out of the parking lot, she saw the Basques' rusty beater of a truck parked off by itself. They were nowhere in sight. She slammed to a stop, jump out of the Land Cuiser with her small Swiss army knife in her fist, and plunged it quickly into the sides of the back tires. *Piss on you, too, boys.*

She wheeled out of the parking lot and drove north and east to Blackstone Canyon still chugging brandy, sensations boiling around that she aided and abetted by punching a Tabernacle Choir tape into the tape deck.

It was midnight when she pulled off the road and parked in the grass near the river. Shoving a ground sheet under the Land Cruiser, she hauled out her sleeping bag, stepped into it, and thrust herself down between the front tires of the vehicle. Jessie tossed and turned under the oil pain. It did not feel to her that she slept at all, but she did not hear and did not see the coyote that trotted up and sniffed one of her tires or the magpies that hop-fluttered within feet of her when the eastern sky woke up.

———

Max had grown annoyed with the no-answer routine on Jessie's telephone line. His annoyance built into a sturdy edifice of anger when he went to the bar and learned she'd wandered off without so much as a hello or a goodbye. Since there was no future in directing the anger at Ben, he hammered it out on the pool table for an hour. When beer and time took the edge off it, he sat himself back down on the bar stool next to a couple of raggedy, weathered-looking drinkers speaking a language he did not know.

"Ben, what's the deal with her anyway?"

"With Jessie? Well, she's an impulse shopper."

Max rolled the thought around in his head and decided to shoot more pool. It didn't help. He went back to his bar stool. "So where has she gone camping? I mean, could I go find her?"

"She's up Blackstone Canyon, hiking the north fork of the creek. If she stayed on the trail, you might could find her. If she goes traipsing back to some other spot, you wouldn't. She's kind of wanked-out at the moment."

"I didn't think she was the moody type," said Max.

"Well, her brother's fiancee died last week. Everybody's taking it hard," said Ben.

Max let the pool cue slide through his fingers, "Last week? When last week?" he asked.

"Last Tuesday," said Ben.

"Jeez!" Max muttered and sat down abruptly. He looked at his own haggard face in the mirror and wondered something that he couldn't articulate. "You know, Ben," he said, "I thought the woman had a thing for me, but I think she just wants my body. Which makes her pretty damned cold."

Ben continued with his beer-glass ministrations.

"I mean, I talked to her twice last week after Tuesday and she never said a word. You'd think she would have said something."

Ben didn't reply.

"Well, wouldn't you?"

"You can't call a thing like that, Max."

"Do me a favor and tell her I'm looking for her when she gets back, OK?"

"OK."

He sat there staring at himself in the mirror, wondering at something about the way his eyes seemed, wondering why the two men sitting next to him were smiling, now at the mirror, now at each other. But he forgot them the instant they slid off their bar stools and slipped out the door.

Twenty-four

Dawn walked in on Jessie's sleep, elbowing past a dream. In the dream Jessie inhabited an unusual disc-shaped boat that cruised as easily through air as it did over water. But the boat would not go. The starter mechanism—flat, round, and somewhat bigger than the palm of her hand—lay broken in two pieces that had to be reconnected and then inserted in a slot in the craft. Jessie didn't know how to fix the starter. She just looked at the pieces and wondered how to manipulate them. Waves washed over the hull as a wind shoved her farther and farther toward the center of a huge lake. It occurred to her as she fingered the starter talisman that there must be a third thing that would hold the pieces together, something that she didn't have. Water sloshed over the boat and her anxiety was rising when faint tracings of light whispered morning in her ear. She awoke grateful. She did not like the dream, the big lake, the strange boat, her immobility.

She crawled out from under the Land Cruiser to begin morning rituals, the small stove out of her pack, set up, and water on to heat for hot chocolate, granola bar for breakfast. She found a secluded place among some juniper bushes to relieve herself and squatted in the dirt. Something so fine about the cool morning air on her flanks. Jessie wondered why she hadn't thought of this before. Why hadn't she high-tailed it from the streets sooner for this solitude? And why should I ever go back? Why don't I just stay up here and live this way forever? To be free from the bonds of possessions, to be free from the grip of other people's expectations—the allure of it whistled sexy promises in her ear. She gathered up her gear, stowed it, and hoisted it up on her willing shoulders, heading up the trail and away.

For the first few hours she hiked steadily following a narrow stream bed, now mostly dry. Jessie's gear weighed close to thirty-five pounds, and she found herself tiring when the trail began a more abrupt ascent through a ravine—a grove of alders and birch. She slowed down, resting when she needed to. At first she thought how much she liked to just go, go, go. But as she stopped to let her lungs catch up, she realized that she didn't need to be in any hurry, that the moment she was in was as good as any moment to come. If she didn't move a foot from the place she now stood, what would it matter? Despite the thought, she pushed on. She realized she had left Bridger behind but she had brought her pushiness along for the ride.

At the top of the steep ravine, the trail gave out onto a rounded hilltop where she stopped and decided lunch would be in order. Bread, hunks of cheese, and grapes did the job they were hired to do, while she looked out upon the sweep of mountains and let the heat settle into her.

She thought about her grandfather, how he had been content to let her stumble upon his life's work. He could have showed her his files while he was alive. How many times had they sat in his office together haggling over conflicting world views? Look, he could have said. Look what I've got here. But he hadn't, had simply, as a final gesture, handed it all over to her and said dinner's ready anytime you are.

She couldn't deny her grandfather's record. Well, she supposed, she could deny it. Perhaps it was all orchestrated lies. Perhaps the files were fakes. Maybe her grandfather had set her up. But no. The thought was ludicrous. He wasn't that kind of man.

What did the evidence tell her? She thought about this a while. The evidence told her that he believed in a system of thought about eternity, knitted together by Joseph Smith, various ministering angels and, later, Brigham Young. By believing in that system, he had tapped into some kind of power that allowed him to see the future. But maybe, thought Jessie, he would have been able to see the future regardless of his religious beliefs. Maybe he was born clairvoyant. These are questions that you can't answer, she reminded herself. You're going around in circles and avoiding the central issue, which is what in sweet holy hell are you gonna do? Enquiring minds want to know.

She settled her shoulders under the weight of the pack and started down into a narrow valley. Sweat trickled between her breasts, cooling her as she walked through a shaded patchwork where the trail meandered through ponderosa pine.

I don't belong there, she said to herself. I belong here, in these quiet reaches. Once a fat pheasant flew out from under the brush as she walked nearby. As she got down to the valley floor, she spied an elk on a southern slope, moving sedately upward, antlers spanning a wide drift. I want to be like that, she thought. Of course it would take a lobotomy. The cool shank of evening brought her to the edge of a small lake.

Shrugging out of the pack, so grateful to be light, so floating, she found a tall pine to pitch her tent under.

She went down to the rocky beach and hallooed the lake, knelt, cupped some water to her face and splashed it over her. The frigid water tingled and tightened her skin. She got out her water bottle and drank down the lukewarm liquid. At this fine and lovely bewitching hour, it was time to be still, time to still herself and watch.

A huge, squat boulder, more than seven feet across, jutted out into the water. Jessie pulled on a sweater and sat on the boulder. The sun had moved below the mountains. Birds skipped across the lake, snicking up insects flitting on the surface. At the north end, where marsh grass grew out of the muddy bottom, she caught sight of a beaver swimming low and ducking away. There was no wind. The air settled around Jessie, who hoped for something tremendous, like a moose to detach itself from the shadows and wade into the water. It didn't happen. Show-off trout leaped high, feeding on insects, like the birds. Mosquitoes checked out Jessie, who pulled a small tube of repellent from her back pocket and spread it on her arms and ankles and over the back of her neck.

The cerulean sky, now growing indigo, offered up the first star of evening. Darkness brought with it a peace. Jessie lay flat on the rock, head cupped in her hands. The night sky seemed to come suddenly upon her, heaven a blaze of stars. The great rampart of the Milky Way telegraphed vast and subtle messages.

She watched the stars, picking out Cygnus the Swan from the points of light above her. A shooting star streaked eastward. A satellite chugged slowly through the bright debris. When the moon pushed up to illuminate the granite peaks above her, she stumbled upon a truth. The universe is immense and I am small. Tiny on this tiny boulder by this tiny lake in this tiny system of mountains on this tiny whirling blue-green planet.

She laughed a little as she compared her own ferocious concerns with the size of the visible universe.

Certain things become irrelevant under a sky like that. It didn't matter whether she was right and her family was wrong or vice versa. It didn't matter whether there was a Celestial Kingdom or life after death or a God in his heaven and all's right with the world. There is no answer, she explained to herself. There are only questions and questions behind questions. What's behind these stars and what's behind those stars and what's behind the other stars? It was a game of the mind to occupy itself with these beyondings when right here in the night sky and right here all around her was everything that was worthy of her attention.

She pictured Ben, his hand on the back of her neck bringing her head down to the rich scent of the blossoms, and she glimpsed a portion of his meaning. I don't need to figure it out. I don't need to keep score. I just need to create a space for myself that doesn't piss me off.

The air had become cold. She crawled into her tent, stripped, slid into the down bag, and drifted into sleep. She dreamed herself into the small high room in the tabernacle. As she looked out the window, she realized that Melody was beside her, relaxed and happy in an old sweater and faded blue jeans.

Melody took her hand and suddenly they were flying out through the window and toward the stars in the velvet night air. Jessie clung to Melody's hand as they raced out and up. She wanted to call out to her to slow down, but she couldn't get her voice to work. The wind of their motion blew past her and soon a garden of stars shimmered about them. Melody let go of her and the two of them tumbled and laughed and fell through the starlight, leaping up to fly among the bright spheres glittering around and through and on them, the starlight seeming to trail about like ocean spray as they played.

Then Melody took her hand again and they were rushing even faster and higher, away from the stars and the sky and toward something that Jessie couldn't anticipate as the night fell away. She grew fearful. She tugged her hand away from Melody's and slowed down. Melody stopped and looked back at her, then slowly disappeared as Jessie sank and sank and sank through the quiet stars and into the tremulous night to wake in her tent, eyes blinking and startled as memories of the vivid dream presented themselves to her waking mind. She curled herself up in the down bag and drifted back to sleep.

Later that morning, shaking out her ground sheet, she pondered heading for the next lake up the valley. But some tugging thing pulled at her, something about Max, about Nephi, about Daniel. The warm hand of the familiar upon her shoulder turned her about. She threaded back through the ravine and up and over the hill and back down the switchbacks riding the crest of a sunny day, calmer than she had been for some time. She relaxed into that calm, which goes some way toward excusing the fact that she didn't notice the two men sitting on the bumper of her Land Cruiser until she was well within sight of them.

And then health and safety issues became the subject of her once-calm mind.

The Basques stood up. She stopped in the middle of the trail and stared at them. They were smiling. She had no weapon in her backpack, just a small pocket knife with a three-inch blade. Oh well. Something is better than nothing.

She reached in her back pocket, got out the knife, and flicked it open then slid it back down. Just tough it out, she said to herself. I'm meaner than them anyway. No, I am not meaner, but I am scareder. And how helpful that is, shaking in my boots and sweating like a dog.

When she got to her car, she went around to the back to stow her pack. They followed, let her shrug out of it.

"Nice day for a drive," said one.

"Yes," said the other. "Nice day."

Jessie went to the driver's side to get in, but they stood in her way.

"You want to come for a drive with us?"

"No," she said.

"Sure you do." One of them grabbed her arm. She yanked it hard away from him, but the other was at her side, grabbing for her. As he tugged her toward him, she pulled out the knife, blade upward, and sliced into the soft underside of his forearm. It wasn't a deep cut or even a debilitating one, just an angry gash oozing blood and an enraged Basque backhanding her, knocking her to the ground.

They must think I'm a football, thought Jessie, a coherent thought, really, because they were kicking her, kicking her in the stomach and in the head. She felt the pain of every blow, no delayed sensation, no numbness, no shock, just hurts like hell and I am screaming bloody blue murder for good reason. As she was about to let loose another blood-curdling yell, she got kicked in the temple. It knocked her clean out.

She lay in the gravel, and the Basques stared at her and then at each other. One leaned over her and eased away the knife that she still held. The other went to the truck and pulled out a length of yellow rope, tying her hands behind her back and her feet together. They took a dirty bandanna that hung from their rear view mirror and tied it around her mouth, and then they picked her up and shoved her onto the floor of the cab of the old pickup, got in and drove west out of the canyon toward Bridger.

Jessie came back to consciousness as the truck jolted along. Disoriented at first, all she could see were work boots. When she tried to move, a hand grabbed her hair and slammed her head back into the floor of the truck. She decided not to try moving anymore. She lay in the dirt, paying attention to various pain messages fighting for attention as her hands went numb and the rope chafed around her wrists. Once she retched up bile, which soaked the bandanna and then dribbled down her chin.

The truck moved along a smooth road and then turned onto a rutted one. When it came to a stop, they got out and left her alone while shadows lengthened across the day and brooded their way into night. At first she couldn't move, and she lay still thinking that she was in big trouble. She had always figured that the worst she could expect from the Basques was rape. But now she realized that rape might be lower down on the list of worsts. Panic rose in her throat, engulfed every bit of her mind. For a long while there was only herself and this fear, and she was horrified when a whimpering sound oozed out around the filthy rag they had used to gag her. She had never made a sound like that in her life. It got her attention.

Then she noticed that she could move, and she began squirming, trying to get her hands from behind her down around her legs and up in front where she might use them. The numbness didn't help. And in the end it turned out not to matter, this small act, because the Basques came back. They opened the cab and looked in at her, shone a bright light on her face. There must have been something about the way the light glinted in her wide eyes or the acrid smell of urine where she had been unable to control herself that satisfied them because they smiled at her as though she had been a very good girl indeed.

They got in and started the engine. The Basque on the passenger side rested his feet on her, pushing down now and then until she moaned in pain as his heavy boots cut off her breathing or pressed into her groin.

I am dead, she thought. Basically, I am about to be dead. And it was silly, really, to be killed because you hadn't given them more money, because you'd stood up to them when they'd assaulted you, because you'd taken a club to them when they'd been playing dirty in the alley. Maybe the tire slashing had been excessive. But boys, boys, isn't this overkill?

They were discussing something in a language she could not understand, disagreeing with each other in elaborate circumlocutions. Then the dispute settled and it seemed that they were happy with her once again because they smiled toothy, mean-spirited smiles lit from the underside by the yellow-green of the dashboard light.

It was dead of night when the truck stopped. One of them leaned down and cut her bonds, using, she could see, her own knife. This seemed to bode well. They wouldn't untie me just to murder me, would they? They dragged her from the truck out onto the pavement where she skinned her knees, too weak to stand. They left the gag in her mouth. In the dark she vaguely realized they had stopped in front of the bar. One of them knelt beside her and shoved something damp and smelly against her nose. Her mind fell down a hole.

The other Basque fitted keys into the lock. Finally the deadbolt came undone and he swung the heavy door open. He helped his pal manhandle Jessie inside. They took her back to the little office, slumped her in the chair, removed the gag, and left her there. Then they went to the truck and pulled a gas can from the back, sloshing gasoline around the door sill. One of them in the driver's seat, the other flicked a lit match into the doorway, ran, and leaped into the truck, which disappeared with a rankled thrash of engine out the alley down the street, toward the highway heading south. They made one stop, however, at a house on the outskirts of the valley, right before the highway runs into the narrow cleft of a canyon. It was a small, sweet house tucked among poplars, hard to spot unless you knew it was there.

A redhead, beautiful by moonlight, waited for them on the porch. She watched as the truck swerved into her driveway, pulled up, and spun around, reversing its direction, before one of the Basques jumped out and walked up to her in the dark.

"It's done?" she said.

"Done," he said.

"You waited till the place was empty, right?"

"Empty," he agreed.

"Because I damn well don't need them digging any charred bodies from the ashes." She saw a hint of a smile as the Basque shook his head.

"Well, here, then," she said and put a wad of cash into his hands. He looked at the money and then he looked at her, stuffed the bills in his front shirt pocket, grabbed her, and kissed her hard, thrusting his tongue deep into her mouth as he ground his hips against hers.

Caroline laughed when he let her go. The horn blared suddenly and he spun around, ran down the steps, and jumped into the moving vehicle. She watched the tail lights until they were gone and then she went back inside the little house, the last person to see the Basques in Willow Valley ever again.

Twenty-five

Ben Cody, head-tripping around his apartment at two in the morning, imagined a universal will pumping the spiritual equivalent of Motown tunes ("ain't no mountain high enough, sing it again! yeah, yeah, yeah ...") through various levels of his being. Oh, Ben, yoo-hoo, guru-man? Your presence is required. Jessie's about dyin' here.

OK, the truth. Ben didn't rescue Jessie from the flames because he saw the fire in a dream vision. He didn't save her rapacious life because a voice from on high woke him from slumber. He didn't read it in his daily horoscope or his coffee grounds. He dragged the drugged, oxygen-deprived little troublemaker out of the flaming bar in the very nick of time because he'd left behind a book he'd been reading and he suddenly wanted it, a numinous nightcap to help put the day behind him.

He hops on his Harley, tools on over to the Tabernacle to discover flames chowing down on the doorway, the wood happily devolving to smoke and cinder. Yikes, dial 911, somebody.

It never occurred to Ben that Jessie would be inside. But the book, the damned book, his first-edition signed-by-the-author *Life and Teaching of the Masters of the Far East* could not be allowed to perish. He'd left it on the office desk.

Fear garbled the many messages his brain sent out to his muscles, but somehow he willed himself across the burning sill and into the bowels of the bar where smoke swirled like dervishes. The shock of Jessie's presence cranked him into overdrive. He stuffed the book inside his shirt, pulled her leaden body forward over his shoulder, and lunged back toward the flames and across the threshold as an unholy wailing split the night in a migraine of sound.

Hacking with the smoke he'd inhaled, staggering under the burden of Jessie, he went down on his knees in the middle of the street. He laid her out, not gently, and slumped beside her, coughing, which is how the fire trucks found them a few seconds later. As water hoses uncoiled and writhed out to do their work, a fireman hovered over the two of them, checking Jessie's pulse, finding it, checking her breathing, finding it, calling dispatch for an ambulance, playing nurse to the played-out souls on the pavement.

The fire ate the building and the water nibbled at the flames. Despite the prompt arrival of the crew, the bar was in big trouble, lots of dry heavy timber eager to conflagrate. Two of the walls, back and side, were brick. They weren't going anywhere. The rest of the building roiled darkly heavenward.

Ben watched it go.

———

The doctors in the emergency room at the hospital had a time figuring out Jessie's various ailments. When she came around, puking, she choked out the various abuses that had been heaped upon her, not too coherently, but they got the picture. Checked her head for concussion (affirmative), checked her chest for broken ribs (one, cracked), dished up heady painkillers, supplied various ointments for the rope burns, and let her snort bucketfuls of unadulterated oxygen. Drugs lopped the top and bottom off the spikes of pain. She checked into unconsciousness as news of the fire rippled out across the valley.

———

Whoops of glee collected enthusiastic signatures from Bridger's devout. God had spoken. The bar had got what it deserved. Don't you mess with the Almighty, Honey. Play that game, you better be prepared to pay.

As members of Jessie's family hovered around her in the hospital, they tried to cope with the extreme ambivalence of their position, Daniel in particular.

He found himself sitting at Jessie's bedside making bizarre deals with God: straight trade—Jessie for Melody. You took the wrong woman, Lord. You took the wrong one. It ought to be Melody recovering. It ought to be Jessie meeting her maker in the hereafter.

Daniel was not proud of these thoughts. He was deeply ashamed of them, something that gave them a tasty repugnance. He fantasized the handoff over and over again and then recoiled from the mental act in much the same way he was drawn occasionally to self-pleasure, only to be disgusted (conveniently afterward) by himself. *I know it's wrong, but I'm weak.*

Jessie did not have to wake to the restrained gloating of her next of kin. She came around when they had wandered off in search of dinner. Ben was sitting beside her, reading.

She coughed and he put down his book.

"Those damned Basques," she said and coughed some more.

"You think they set the fire?" said Ben.

"What fire?" said Jessie.

Ben would not have tried to predict her reaction to the fate of the bar, but he was surprised at the silence, the stillness of Jessie's body as he described how he had found her and what had happened.

Her eyes traveled around the hospital room as though she were looking for flaws in the structure. She stared at her hands for a while, particularly at the place where a tube went into one of them. She looked at him. She looked away.

"So. The whole thing is just ... gone?"

"Yes."

"Shit."

She sat with the idea for a while longer and Ben let her have her thoughts about it.

"So. Essentially, they tried to kill me."

"Apparently."

"Ha! Those fuckers." And then another thought came to her. "And why did you show up again? Hadn't you shut it down for the night?"

Ben described the book he'd gone back for. As Jessie realized how near she had come to being reduced to basic carbon, Daniel came in. He looked pale, as though he hadn't slept much. Ben excused himself as her father and mother came through the door.

"I guess we're going to have to drum up new things to fight about," Jessie said. They expressed relief, father, mother, brother, but Jessie poked about between the words and found other meanings. She didn't buy their sincerity. Awkwardness stomped around the room, a strange dissociative feeling. *Who are you people?* That's what it felt like to each of them. *Who are you and what am I doing here?* Jessie feigned exhaustion and they went away.

She called Max. He didn't answer his phone.

———

Nephi had not had a drink in four days and it was making him nuts. John Tyhee had told him to lay off the booze and he was giving it his best shot, but he had been relying on its restorative powers for so long that letting go now was like asking him to cut off an arm or a leg. Weird how Tyhee had taken over his brain, how Nephi had let him come in and start giving orders. Not drinking occupied most of Nephi's energy. It seemed strange to be caught up in a process of inaction.

165

When he came in from various chores that evening, he cranked on the news and was stunned to learn the fate of the bar, the near-fate of his former true love.

Christ. He got the urge for a big shot of something. He wanted to go see Jessie. And he wanted a bellyful of alcohol on his way. He called Tyhee.

"Your sanity is what you're after," Tyhee said to him. "Does she contribute to it or detract from it?"

It was a tough call. Nephi had to mull the question over a little. "Overall," he said, as the recent past won out over more distant, less painful times, "overall, I'd have to say she's kind of crazy-making."

"A crazy-making woman? I have known one or two of them," said Tyhee and rumbling laughter accompanied the comment. "You got to let her go. Otherwise you will be back where you've been before. If you like it, there, fine. If you want something different, you have to start crawling out of it."

"What am I doing this for?" said Nephi.

"Go clean out your barn. Call me back when you're done."

And although Nephi resented the commanding tone that Tyhee took with him, he went and did as he was told.

———

Ben went back to his apartment curiously elated, curiously free. He didn't need a vision or a dream or advice from Felice. He knew. If it was possible for cells to sing then Ben sang in all his reaches, from the top of his head down through his hair follicles and all the way out through the calloused soles of his feet. Stick a fork in me, I'm done. I'm through. I'm outta this sorry little backward burg with its self-righteous people and its holier-than-the-entire-universe attitude. I'm walkin'.

166

Twenty-six

Who gets to live long and who gets to die young, an endless, blistering conundrum, one Jessie pondered as she discharged herself from the hospital and headed home. Should be dead, but I'm not. Melody should be alive, but she's not. She got hung up on this thought and didn't stray far from it, as she waited for her body to deal out repairs. Days went by. Her bruises metamorphosed from purple scarlet to yellow brown. The aches subsided. She spent time sitting on the front porch reading the newspaper, reading detective novels, staring out at the street, working on a late-August tan as though it mattered.

As she felt better, she took an interest in her grandmother's neglected flower beds. Internally, she worked the riff, various themes composing themselves around the fact of her life. And on those occasions when the mental music danced her toward the why and the how of her rescue, all her physical motion stopped. She might be digging out the tough, burrowing root of a dandelion only to set back on her haunches, arms slack, eyes looking off somewhere. She might be washing up the dinner dishes and realize that for some unclear period of time her hands had been resting in the dishwater, which was now lukewarm. She might be sitting in a patch of sunlight, sweaty, torpid, only to discover the sun had long since deserted her.

Even with Max, although she drifted, she cycled back. Once she asked him if he believed in God.

"Excuse me?" he responded, but not unkindly.

"Let me ask it a different way," she said. "Have you ever seen any evidence that there's more to life than just what we can experience with our senses?"

"Angel, sensory experience is my idea of God. And some sensory experiences more than others."

"Oh."

Max got out of the bed and went to the kitchen where he ran a tall glass of water and brought it back. When he sat down and handed it to her, he said, "Once I was standing on a submarine deck with about half a dozen other guys. There was some construction going on in the dock yard that day, a big crane moving steel girders around. We weren't paying a lot of attention, just taking a break and having a smoke. All of a sudden the crane swings loose and drops the girder and it hits two guys standing right beside me. It missed me by about a foot, I'd say. It killed them. They were both married and had families. I was single, had a nutcase girlfriend couldn't stand me half the time, couldn't live without me the other half.

"Another time I was driving to the base along this twisty-turny two-laner. It was a wet, slick day. I was going kind of slow and there was this guy behind me trying to haul ass. Normally I'd be in a hurry, too, but I wasn't on this particular morning. So this guy is right on my tail and I finally pulled over and let him scream on by me. About a mile down the road I catch up with him. He's been in a head-on collision with another car. They're just two twisted hulks hanging off the road about to fall into the river. Any other day it would have been me. I don't know what to tell you. Am I just lucky, or is the universe looking out for me? I try not to think about it."

Jessie tried not to think about it, too, but the more she tried, the more her mind circled its wagons around the fact of her survival and refused to budge.

She had no energy to go back to work. The long-neglected real estate office did not beckon. She didn't care what she did. She didn't notice how she passed the days, or even that days—several of them—were passing. When the insurance people came out to settle on a payment over the fire, she didn't argue with them at all, just nodded, signed a bunch of things, and took the check. When the police came by to resurrect Jessie's memories about the various injustices visited upon her person, she didn't go into a vengeful tirade. She didn't rant about inept investigators or vow retribution. She dredged up details for them as though she were describing the plot of someone else's story. Oh, yes, officer, then they kicked me senseless and when I came to I was hog-tied and dumped like a sack of flour on the floorboards of their truck. You want some coffee or something?

Her lawyer, Marianne Meecham, called to say someone wanted to buy the scorched property. Jessie muttered a vague response. Marianne said she'd call back later.

Alden dropped in on her one afternoon when she was stuttering around the garden, and she went right into it with him.

"So if I've been spared," she said as he knelt beside her in the dirt, "what is it I'm supposed to do?"

"Well, Paul went out and preached the gospel," said Alden, and although he'd meant it as a joke, she didn't laugh.

"But what gospel, Uncle Alden? What gospel? The gospel according to Matthew, Mark, Luke, and John? The gospel according to Joseph Smith? The gospel according to Buddha? I mean, Ben's the one who rescued me, and he believes in some weird Zen deal: Be happy, don't worry, ain't life grand."

"You've been playing around the edges most of your life," said Alden. "You've been getting your kicks by not being and not doing things. You like living on the rim of the family. You get a lot of pleasure showing up and then pointing and laughing. Seems like that's what you've done with Nephi. Just when you guys get close and comfortable, you blow him off for somebody new. When that gets close and comfortable, you're gone again. You make a lot of money moving property from one person's hands to another's. You're on the outside looking in. Why don't you jump into the pool instead of running around splashing water on everybody else?"

"What do you mean?"

"What do *you* want? Figure it out. You've been screaming for years about what you don't want and what you don't believe. What do you want? What do you believe?"

"I believe I'm tired," she said. "I believe I'd like a little respect. I believe I'd like to have a context where everybody isn't down on me just because I don't pray and dress up nice on Sunday. I believe I'd like my goddamn brother not to hate me because I'm alive and his fiancee isn't. I believe I'd like my mother to stop looking at me like I'm her worst mistake."

"Jessie, that's like going into the grocery store and telling the produce clerk you want artichokes and the grocery clerk tells you he's sorry, but he doesn't have artichokes at his store. Then you start stamping your foot and screaming that you want to buy artichokes from him. There are things your family can't give you. If you want respect for being the black sheep, you're going to have to go someplace where people respect black sheep. That wouldn't be this family. And it wouldn't be this valley. Obedience and conformity get respect around here."

"Are you trying to tell me I don't belong?" she said.

"I don't need to. You've been telling yourself that for years. But you haven't done anything about it except blame everybody else because you can't get what you want."

"I'm overwhelmed by your insight," she said.

"Don't get smart with me," he said, in a tone he'd never used with her before and went away.

But he'd given her something to think about, a shift in the plates of her cogitative repertoire that carved a rift of a valley, a way out. I don't have to do this shit no more. There's other places I can go, other people I can be. She conjured a bright new elsewhere, and the fantasy provided the same intoxications of an imaginary lover, perfect in all ways. All her whims catered to, no one to annoy her, people who were like she was, threads of wildness running through them, people not afraid to get down and dirty with life, to muck around on the dark side. Like the good fantasy it was, it distracted her from the other junk, the big questions, the what-was-I-spared-for dilemma.

As she indulged in it late one afternoon, her phone rang. She was so surprised by the voice on the line, it took her a minute to believe that it really did belong to Nephi. He sounded brusque. She realized he was talking about Daniel.

"What?" she said. "I missed the first part. You say he's down by the orchard?"

"I think, I'm not sure, but I think he's blitzed," Nephi said.

"Blitzed? You mean, like, he's been drinking?"

"Well, he's down there kind of staggering around, anyway."

"Holy smokes. Huh. Listen, thanks Nephi. I'll come down. ... No. I don't think I'll need any help, but if I do, I'll come get you. Thanks again."

Her grandfather's orchard abutted Nephi's land. Jessie had no difficulty finding her brother. When she parked the Land Cruiser, she followed the sound of a voice doing a rather uncertain rendition of "Stardust Melody." She caught up with Daniel wandering among the peach trees, a quart of 100-proof vodka in his hand. It was a third empty. For a first-time drunk, he seemed remarkably upright. He paused when he saw her coming toward him, then held the bottle out. She took it from him, twisted off the top, and let the vodka roll down her throat. "Come on with me," she said and took Daniel's hand. It was the sort of scene their mother would have cherished, adult children mimicking the rituals of childhood, the days when Jessie had taken Daniel to play on the swings at the park, or had leaned over him to dry his eyes after he'd skinned a knee. They walked among the small trees, Jessie steering them up the sloping ground to the edge of the property where a barbed wire fence separated it from Forest Service land. When they got to the fence, Jessie pulled up on a strand of wire and Daniel slipped through. She followed him into a stand of pines along a narrow path, one they'd known since childhood. Daniel faltered and she took his hand again, walking a little in front of him until they came out of the trees along the rocky bank of a stream.

They had no trouble finding the place they had always come to, a smooth boulder with a depression in it, just big enough for two small bottoms, warm in the sunlight. They sat, pulled off shoes and socks, and dangled their toes in the frigid water. Daniel reached for the bottle again and Jessie let him have it.

"It turns things in my head," he said.

"What?"

"Turns hard things soft."

"Yes," she said. "It will do that."

It also appeared to be turning things soft in Daniel's eyes. Moisture glimmered at the corners, then began to spill out and down his cheeks, a drift of tears that got stranded in the stubble of a three-day growth of beard. It was not that Daniel sobbed. It was that he sat breathing heavily while grief trickled down his face. It made Jessie clutch inside. He wrenched himself suddenly off the boulder and fell over in the grass, guts heaving the poisonous booze back out of him. He puked the stuff up a good long while.

Jessie spent the interlude dumping the rest of the vodka out of the bottle and then rinsing it in the clear water of the stream. When it seemed to have lost the worst of its smell, she dunked it under water and let it fill. When Daniel sat back on his heels, she held it out to him. He pushed it away.

"No, it's just water, now," she said. "Drink some."

The throwing up had turned Daniel's venture with the world of alcohol into the unpleasant experience he had been warned about, and it took Jessie quite a while to get her now-sloppy sibling back to the road and her vehicle. When she had him safely loaded in, she hauled him off to Aunt Claire and Uncle Alden's. Let him sleep it off there, she figured. No point in making her parents suffer.

She drove home thoughtful, the incongruence of her righteous inebriated brother fluttering around. It's weird, how wrong it is, she thought as she scrambled eggs for dinner. It may be me, but it's definitely not him. She dumped salsa over the eggs and sat down at the kitchen table, pushing piles of bills and old newspapers out of the way. As she ate, she noticed an edge of onion-skin paper sticking out of the pile. She pulled it toward her. It was Daniel's blessing. She read through it again.

The eggs and salsa were abandoned to congeal. Jessie went back to her aunt and uncle's, pushed in through the front door, and found her aunt in the living room.

"Where's Daniel?" she asked.

"Asleep in the guest room," said Claire, "and I have to tell you, Jessie, I don't think getting him drunk did him any favors."

She didn't feel like arguing. She just went to the back bedroom where Daniel slept curled around a pillow, snoring. She pulled his billfold from the pocket of his jeans, wrapped it around the folded blessing, and set it on the dresser.

Got to go. Where? Don't know, but I got to go: The essence of Jessie's thoughts that night as she made a stab at cleaning up the kitchen. No more mind games, no more fantasies, let's just get this sucker in gear and get rolling.

In the morning she got Marianne on the phone and said, "Yes, sell that property. Just make sure they pay. I'm not giving it away."

She got Claire on the phone and told her if anybody wanted to rent William Moroni's house, to have at it. The news of her imminent departure got positive reviews in the family. Subdued, but positive. Jessie's leaving town? Yes! I mean, probably healthy for her to get away. Big sighs of relief. Daniel, still one large walking tear duct, cried for reasons he didn't bother to sort through. Her parents went into round two with ambivalence, expressing a small iceberg of feeling while larger, truer, darker stuff plowed beneath their words.

Jessie couldn't decide where to go. She just woke up one morning cursing happily because the destination was irrelevant. It doesn't matter where I go, I just have to take a run at it. The world is my oyster. She tied up loose ends, giving her lawyer power of attorney, shutting down the real estate office, arguing with Max, recording cassette tapes full of road tunes. Can this be me? she asked herself frequently. Can I be leaving? Yes! I can.

On a particular morning in late September, the departure train appeared ready to roll. She loaded gear into the Land Cruiser, camping supplies, clothes, music, passport (who knows?). She kissed a glowering Max goodbye and hit the road.

On the other side of town less resentful farewells were being exchanged. Felice stood beside Ben who straddled his motorcycle and tried not to sound sentimental.

"I can't think of any good words to say," he said. "You know what you've meant to me."

She smiled at him, reached out, and cupped his cheek in her hand. He hesitated, something hovering on the outside of his consciousness wanting expression. He couldn't pull it up. "You never did tell me how old you are," he said, stalling.

"That's true," she replied. "I never did."

"You aren't going to, are you?"

"If it mattered, I would," she said.

"Felice, there's something about it that matters to me."

"Well, then. All right. Wait here." She went into her house and came back out with a big, worn leather-bound Bible. She opened it to the front page where faded ink listed names and birth dates. She pointed to her own. Beside it, in pale blue ink was the date April 1, 1877.

Ben whistled. "Good Lord, woman. Is that you? That makes you ..." he paused to do the math.

"Yes, yes, yes," she said. "105 years old. I know."

"How did you live so long?"

"I did it by not dying."

"No. I mean really," said Ben. "How have you stayed so healthy?"

"And I'm really telling you," she replied. "I have let myself be alive. Alive to everything." She began laughing. "I didn't do it by hoarding any of my energy, either. I hope when you get wherever you're going, you let yourself go a little. You can back your semen up into your brain if you want to, but it's not going to give you eternal life."

Staring at his hands on the shiny black of his helmet, the fifty-year-old Ben actually blushed. "I want to say I'll see you later, but I won't be coming back here. I know it."

"It's a surprising world," she said. "We never know what will happen."

"I'll send word when I land," he said and started his engine.

"Goodbye," she said, smiling. "Godspeed."

173

Twenty-seven

A smoking curl of highway wound across the valley floor to snake through the narrow eastward canyon and deliver drivers out to the interstate. Ben let the Harley follow its westward inclination. He didn't carry much in his saddlebags: jeans, a few shirts, a couple of precious books. The spareness of it pleased him. By late September the shift in temperature whipped the air around him into a chill confluence. He was glad for the leather, for the feeling of calm, for the motion of the highway racing away from him. He started the long climb out of the valley and into the canyon. When he got to the last pullout, he ran his bike to the scenic overlook to gaze upon the valley that had sheltered him, that he'd sheltered.

Already parked there was a familiar tan Land Cruiser, a familiar body leaning against the front bumper looking out over the morning washing up the Wasatch Mountains as the sun cleared the peaks.

He coasted to a stop and pulled off his helmet. She looked at him, her eyes squinting against the sun.

"It's so strange," she said. "It's so beautiful and yet we have to go."

"Where are you going?" Ben asked.

Jessie snorted, "I don't know. No idea at all. I thought I'd drive out to the interstate and then see what hit, the urge to go north or south or west. I don't think I could go east. I don't think I could stand anything east of Colorado."

"Have you ever been east of Colorado?" asked Ben.

"No."

"So you're just driving off into the sunset, or," he tilted his head toward the eastern sky, "sunrise?"

"Uh huh. Where are you going?" she asked.

"To the coast," he said.

"California?"

"Oregon."

"I hear it rains a lot in Oregon," she said.

"True," he said.

"Well," she said.

"I've got to get moving," he said. They hugged each other in a shy way, as though they were new to the business of hugging and unclear about its intricacies. Ben got back on his bike and Jessie swung up into the Land Cruiser. She trailed him down the graceful curves of the Thunder Mountains. When the highway spit them out at the junction with Interstate 15, Ben took the north entrance that would lead him on to Interstate 84 for points west. He watched in his rear-view mirror as Jessie slowed to a crawl. As she got smaller and smaller in the distance, he saw her make a choice. In a burst of speed she blitzed onto the four-lane heading south. He smiled at the thought of her in the burning-bright desert, and then his thoughts of Jessie faded as his vision ran toward the misty vales of the forested coast.

———

An entire other tale could be built around Jessie's peregrinations southward, the ruckus she raised dancing in Salt Lake City bars; the Kennecott miner whose heart she held hostage for a night and a day; the afternoon she spent lounging on the quad at Brigham Young University before security escorted her and her bottle of tequila off campus; her two-week infatuation with Devil's Garden in Arches National Park; the alcohol-induced epiphany she experienced when she hiked into the bowels of the Grand Canyon and which she did not recall in the hangover-daze of the next morning; the psychic in Sedona who took a look at her, muttered over some tarot cards, and said, "Well, you've certainly been a pain in the ass to somebody"; also countless little escapades in dreams, lots of wild flying, mythical beasts, and the cranky noise of some bird she couldn't identify.

But full as she made her days and nights, some missing ingredient interfered, some restless thing driving her southward and southward but unplacated by the journey. The thing was, she kept calling Max. And Max, God help him, kept letting her. They both knew better. These long-distance dalliances were worse than fantasy. But they couldn't help themselves. And still she moved south.

One morning, hovering on the brink of Mexico, her eye on Baja, she hallooed herself to a stop at the side of the road. Just a doggone second, here.

She sat still and an image from the past presented itself front and center for inspection. It was the day she and Max had hiked high up into the mountains. She saw the sea of peaks, the way she could almost feel them spiking roughly against her skin, the incandescent blue of the sky, the hot, dry air, the spindly aspens of the lower meadow, flashes of all the things that belonged to her, that she belonged to—the long, high valley, the mountains, the canyons, the night sky.

Just a dad-blasted second, here. Alden's question fired again inside her: *What do you want?* It produced another image from the past: that drive back from Pocatello, angel loaded on the seat beside her, heading toward various things she loved.

The heat in the parked Land Cruiser sucked sweat out of her. A dark bird with a flick of white marking flashed across the road, railing like the bird of recent dreams. Iridescent, long-tailed cranky scrounge. Unwelcome magpies squawking at a funeral.

Home. *My home, goddamn it.* Why should I be running away? Then something her uncle had said came back to her: You get to be who you are. One of life's little gifts, if you care to accept it. Jessie felt the confluence of her selves—the rebel, the seeker, the adult, the child—for the first time as a single entity. None of them needed to be excluded. They were all what she was, life's gift to her.

The Land Cruiser engine fired up suddenly, tires sputtering gravel as the square vehicle pushed up on the pavement and made a U-turn. At a 7-Eleven on the outskirts of Yuma, it came to a stop. Jessie jumped out and trotted to a pay phone. She dropped several quarters in and dialed, tapping her fingers impatiently on the wall as she waited for the call to go through.

"Marianne? Jessie. Have you closed on the deal on that property, yet? No? Good. Listen, you call those people and tell them the deal is off. I'm not selling anything. Marianne, damn it, I don't care if they'll be pissed. They'll get over it. ... I don't care. I don't care about any of that. Listen, isn't that cousin of yours over in Tremonton a contractor? Fine. You call him up and tell him I've got a job for him. ... What? I can't hear you. There's damn eighteen-wheelers gearing down right across the street from me. What? What? Oh, yeah, you bet your sweet ass, girl. Phoenix from the ashes. Absolutely."

And with that, Jessie got back into the Land Cruiser, laughed as she put it in gear, punched Roseanne Cash into her tape deck, and headed up the highway, back the way she had come.

Epilogue

Nephi stood on the high bench that pushed up against a sag of mountain. At the western rim of the sky, pinks and oranges bled down the horizon and off the map of his sight. Baby waited at his side, bumping her head now and then against his arm. He followed the bowl of the sky around to the northeast where in the fading light a bloated pale moon fumbled into view.

The eruption of various emotions occupied Nephi. The numbing effect of alcohol and marijuana had worn clean away. The numbing effect of his careful inattention to detail had begun to fade. Like lightning in the night sky, like the violent shift of tectonic plates, like a flash flood through Monument Valley, the emotions Nephi had screened from awareness ripped now across his conscious mind. Some days he staggered under the weight of sorrows. Some days he could not burrow out of the rage. Some days fear slithered up his spine and whispered evil, wretched things in his ear.

He made a point of looking long at the sky.

John Tyhee said he had a lot of catching up to do. Tyhee said he would flounder around in feelings until he thought he would drown in them. Tyhee was right. But every day Nephi made this brief pilgrimage to watch the sun slip away from him and to acknowledge that he hadn't drowned yet. It was the sea of the past. Everything that he had skirted, run away from, minimized, or outright lied to himself about washed up against him demanding his attention. All he had to do was keep breathing, keep looking at the sky, and breathe.

Tyhee swore that if he let it all come and honored it that one day he would awaken in a different world. The evil, wretched things no longer whispering, the sorrow shrunk to proper size. Tyhee promised joy. He said it quietly over lemon grass tea. Nephi didn't believe him. Except.

Except that he had nothing else. The only thing of value Nephi acknowledged was the calm, uncluttered way Tyhee went about his days and nights.

The sky was dark now and heavy with stars. Nephi sighed as the canyon breeze ruffled his hair sweetly. He swung up onto Baby and rode down toward the warm lights of his home.